WHITE CRANES DANCING

Fiona Cameron

Flying Swan Press

PART ONE: PRELUDIO

St Petersburg, Russian Federation, 16th June, 1997

Dee is still furious over the Captain's Table incident last night.

She had her eye on Captain Paolo Conti before we set foot on the gangway. When we arrived at Leith, he was out on the docking bridge, checking to see if he'd scratched his boat parking; he glanced down at us with those deep, dark eyes and smiled. It would have been no surprise if Dee had shinned up one of the mooring ropes, like a hungry rat. The trouble is, her hopes were raised the minute the smart gold-embossed invitation was delivered to our cabin (a very expensive cabin; she doesn't do things by halves, and her business has been doing well recently).

But of course, I found myself seated next to Paolo, with the only fanciable unattached man from among the passengers on my other side. Dee sat fuming at the far end of the table, flanked by a seagoing flunkey with much less gold braid, and a retired bishop. She won't believe I didn't use underhand tactics to set this up. She probably thinks it's my revenge for schooldays, when my only useful role was as foil to her plump, blonde good looks on double dates.

'It was pure coincidence,' I tell her. 'I'm sure he doesn't concern himself with the seating arrangements. The maître d' does that. Maybe he thought Paolo needed tips on dealing with journalists more than advice on interior design.'

Trying to jolly her out of it. No chance.

'And was it pure coincidence that you and *Paolo* disappeared the moment the meal was over, and you weren't seen again for hours?'

'Naw, that was a set-up, I confess. We sent the officer of the watch on his way, so *il capitano* could ravish me on the chart table.'

She snorts. 'Must have anaesthetised you then, if your past performance is anything to go by.'

'Dee, they're not allowed to have affairs with the passengers. Paolo's never going to do anything to jeopardise his job, you idiot.'

'Why was your hair all messed up when you came back to the cabin in the middle of the night then?'

'It was breezy out on deck. And it wasn't the middle of the night. It was about ten minutes after you got back, because we saw you. Absolutely nothing happened, I assure you.'

'Not out of any loyalty to me, Serena. I don't know why you have to be so selfish. It's not as if you're looking for a man anyway. You've newly managed to get shot of the last one.'

I'm trying to remember to be charitable, because we still have another ten days of this damn cruise to get through – and after all, the whole reason for it was to take her mind off the fact she'd been jilted three weeks before her wedding. I, on the other hand, am celebrating my divorce. I'd maybe have chosen a different destination, but we're only here for two and a half days, and after all a dozen years have flowed under the bridge since the ghastly school trip in 1985.

Dee's an interior designer and money's no object as far as she is concerned. The cruise has put me in hock up to my eyeballs. But I've convinced myself I deserve a treat. It's only three years to the Millennium, and I'm well past the stage where I can think of myself as a "girl". I need an adventure, so I'm going for it. I'll stand once again in the places my father loved, which I've loved since I was tiny, where I've always known I'd find the Prince from the films of the Kirov Ballet Aunt Peigi used to take me to see after she came home from Canada – *Swan Lake* and *Sleeping Beauty* (though my Prince is the antithesis of Sergei Berezhnoi with his black hair and dark eyes and very tight tights).

'This is the anniversary of the date Nureyev defected in 1961,' I say. Sheer force of habit. In the newsroom, we're forever checking out the *Book of Days*; insurance against slow news weekends in summer. It's also the anniversary of the day they hanged Imre Nagy. I decide to stick to cheerful thoughts, keep my father's ghost onside.

'Do I care?' snaps Dee.

The first day here is almost gone; tomorrow will be taken up with a full-day excursion to Pertodvoretz and Oranienbaum. All my chores are complete; the picture postcards are bought and written and mailed – though who knows if they'll ever reach their destinations? The tawdry souvenirs have been acquired. I have a single evening to say goodbye to Peter's city one final time. I don't expect to be back.

We've arrived at the height of an unaccustomed heat-wave, but it rained two days ago, so the air has the soft, fresh-washed texture of swansdown – subtly different to the breeze in Balvaig after rain; that's a silk chiffon scarf drawn gently across the skin. West Highland and Baltic summers are sweeter because they're nearer the bone. I want to rest my cheek against the night air of St Petersburg, and cry.

'I wish we had longer here. Two days isn't enough. Wait here a mo,' I tell Dee. 'I have a book at home with this exact same view in it.'

On my fifth birthday, Frank, my father, pressed a picture book into my sweaty, dubious hands; hands that would have preferred a toy. 'This is my most precious possession I'm entrusting to you, sweetheart,' he said, 'so you'll grow to love the place as I do.'

He bought it when he was a Young Communist League envoy to this city's Jubilee celebrations. He'd written his name carefully inside the front cover: *Frank Stuart, Leningrad, June 1957*; a decade before I was born. The captions were in quaint, archaic English and in Russian. I traced the elegant Cyrillic script with my finger, and knew in my heart I'd be able to read it one day (though Frank never learned). I opened the book at random, to a panorama of river and bridge and steeple: *View from the Lieutenant Schmidt*

Bridge. Love hit me like a train. I recognised the place where the Prince would find me; on an iron-lace bridge over the Neva, in the city originally named for a man called Peter, like my Granda, although not so severe as him. There I'd wake up, and live happily ever after.

'That's one of the bridges they open up at night to let the ships through,' Frank said, looking over my shoulder.

'What – when people are on it? Like the bridge of San Luis Rey?' (One of the volumes on my Aunt Peigi's shelf, beside the well-thumbed Oxford Book of English Verse, which falls open automatically at Hogg's *Bonnie Kilmeny*.)

'No, they warn you, silly.'

As I begin to cross the bridge, I realise it's wider than I'd remembered. I assumed the river of traffic would slow, or swerve, or take some action to avoid running me down, the way it would on Princes Street. But I have to gallop when it doesn't. I'm not paying enough attention, and the right heel of the uncomfortable sandals Dee persuaded me to buy for my holiday wedges itself firmly between the inner edge of a tramline and the decrepit tarmac. Then I hear the tram coming. *Clickety-clack. Who's that trip-trapping over my bridge?*

My name rings in my ears, as if someone is calling me. *Ser-eee-na.* Morag's voice this time; my mother. It's run in my head on an endless-loop tape all my life. Its batteries didn't run out when hers did. *Can't you do anything right? What a stupid, ugly way to die. Who's going to weep over your warm, mangled body, or remember that your eyes were still open and go off to war to forget? Never mind. Come to me. You'll be better off here. It's hot all year round.*

God, there's another tram coming the other way now. I'm stuck between them. I stand up straight, wiggling my foot frantically as my greasy bell-clanging Nemeses trundle and scrape towards me. I don't want to risk the indignity of dying with my arse in the air if I bend to unfasten the small, fiddly buckle.

I've no knowledge of how he arrives beside me, only the sensation of strong arms. I'm swung round and over the edge of the metal track, and my foot snaps free of its flimsy strap. He clasps me tight against a pale-blue-shirted chest that smells of clean laundry and fresh cigarette smoke. The trams pass so close one brushes against my hair, and I feel the draught of the driver's breath as she swears at me – 'Cretin! Do you want to get yourself killed?' (And who has the correct answer to that?)

I cling to the edges of a leather jacket.

'I've got you,' he says. 'You're safe. Keep still.'

A deeper voice than I'd expected in a prince, with a rough edge to it, a husky quality like Rod Stewart's. I look up at him, and think, *I know who* you *are!* He hugs me to him as if I've been there most of his life too. Then he scoops me up and dodges between cars till we reach the pavement. He's tall, muscular, slender: thin. His hair is very blond.

'Excuse me,' he says, setting me down on my feet, holding me steady. 'You were so scared I didn't know if you'd be able to run.'

'Probably not. It hurts.'

'So you do speak Russian? I wondered if you

understood what I was saying. I figured even if I broke your ankle it was better than your neck. What were you *thinking* of?'

'I was actually wondering if tram wheels are hot because of the friction, or cold and sharp.' Like Lizzie Borden's axe.

'That's not what I meant.'

'I know. I'm sorry, it was a silly thing to do. Thank you for saving my life anyway.'

This is no doubt an exaggeration. The tram would probably have stopped in time, or I'd have found the strength to free my foot. He keeps hold of me. The feel of his hand is familiar; the warmth of the skin, the way his palm is firm and smooth and without hint of sweat, the way his long fingers curl round mine.

He says sternly, 'I was watching you. I couldn't believe my eyes when you just stepped off the pavement.'

He's had to take a risk too.

'I should have used the proper crossing,' I mutter humbly. 'It's not as if I haven't been here before, I should have remembered what the traffic's like.'

Though in 1985, I'm sure there weren't nearly so many cars. Moments ago, I was ranting to Dee that nowhere feels foreign nowadays; it's all Coca-Cola signs. Even the black and white striped street crossings are the same.

'Merely helps them take aim,' he says. 'Do you feel calmer now? Can you put your weight on it?'

'Why were you watching me?'

'You're beautiful.'

As shallow as the rest, then. I'd hoped he could see deeper.

Dee arrives precipitately beside us.

'Stand right here,' the stranger says. 'Promise me you won't do anything silly?'

I nod obediently, and he dodges back into the traffic to haul my shoe from its grave.

'It's scuffed, but only the strap's broken. I have a pin.'

He kneels on the pavement, produces a safety pin from his pocket and fastens the thin leather to the side with meticulous care, then runs competent, professional fingers over my ankle. I decide he must be a doctor.

'I don't think it's even sprained,' he says, 'just bruised. You'll allow me to buy you a drink.' Even allowing for the fact Russian speakers place the stress differently, it isn't a question. 'My name is Maksim Grigoriev. Most people call me Max.'

Well, of course. I always knew in my heart it would be like this. Two princes in one.

He extends a much more formal hand. 'And you?'

Cinderella. 'Serena Stuart MacKenzie. And this is Deirdre McCulloch. Dee.'

'I need a drink,' Dee says, 'after watching Serena's party trick. Where's the Nevsky thingie? We want to go to the Literaturnoe Café.'

And even before we reach there, I want to check if they've left the blue and white stencilled notice on the wall, lest we forget: *Citizens! In the event of artillery fire this side of the street is the most dangerous.*

Max shrugs dismissively. 'It's obscenely expensive and it's full of tourists. It closes early anyway. Let me take you to a bar where you'll meet real Russians.'

As we begin to walk, he falls into step beside me.

'I should really go back to the ship and put on some sensible footwear,' I say, unconvincingly.

If I go back so early, Paolo will be watching for me, I'm in no doubt. He's too self-assured to make the type of mistake that could cost him his career. It wouldn't go further than another few very chaste kisses, but a line would have been crossed. *If this is not meant to happen, block it*, I chanted inside my head a few hours ago while Dee and I wandered aimlessly among Vasilievsky Island's sinister streets-with-no-names. *Let everything turn out for the highest good of all concerned, as recommended by Shakti Gawain. Amen.*

'Anyway,' I add, 'we need to get back to the ship before they open the bridges for the night.'

Everyone going ashore (few of us opted to, under our own steam) was warned: it's essential to be back on the correct side of the river, and in the right district, by the time that happens, if we don't want to find ourselves stranded until tomorrow morning.

Max consults an empty wrist.

'Speak English, you two. It's very rude not to,' says Dee. 'It's just after ten.'

'Plenty of time,' he says. 'Several hours. Isn't the river beautiful with the moon almost full and the daylight still with us? I often walk across to the Strelka just to savour it. It's the scene the ones who've left dream of.'

And even with the Communist paint flaking, it is stunning. Drifts of amethyst mist over the Neva, the elegant three-branched streetlights on the bridges and along the embankment, casting superfluous pools of tawny light as atmospheric as anything you'd see in Paris; lacy bridges and clipped limes silhouetted against a peach-and-lemon sky. It would take a Philistine to notice the rusting sub moored opposite us.

"Our White Nights," the locals say, as if they'd invented the endless twilight, getting-out-of-school sensation the Scots call *the simmer dim*.

'You'll be fine with these shoes,' Max adds. 'It's not far. Your injury is slight.'

'Are you a doctor?'

'No! But I have healing hands.' He smiles down at me; a sweet-enough-to-eat smile that makes the earth spin beneath my feet. 'I'm a cellist. Did you know it's Stravinsky's birthday tomorrow?'

'For Christ's sake!' says Dee. 'Get a move on, Serena.'

Max doesn't quicken his pace. 'Although you speak my language with an excellent accent, I can tell you're not from here. You're on a cruise holiday?'

'The ship across there: the *Fortuna*.' I point to it, wondering if Paolo's on the bridge with powerful field glasses. Wouldn't put it past him. 'We're only here till tomorrow evening. Not really long enough.'

She looks so normal and safe, tied up on the Vasilievsky Island side, her rakish blue and white funnel towering above the quay, although she isn't the largest of cruise ships. Only a moment away; as long as we don't stray too far, no reason to worry.

'She only looks the quiet type,' Dee snarls, over her shoulder. 'Captain's had her lashed to the wheel since Copenhagen, but don't get your hopes up, or anything else.

She doesn't go for fair-haired men. Though she's always had a thing about Russians, since primary school, so maybe you're in with a chance. Better not ask her too many questions about the one she had the hots for when she was here before.'

Max is pretending not to hear Dee, or not to understand her.

'Dee's not rational,' I say, just in case he has. 'We got lost down the side-streets earlier.'

Just before dinner, we strayed into a time warp of 1960s Leningrad. There were few people around, and those we met sized us up like cannibals. The buildings were faded to water-colour-left-in-sun shades even the classiest paint firms couldn't reproduce: only time and climate gives such an effect. Every available wall was covered in peeling posters advertising long-finished theatre performances, circuses, and English classes; dozens of these. Everyone wants to learn English; everyone wants to get out. It reminded me of the pictures in the old *National Geographics* Frank insisted on keeping. The ones Morag scoffed at: *The Red Menace*. The Enemy.

'You couldn't get lost in Peter,' Max says, 'the streets are all on a grid.' And he catches my hand again, drawing me back from the path of a speeding car. 'Careful! They'll hit you rather than risk getting rammed. Less damage to the bodywork. Don't they have traffic in England?'

'Scottish drivers aren't homicidal.'

He gives me his oblique and secret smile again, while I register a surprising fact: he has the most perfect teeth. No sweeties when he was young.

'So – Serena Stuart MacKenzie from Scotland. A beautiful name. Serena.' *And in his sexy accent, indeed it is.* 'Whereabouts in Scotland?'

'I was born in the Highlands, on the Isle of Soma – it's not a large island – in a tiny village called Balvaig. I live in Edinburgh now.'

'I was born in this wonderful city,' he says. 'It's marvellous that you speak my language. You learnt when you visited before?'

'I was only here for a week, a dozen years ago. Leningrad. I learnt the language at school.'

Hazelpark had a history teacher as besotted with the place as I was, but she didn't speak Russian – the only reason I'd found myself on a sixth year history trip. The school had found a discreet way to pay for me.

'Is it any different?'

More run-down. Still beautiful. In 1985 it was austere and scarcely free, but the paint wasn't flaking, and people had work. There was more grace about it. Strangers, even young people, didn't call each other 'ti' from the first meeting, and they still used the patronymic. But the city's heart is the same as ever. Fabergé bling and mud.

'The churches are churches again,' I say.

The women can get religion while the men hit the booze. Just like home. Superstition masquerading as religion; fatalism, cruel gods, hospitality verging on masochism. None of it makes sense. And plenty in both countries think the answer to it all is a message at the bottom of a bottle, if only they could find the right one; best drain them all, just in case.

We catch up with Dee, and Max leads us to a shabby pub along from the Gostiniy Dvor. The way he flicks each note surreptitiously between his fingers tells me he can ill afford to be hospitable, so I sip my drink. Dee downs hers in one gulp. She's been on the booze since we left Leith and I've been suffering guilt-pangs over neglecting her while she went through the trauma of being dumped by a banker five weeks after reaching her thirty-second year, and deciding maybe she'd better have some of her eggs frozen. We are both adults. She's not my responsibility any more.

I study Maksim Grigoriev, closely and stealthily. He has a forelock that falls across his eyes, and a mannerism of sweeping it aside with the back of his hand, like a wee boy needing a trim. His nose is a shade too large to be classical, but it suits his lankiness and makes him look distinguished. A sensitive mouth – no: sensual – and lacking the sullen downturn I've grown accustomed to again over one short day in Peter. Eyes the colour of a peaty burn in spate; warm brown with gold flecks. Dangerous eyes. A narrow, high-cheekboned face with the most exquisite ellipse of jaw line; the curve the Pre-Raphaelites gave their knights. I experience a powerful urge to trace it with my finger, and clench my hands under the table.

I'm being inspected too. Men gawp at me and notice my hair and my eyes and my fashionable lack of boobs, and my neat wee bum. Maksim looks into me rather than at me, as if he can see through my skin. I couldn't be offended.

'You want to go on to another bar? Maybe this one isn't very smart,' he says anxiously.

'It's fine.'

Dee is halfway to the door. 'This is a dump. Let's go somewhere we might meet interesting people.'

'We'll walk a little first. Let you work up a thirst again.'

We end up in a larger, noisier pub near the Mariinsky.

'Stop fretting,' Max says, 'it's still only three minutes to your ship from here.'

It's a bad move all the same.

'Ah, Grishkin! You'll introduce me to your friends?'

The man who elbows his way through the crowd towards us isn't so tall as Max, but more powerfully built. Black hair, black eyes, luxuriant moustache, a wide face with more than a touch of Asia in it; an artist's impression of Genghis Khan. Although he is smartly dressed he has an aura of thuggery and I register that Max isn't deliriously pleased to see him.

'These are my guests, Zhenya,' he says. 'Visitors. Behave yourself.'

'Don't be greedy, you dirty bugger. You can't screw two women at the same time. I'm getting a boner just looking at the dark one.'

'The dark one speaks excellent Russian. Yours is the blonde.'

Genghis blushes, and I can see that he's handsome, or at least striking. His almond eyes glow like coals.

'Sorry. I only meant to be friendly. Joking with my old comrade-in-arms.' He turns his attention to Dee, seizes both her hands in one of his paws. 'I like very much to practise my English. Yevgeny Kutozov. Zhenya. But my friends call me Kuzkuz.'

'The stuff they eat in Morocco,' says Dee.

'That's me. Wholesome and filling, but you won't put on weight unless you're greedy.'

Canned laughter from a weasel-faced spiv at his back signals that he hasn't arrived alone. The hair on the back of my neck prickles. I press closer to Max, and he doesn't draw away.

'Tourists!' says Zhenya. 'And what have you found to gawp at today, my lovelies?'

'The Biggest Museum in the World,' Dee tells him. 'And a turquoise palace. The one where they keep going on about who stole their bloody amber.'

They all laugh. It made me sad, though. Yes, they've brought back all the treasures they'd carried away for protection in the 1940s, and they allow the herds of tourists in to gaze on them, briefly, before they're shepherded back onto their buses. The guides brandish folding umbrellas above their heads like crucifixes. So many tourists, so many guides, so many umbrellas all the same, so many buses parked in Palace Square; such a risk of getting lost. Most don't. They're safely decanted back to their hotels, their cruise-ships, the airport, and they go home to bore their friends with stories of: *when I was in Russia*. But they're deluded. St Petersburg's not Russia, any more than Balvaig's Scotland. It's all veneer, the lapis lazuli and malachite and amber and gold, gold, gold – wherever you look, everything drips with gold (even the smiles). And the Catherine Palace! Couples in eighteenth-century gear strolling in the gardens. What will they have next – Nicholas and Alexandra on ice? I've read that factory workers are being paid in anything from rat poison to jars of pickled gherkins. How many gherkins to dress up and pose for photos with the tourists?

When the Hazelpark party visited Pushkin all those years ago, our bus broke down halfway, and KGB minders' cars circled it like sharks. Might as well toss a coin to decide which was the better outcome.

I refuse Zhenya's offer of more alcohol, and demand coffee; one of us has to keep a clear head. Max's frown subsides. He stretches his elegant legs under the table; I can feel his warmth.

I watch Kuzkuz. An old friend, he said, and Max didn't deny it. Dee's thigh is pressed against his, and her skirt has ridden up so that her pants show. Fergus, my ex, says there's a point with her when it ceases to matter: animal, vegetable or mineral. It's insecurity, but I'll never let her know that I know. 'My mother says your family's dysfunctional,' she announced confidentially when we were eleven. I looked it up in the school library, but I was none the wiser. I'm still not sure I know what it means, other than "different". Dee thinks her family's normal? She's babbling now, because she's jealous.

'The girls here are smart. Quite fashionable.'

The sole female in Kuzkuz's entourage is dark and handsome rather than pretty, but the passing blondes, perched on their stiletto heels, all high cheekbones and elegance, have the colouring Dee's obliged to buy from a hairdresser and the Estée Lauder counter in Jenners.

'It's another baby-pigeons mystery,' she burbles. 'These dreadful old women in black coats, and the young girls. No gradations between.'

'What did you expect?' asks Zhenya. 'Deformities

because of Chernobyl?' The alteration in his voice makes my throat constrict. 'People dressed in rags? In your country, do the girls not have pretty dresses? Very good, Catherine's Palace. No matter that the people have no food. They've repaired it for the western tourists who come to stare, even busloads of Germans. You know how many millions of our civilians died in the Occupation? And we've repaired it for the Germans to see.'

'You'd have repaired it anyway,' I say, hoping to defuse a fight, 'out of cussedness.'

In a blink, he's affable again.

'We repaired it? The Russians repaired it. We're just mongrels, Max and me. Not pure-bred. Anyway, no need to fall out. Why don't you come for a drive with me? I can show you the sights. Take you to a nightclub. You think this is the third world? Of course we have nightclubs, excellent ones. I'll give you a good time, Dee-Dee.'

'Only if you have a decent car.'

Car-daft. She'd agree to copulate with Jeremy Clarkson if the deal included a spin in something fast and dangerous. But surely Dee would balk at a madman, even if he is a looker?

Zhenya jerks his thumb carelessly towards the silver 600 Mercedes parked at the door. 'My company car.'

I had a good look at it on the way in.

'No chance.' Max is angry. 'You can play that game on your own.'

'What's the harm? He wouldn't mind. He left the keys for me.' He pats his pocket. 'Anyway – your girl can come too. I won't invite you, since you're so critical, Grishkin.

It'll be fun.'

'It's too late. We have to get back to the ship.'

'Your pal said it's hours yet. Anyway, Kuzkuz can give us a lift.' Dee's already slightly unsteady on her feet. I pull her down again.

'No way you're getting in that,' I say. 'Have you seen the tyres?'

'The big problem with these foreign models,' says Zhenya. 'Can't get the parts. If you find a single car in this city with tread on the tyres it'd be a miracle. The wheels would be worth more than the entire article. It's the same as the dodgems, sweetheart – safe, because we all know it's dangerous. Come on, Serena, or whatever your name is. I can satisfy two women. I'm not a cello-player.'

'No thank you. Dee – you don't have time to go for a drive.' I can't believe she's being so foolhardy, this woman who dons rubber gloves to arrange the soft furnishings of douce middle-aged Edinburgh lawyers. She's positively glorying in the fact she's picked up the guy who has a car.

'Serena's in a hurry to get back,' she says. 'Hot date with a sailor. I thought she was going to get more than her dinner at the captain's table tonight.'

She puts her fist under the edge of the café table and lifts it an inch or two. She can make folding a hankie look obscene, and people always laugh. Even Max smirks.

'She's desperate to be there when he gets his anchor up.'

Before I can stop her, she's out to the Merc and snuggling into the leather seat. I sigh and put my hand on the door-handle. *You have to play what Deirdre wants to play,* chants the Morag-tape in my head, *we owe the McCullochs so much…*

Max's hand is on my arm; a firm grasp, designed to persuade. 'If she's determined, let her go. I'll walk you back.'

'I'm completely sober, and I'm capable of looking after myself.'

'All the same, I'm not allowing you to get into that car.'

Damn the man, acting like any other, thinking he can tell me what to do.

'Please, I feel responsible,' he says. 'I brought you here as my guest.'

And he looks so troubled and young and sincere that the resentment evaporates and I stand back from the Merc. Dee's a big girl now, and she's not what you'd call *drunk*.

'Remember, we have to be back at the ship soon,' I call after her.

'What did she say she does for a living?' Max asks, watching the tail-lights vanish at the corner.

'She's an interior designer.'

He looks blank.

'She advises people on how to decorate their houses, and what curtains and sofas to buy.'

He pulls a face. 'She's a decorator, in other words?'

'God no, she doesn't get her hands dirty. She decides on the colour schemes and hires other people to do the real work. She's an extremely successful businesswoman. If we get our Scottish Parliament she reckons she's made because the new MPs will want their flats done up.'

Max leads me back into the bar.

'And she's your friend? Close friends, I think, to vacation together.'

The truth of it is, I was probably near the bottom of her list. But everyone else we know is encumbered with a current man, or kids, or both.

'She's had a very distressing experience recently, and I had loads of leave due, because I never use up my full quota, so we booked this at the last minute. Got quite a bargain.'

Even though I'll have to avoid the bank manager for quite some time to come.

Max rolls his eyes. 'Anyway, it's you I want to talk about.'

'Explain the joke about cello players.'

'He's being vulgar. Zhenya plays the viola. They claim to have more stamina with women.'

He blushes. (The first time I see how easily it happens. It makes me want to redden his cheeks even more.)

'So where's your cello?' I pretend to look under the table.

'Sold, months ago. I couldn't afford to keep it.'

I'd swear there are tears in his eyes. I feel awful. I didn't mean to upset him.

'Cellos are so expensive to feed,' I say, trying to lighten his mood.

He shrugs, but his eyes are still sad. 'The problem is I have to eat occasionally. It's a pity. I could have made good money busking in the streets with all the others for tourists like you. I trained at the Leningrad Conservatory, the finest music school in the world.'

'What did Zhenya mean, you're both mongrels?'

He gives his lop-sided grin (the private one; I know already it will be only for our jokes). I prefer cheerful to sad.

'He's talking for the sake of talking. His mother was Tajik, mine's Ukrainian. Anyway, tell me more about what work it is you do. You work on a newspaper?'

The standard glazed expression as I fill in the detail of what I do to earn a crust.

'You're on TV?' he says.

'It's no big deal. It's only the news. I'm rarely seen. I'm usually the voice reading the script while a video clip's shown. It's a commercial channel called Albion. It's not as if it's the BBC. It's a mundane job, not at all glamorous. The Merc – it's not Zhenya's, is it?'

'It'll be fine. You must meet famous people though?'

'Minor politicians, middle rank policemen, local businessmen, the odd footballer. Very occasionally some celebrity or science guru who's visiting. All very mundane.'

Weasel-face has disappeared. The dark girl stares morosely into her glass. Down a side street I can see the elegant rake of the *Fortuna's* bow. Less than five minutes it will take to walk across the bridge.

'I think I should start heading back,' I say.

Another endearing smile. 'There's no rush, surely.'

Grishkin, the others call him. A sweet, innocent name; a child's name from a fairy tale. Deceptive, like the city. The sinews on the backs of his hands are as symmetrical as the spokes of a wheel; strong hands.

'So – the car – is it Zhenya's?'

'It belongs to a man called Mayakovsky. Local businessman. You want me to arrange an interview with him?'

'So he's stolen it?'

'He's – borrowed it. He only wants a little fun.'

'I've let Deirdre leave with a mad rapist in a stolen car?' *Oh God, what will I tell her mother?*

'Rapist?' Max laughs. 'She'd have lain down on the floor with him here if there'd been space.'

'The car – what will the owner do?'

'Shoot the pair of them. I'm teasing you. They'll be back before he ever notices.'

He lights a cigarette, stubs it out again after one drag, as I sling him The Look I zap smokers with.

'Zhenya knows him?'

'You're bored here? Let's take another walk.'

'Where is this man? He must be nearby. Or did your pal steal his car elsewhere?'

'Zhenya has the sense not to stay away too long.'

But does Dee? We sit in the bar for what seems like hours.

'Let's go and look for them,' I suggest.

Max shrugs again. 'They won't come to any harm. Zhenya's a little strange, but he's not a bad person. He'll look after her.'

'Maybe he already dropped her at the ship? I should go back too.'

'Too late. The bridges are opening. You can't get back over till the morning. Look.'

There's my picture-book bridge, upending itself, streetlamps at a crazy angle, like the freeway in a Californian earthquake.

'Damn, what on earth can I do now?'

'Come home with me for the rest of the night,' he says.

'I can't. Max, this isn't funny.'

The Russian shrug again. It still drives me mad. I thought I'd forgotten it, the way they'd act thoughtlessly, leaving doors open so all the heat got out, and shrug: 'Nothing to do with me, comrade.' The paradox is the love I feel. Damn Frank. Damn the Soviet-Scottish Friendship Society that fed his illusions.

'Isn't there a hotel near here?'

'I don't think a respectable hotel is going to take you at this hour!'

'Well, is there nowhere we can sit for a few hours?'

'We could sit on a bench and watch the river – but it's cold. You don't have a coat.'

I'm already shivering.

'Don't frown,' says Max. 'You'll get wrinkles. You'll be safe at my home until the bridges go back down in the morning.'

'You live with your parents?'

'Of course not. My father died ten years ago, and my mother went back to work in Kiev, where she comes from.'

'What does she do?'

'Doctor,' he says casually. 'Women's reproductive problems. It's quite a large hospital. She's pretty senior. She delivers babies too, if there's a hitch.'

'She's a consultant?'

'You assumed I was from an uneducated family?'

'I'm surprised.'

'What age are you?'

Hard to get used to such directness. Next he'll ask me what my salary is. I toy with the idea of lying because I hate the finality of it.

'Thirty. And you?'

'Twenty-nine. Well, nearly. October.'

On my birthday in April, I wrote down a list of all my fears, ranked in order of magnitude. I discovered that finding myself in a falling plane or a sinking ship is a less scary prospect than another three decades with no change; skating on the thin ice of my life till it's over. I resolved then not to let another chance of finding the glass slipper slip by.

'So you live on your own?' I say.

He hits me with the attractive naughty-child's giggle that could break my heart. 'Yes and no. Reserve judgement till you see it. I share a flat with others. You weren't really going to bed with your ship-captain tonight?'

'Only in Dee's fertile imagination.'

'Your friend mentioned you met a man here last time? You had a romance?'

'Not at all! I was with a school group. One of the waiters in the hotel was rather good-looking. Dee imagines I liked him.'

Sergei Timochenko. Seriozha. I try to blot out the memory of what a coward I was in 1985. The other girls were smitten, so I decided to give him the come-on; he didn't need much encouragement. Nothing untoward happened. Merely some fumbling and inexpert kissing in the Summer Gardens, on his afternoon off. God knows who clyped on us, but he got into terrible trouble. I was too naïve to realise that giving the Hazelpark teachers the slip hadn't been the issue. Dragon-woman who managed the catering staff was the real threat. Seriozha may have lost his job because I was so vain.

'But you have someone special at home?' asks Max.

I shake my head. 'I used to be married.'

He stops walking and gazes in my face. 'What happened – he died or he left you?'

'I'm divorcing him. Well – the divorce is just newly through.'

'MacKenzie – this is his name or your own?'

'Mine.' *Though not my father's.* 'His is Learmonth. Like Lermontov.'

'Will you marry again?'

'I don't have anyone I intend to settle down with. Do you?'

'No, I'm the same; there's no one.'

I've never experienced a full-blown holiday romance, the one where you don't learn his second name, possibly lack a common language and have nothing more than a quick and casual liaison in a doorway or on a beach. (Sand in your underwear, unspeakable horrors in your bloodstream and no clear memory of what he looks like in daylight.) Dee's different; unnecessary for the man to buy her a drink, never mind a meal. *I can't be bought for the cost of a fancy fish supper,* she'll say. *I am a virtuous woman, and my price is above Harry Ramsden's.*

'Maksim, I know you reckon Dee's a woman with lax

morals, but I can assure you I'm not.'

'What a high opinion you have of me! If I thought you were like your friend, I wouldn't have invited you to my home. You should know I wouldn't take advantage.'

'This Mayakovsky, what sort of business is he in? I thought the Mafia hype was only in books?'

'Some of it's true. He runs what the Western media – you – choose to call a protection racket.'

'So he takes money from the bar owners?'

'He takes money from anyone who's raking cash off the tourist trade. That's what gets Kuzkuz so wound up. Mayakovsky is a rich man because of Westerners. Even the stallholders in the street. I bet some had set up beside your ship before the gangway was down – how do you think they managed to be there when the police move the others on all the time?'

He suddenly seizes both my hands and waltzes me round on the pavement.

'They were no more than seventeen or eighteen most of them,' I say. 'It's small change they get for their junk.'

('Bet there's not much these girls wouldn't do for dollars,' Dee said as we left the ship. 'Probably the boys too. A few of the old geezers on board might get lucky. Presumably why they call it hard currency.')

'A cut out of enough change adds up,' says Max. 'And he supplies the crap they sell. You don't imagine there's a posse of craftsmen making matriochka dolls of Clinton and Yeltsin, or that all these Red Army hats came off real soldiers?'

'So how does Zhenya know him?'

'Used to work for him, so did I. We were musicians, in one of the big hotels. Not the sort of place I could have afforded to have a beer, never mind eat there. But the western tourists wanted Tchaikovsky while they stuffed their mouths.'

'And you quit on such a promising career?'

No smile. The waltz ends.

'Mayakovsky owned the instruments. He wouldn't let us practise. Said the punters wouldn't know the difference if we played a few bum notes. I wouldn't work that way, neither would Zhenya. We cling to the remnants of pride.'

'So this Mayakovsky is who you sold the cello to? If he'd let you practise you'd still have been working for him?'

'Don't take that tone. You'd have done the same. It's not fun to be hungry, Serena. Let's change the subject. We're nearly home. You'll soon be warm.'

Now it's Grannie's voice running in my head. *Men were put in the world to cause women pain, and women were put in the world to tempt men from the straight but narrow path. The very first book of the Bible tells us this. You're living proof, aren't you, look at the harm you've caused, and you barely ten years old…*

Baltiyskaya District, St Petersburg 17th June, 3:00 am
'Home,' announces Maksim, leading me to the doorway of an exquisite Empire-style building with faded primrose walls. I've become increasingly dismayed as we left the smart centre of the city. I'd call this a slum, not at all what I'd expected. But at least there are people about. That's what troubled me earlier, among the deserted streets of Vasilievsky Island; the feeling nobody's at home, or if they

are they certainly won't answer the door; they watch, from behind half-closed shutters.

He opens the street door, the posh entrance, and motions me into a soot-dark hallway.

Rape, abduction, white slavery, embarrassing diseases; you know nothing about him, he may be a criminal, an anarchist-communist-drug-dealing-abortionist, filthy creatures, blah, blah, blah, sings Morag-in-my-head.

Max releases my hand, and moves away from me. 'I won't be long.'

'Don't leave me here in the dark. Where are you going?'

'Out the back. Call of nature.'

'Isn't there a toilet?'

He's laughing at my panic. 'Of course there is. A lot of us have to share though.'

Russian chivalry. When he comes back he draws my hand into his again, and must feel how I recoil.

Another of my mother's phobias: ice cream that wasn't from a shop. *Where do they do their business when they're out in these vans all day? They pee in empty lemonade bottles and throw them out the window. And do they wash their hands? You're much mistaken, my girl, if you think I'm letting you put anything in your mouth after they've touched* that.

I grip Max's fingers firmly.

'It's so dark. Isn't there lighting?'

'People borrow the bulbs. You're not afraid of the dark, surely?'

He holds my hand reassuringly while we climb four flights that smell of cooked cabbage and raw tomcat. At the triple-locked front door he produces a jailer-sized bunch of keys. Once inside it's a haven of panelled mahogany and parquet floors. Max takes his shoes off at once, and I pad along the corridor after him. Memory sinks its claws in small details: Proust and his tea-dipped madeleines, soft footfalls in Russian homes.

'You live in a mansion and I live in a wee house built for artisans,' I say. 'Communism's alive and well!'

But Max's territory is rather less than half of a larger room, partitioned with plywood, austere enough to make me shudder. A mattress on a wooden frame – you couldn't call it a bedstead, but it looks clean – and two insubstantial blankets neatly folded on top. A narrow cupboard, a small table with a lamp, a wooden chair and a dilapidated armchair. No visible source of heating. Numbing to think this is all he has.

'Don't you like it?' he says. 'I am a free man. There's nothing to steal. In the suburbs I could have a flat of my own. But I love the old city. Life must be about more than living space. My home has soul.'

'It must be freezing here in winter. How do you keep warm?'

'We're very civilised. We have central heating. Look.'

He reaches up to tap a set of hideously corroded pipes I hadn't noticed, because for some reason they're almost at ceiling-height. They don't look as if they'd retain liquid.

'I wouldn't like to be near one of these with hot water passing through it,' I say.

'It's quite safe. They test them every few years, under pressure. Usually only a handful of fatalities.'

I know he's teasing me, but it makes my flesh creep to

picture him there in December, shivering under a thin blanket, or scalded by a boiling jet from a burst pipe.

'My feet are filthy,' I say. 'Where's the bathroom?'

I noticed on the way past it's a Virginia Woolf loo, with a Room of its Own.

'Sit down. I'll bring water.'

He kneels on the floor and washes my feet gently, stroking my ankle.

'It's only bruised,' he says.

'Have I got tar on my toes, from the tramline?'

I used to all the time when I was a child, off the road. When my Aunt Peigi was home in the summer, she'd rub my feet with butter to get it off, the same as she'd do to the cat's paws. *Tinker's child*, Morag would say. *Do you think I want the whole village saying I can't afford to put shoes on you?*

Maksim caresses my feet fleetingly as he dries them.

'No tar. You have very pretty toes. All yours.' He gestures to the bed. 'Make yourself at home. Take both blankets. I've slept on a chair often enough, I'll be fine, I'll put a jacket over me.'

'Who's next door?'

I can hear them talking quietly to each other, a man's voice and a woman's. The walls must be the thinnest ply money can buy.

'Oleg and Maria; ordinary people, about our age. Brush out your hair. It's bad for you to sleep with it plaited.'

I've never grown out of wearing it like this, even though Fergus used to say we looked like Willy and Colette.

'Have you a brush?' asks Max.

I grab my bag. 'Yes. Here.'

He kneels on the bed and grooms my hair, the way no one has done since I was ten. He runs his fingers through it, weighs it in his hands, strokes it. My throat is tight with conflicting emotions.

'Serena,' he whispers, 'I love the sound of your name. Serena with the mermaid's hair. Did you know that's what it means in Russian? Mermaid.'

Does it hell. There's a world of difference between a siren and a mermaid. I lure sailors to their deaths in any case. I'm trembling. I'm afraid he'll notice. He stops brushing.

'Lie down now,' he says sternly. 'Take off some of your clothes, or you'll be uncomfortable. I'll leave you for a moment.'

And he leaves abruptly, while I struggle to think what I've done to offend him.

When he comes back, he switches off the lamp at once. I try to sleep, but the neighbours are still chattering. Besides, I feel guilty and miserable.

'You could lie down here too, Maksim,' I say in a small voice. 'There's plenty of room.'

'You wouldn't mind?'

'I'm stealing your bed. You saved my life. How could I mind?'

I hear him unbuckle his belt, and remove clothing, and then he stretches beside me, gingerly, on top of the covers. I turn my head to try to see him in the dark, very close, for there's only one pillow.

'You know what,' he whispers, 'if you save someone's life you're responsible for them. Do they believe this in

Scotland too?'

'We just pass by on the other side to avoid thinking about it. Goodnight. I'm tremendously grateful to you.'

There's a disconcerting scrabbling and rattle of claws on wood, loud in the darkness.

'Is that a rat?'

'It can't get inside the room. It's in the wall. It's only a small mouse.'

I know a rat when I hear one. But I lie down again, and he settles at my back.

'You'll be cold,' I say. 'Please – you must get under at least one blanket.'

He wraps his arm round my waist in a way that invites no argument and holds me tight and secure.

'There. No mouse can come near you.' He sighs a little, wondering, no doubt, who decreed it was his duty to snatch me from the path of trams, protect me from rodents, give me his bedclothes. Suddenly he sits up, leans over and kisses me gently and briefly on the mouth.

'Goodnight,' he whispers.

My hormonal system gets stuck in overdrive. Spontaneous human combustion. All that'll be left in twenty minutes will be a wee pile of ashes and my feet, which are always too cold to burn. I don't know which of us is more startled when I squirm around to kiss him back, not a friendly kiss or a grateful one, but hungry, thirsty. I seek him the way firelighters seek flames, craving the sensation of his bare skin against mine, all over, outside, inside, everywhere.

The couple next door choose this moment to begin.

Squeaky bedsprings and heavy breathing I might have coped with, but not running commentary peppered with exhortations.

Sweet God, they'd hear us too. The entire building must be able to hear. Possibly my impromptu bout of lust set them off. Oleg was just faster on the draw. An alternative version of the gunfight scene from *High Noon* begins rolling in my head, and I draw away from Maksim so precipitately I roll off the bed and lie there while Maria caterwauls and yelps, my fist stuffed in my mouth to drown the laughter.

Poor Oleg doesn't get any good lines, just stage directions. *Slower. There. Yes! Yes! Hold onto it. Yes, yes, yes!* Making up for lost time, if the *Cosmo* article Dee was quoting at me earlier has its facts straight. Or else she's popping her cork for the entire Russian nation.

I sit up, struggling to fight down the vibrations in my throat. Max leans across without speaking, pulls me back onto the bed, swaddles me as if I'm a baby, and lies cuddled against my back. He draws his fingers gently over the side of my face. When he realises I'm giggling rather than weeping, it sets him off too.

'Joke,' he whispers in English. 'The police arrest a man, and say: "Are you going to come quietly?" "I always do," he says, "I live in a communal flat." '

What a man. All the expensive education I got, and there's no way my command of colloquial Russian holds a candle to his of my language. How on earth did he manage to learn so well? We lie like naughty kids, blanket stuffed in our mouths. I could never laugh in bed with Fergus. It's more intimate than sex. But I grow sad imagining how it must be to lie alone night after night, listening to the neighbour having her pipes reamed less than a yard away.

'Are you OK?'

'Yes,' says Max sleepily.

I don't have (will never have until it's too late) the words in either language to explain to him how it is with me. That the fact I baulk at *doing* it doesn't mean I don't feel the urge to.

Sins of the flesh. What the MacKenzies called any impulse for loving that wasn't a story in a romantic novel or a soap opera on TV. My mother had a Cairn terrier bitch; Terry she called it. She'd not have her spayed, so the creature came into season every month or two, and all the dogs in Balvaig would arrive at the house, howl, pee on the walls. They'd smell her on me too, if I went out. When I was four or five a collie set its huge black paws on my shoulders and humped my leg. I screamed louder than ever when I saw white globs running down over my sock.

'Mammy, the poor dog's burst, its insides are coming out.'

She told all her pals, and I heard them snigger together. But clearest of all I remember the wee bitch herself, rubbing her belly along the carpet with her inflamed crotch stuck in the air. Morag the man-hater would kick her hard. 'Quit it, you disgusting brute.' And she'd lock Terry in the cold, dark shed.

I can't sleep, wondering where Dee is – back on the *Fortuna*, cursing me for a double-standard slut, or lying with Kuzkuz in another bed, crushed under the weight of his big body, or astride him, a mad horsewoman, acting out one of her fantasies, the sex-goddess who can't get enough of it.

'Do you think Dee's gone home with Zhenya?'

Max grunts.

'She would, you know.'

'You came home with me.'

'It's not the same.'

'I know. Sleep now. We'll find them later.'

I fight to stay awake – for God's sake, I don't know whether my friend's safe back in our cabin or out in the night with a maniac – but I'm so comfortable, I doze in the warm circle of Max's arm, letting my fickle, treacherous body mould itself against his, while I dream I'm at home in Balvaig, in Granda's house, in my own bed, and this man with me…

When we were all at Kingdom, the MacKenzie family home in Balvaig, Granda wouldn't let my mother sleep with her husband. Better to marry than to burn, is it indeed? Well, Peter MacKenzie was the man who knew all about putting out fires. So in my earliest memories, when my father visited us in Balvaig, he was banished to a narrow iron bed in the wee back room where Grannie usually slept. Morag and I slept upstairs, in what had been Aunt Peigi's bed till she went to Canada, across the landing from Granda's room. Even once we moved to Glasgow, Frank's periods of residence were sporadic. It wasn't until I was transformed into an urban child and befriended by Deirdre McCulloch I learnt that other people's parents slept in the same room in the same house, never mind the same bed. She questioned me closely about Frank and Morag.

'He doesn't live with you?'

'Not all the time.'

'And you call him Frank, not Daddy?'

'I've always called him Frank.'

She puffed out her cheeks. 'I'd say he's not your father then.'

But of course he was my father.

'My family's not the same as yours,' I said.

I don't blame the old folks. The tenderness was bred out of them from the days their ancestors were herded like beasts and their homes burnt over their heads while the police and the factor looked on. A raw religion, theirs, and its kirks nearly empty now, though it still has its claws in me.

What mattered most when I was a child was that I didn't get an Easter egg when the kids whose grandfathers weren't Free Kirk catechists got theirs. *It is a solemn time*, Granda would say. *Your Saviour has spent His death-agony for you, His precious blood running down, and you wheenging for sweeties to rot the teeth God gave you.* And I knew if I as much as opened my mouth to protest he'd lock me in the old shed that used to be the toilet and still smelled of it, so I wouldn't grow up thirled to the sin of anger.

I know fine what they said in the village when Fergus and I parted, though Peigi, her face white as bone, tried to make me believe it was someone else they were sniggering over. Old Peter put a hex on his daughters, they said, he cursed them so they'd never find happiness in a man's bed. And there's Morag's daughter gone the same path. Even unto the second generation.

They pulled down his tinpot church last year.

I wake with a start. I'm desperately hungry; I could just murder a slab of *Dairy Milk*. Max sleeps so silently and still, I have to lay my hand across his chest to reassure myself he's still breathing. It's enough to waken him.

'Max – I don't suppose you have any chocolate?'

'Chocolate? No, sorry.'

Then I remember I've half a bar hidden in my bag, because Dee doesn't approve of sweeties either. I slip from the covers and fetch it. 'Want some?'

I can sense him smiling in the darkness. 'You can't eat chocolate in the middle of the night.'

'I'm hungry. Do you want a piece?'

He nuzzles my fingers as I slide the chunks into his mouth, and I find I've managed to burrow under his bit of blanket as well as my own. He turns his back to me, and draws my arm round his waist, clasping my hand. So very thin. I can feel his ribs.

We doze again with our heads pressed together on the pillow, united by the safe, comforting taste of milk chocolate.

Max shakes me awake softly. I'm disoriented. I haven't slept so soundly since… since I can't remember when.

'Come with me. We'll get clean before the others are up.'

In the kitchen, we wash and dry each other as

innocently as cats, still half-clothed. He cleans his teeth, and proffers the brush hesitantly.

'You don't mind?'

'Certainly not, if you don't.'

Not another person in the world I could share a toothbrush with, not my mother, not my friends, never Fergus or any other man. But this is how it seems to be with Maksim.

'You have the most beautiful eyes,' he says. 'They're like flowers.'

I revise my opinion of the colour of his. Warm amber. Even his skin is far too smooth and beautiful and tawny golden to belong to a man.

'How do you keep so clean in a place like this?' I ask him.

'The banya. The one Russian tradition worth keeping. Shall I take you there later? Surely you have them in Scotland. Saunas? The best thing in the world for your health. It's where the babies would be born in Karelia. The cleanest place in the village.'

I grin to myself, thinking about the alleged health benefits of Edinburgh's saunas.

In his room once more, he dresses modestly, with his back to me.

'Hasn't Zhenya got a mobile phone?' I ask.

Max smiles and shrugs. 'We don't go in for such things.'

I've been trying Dee's over and over; it goes straight to voicemail.

'The battery's probably flat,' says Max. 'Please stop

worrying. I know Zhenya, and he won't let her come to any harm. They're probably still out enjoying themselves.'

17ᵗʰ June, Vasilievsky Island, St Petersburg, 10:00 am
Dee hasn't been back to the ship; no one's heard from her, but the tour manager doesn't seem perturbed.

'It happens,' he says. 'As long as both of you are here before we sail tonight. Aren't you coming with us on today's tours?'

It's a little eerie to be in our cabin, just me and Dee's shoes. I have to wipe my eyes as I survey the collection. I put on my own most comfortable pair, after toying with the idea of borrowing some of hers. Twelve pairs. On school trips, when pupils were restricted to one case each, Dee would make everyone pack a pair of her shoes, and she'd be late down every morning, deciding which to wear. She'd rate a change of shoes higher than clean knickers.

Automatically, I replace the top on her pot of Guerlain Hydrabella, which I know cost her more than my mother ever earned in half a month's work. It's lying open as usual. I keep telling myself I'd *know* if anything bad had happened to her. We've been friends since we were ten, after all. Never so terribly close, but still…

Because I can't see any alternative to waiting patiently for Dee to turn up, I let Maksim Grigoriev take me on a city-centre sightseeing tour. We visit Peter the Great's log cabin.

'He married a woman who'd been a slave,' says Max,

shining-eyed, 'and he was miserable if he wasn't working. Kings, diplomats, no matter who, they had to talk to him while he worked in his shirtsleeves at the lathe.'

I smile politely, caught up in how clever I am to have bitten my tongue before telling him: *I know*. Peter's city. Its citizens call it that again — they always did, in their hearts. "Peter", they say, and there's devotion in their voices, laced with cynicism. Not another city on earth so entrancing, though as many people live in it as in the whole of Scotland, and its maker was no saint. The new brides still lay their flowers at his feet, Peter, the rock, on his high rough plinth of granite, his horse rearing, trampling the serpent for ever and ever and ever, as he gazes out across the Neva at what he started.

Strange that he's Max's hero. Big Peter. A huge man with coarse, calloused hands and a coarse, callous sense of humour; an enormous, perambulating stick of testosterone. And he was a cruel man, but it's part of the attraction, always has been. I've read about the Polish officers at Katyn, and the collaborators at Babi Yar, and I know what they did in Hungary, in Czechoslovakia, in Berlin. I've seen the documentary pictures of the German prisoners face down in the mud with their balls hacked off, and I know it's bad still and there's worse to come. History judges them harshly; in my eyes, they can do no wrong. *Frank Stuart must be the only man in the Western hemisphere who gets a hard-on reading about Stalin's purges*, I overheard my mother say to Peigi when she believed I was too young to understand. Mine is a dangerous heredity on every side.

Max and I climb the three hundred steps to the viewing

platform of St Isaac's, and study the old city spread beneath as intricate as a tapestry (it's possible to avert the eyes from the drear grey high-rises beyond). So much silent water, where Peter made them manhandle the Neva into an elegant open granite coffin, and all the other water of the swamp too, until there are fifty artificial rivers, somnolent and vindictive and trapped in prisons whose walls offer no grip to the nails. How can you contain the waters that lie under the earth? Fifty waterways, forty-two islands, with almost three hundred and fifty bridges tying them together like rafts. So many bridges, so much misery, so many ghosts.

'Built on bones,' the geography teacher from Hazelpark told us in 1985. 'Peter the Great, Stalin, the war. Built on bones.'

For years after, my dreams swam in canals filled with enormous blind carp which had gorged on eyeballs and human flesh. No good can come from imprisoning rivers. A suicide's paradise, as long as you're not wearing anything to catch on the wrought iron as you clamber over, trapping you like an inept acrobat. You could stand swaying on a parapet and no one would intervene. It's not London where a stranger might cajole you down and buy you a cup of tea, or Amsterdam where a jovial Dutchman would fish you out with a boat-hook, or Bruges, where Japanese tourists would click cameras while you drowned; *Look – a pageant. A re-enactment of the tragic lovers in the Minnewater.*

In St Petersburg no one would push you. They'd pause a moment to give you an opaque, calculating, sideways glance – same as New York; no eye contact. Then the shrug. People with money in their pockets don't jump in the river. They'd walk on. Not a head would turn when the splash came. And I used to wonder why no one prevented Anna Karenina from going too near the edge in the first place!

Max's fingers are warm as life round mine.

'It's so beautiful,' I say. 'You love this city, don't you?'

He picks up the regret in my voice, and smiles wistfully.

'I adore it. I've never lived anywhere else. If it doesn't break your heart you're lacking one. Built in heaven and dropped on the earth in one piece, that's what they say.'

'We should go back to looking for Dee. I suppose you know Zhenya from the Conservatory, if he's a musician?'

He looks surprised. 'No, he's a lot older than me. We met in the army.'

'You were a soldier?'

'For a little while. Practically all of us were, in Chechnya. We weren't given much choice.'

'I wouldn't have thought you'd approve of that war.'

'I'm not a coward.'

'So Zhenya and you killed people?'

'Nearly got killed, most of the time. He helped me out of a few spots before we both took ourselves the hell out of it. I owe him. OK? Let's change the subject.'

'How do you mean "took ourselves out of it"? You mean you deserted?'

He glowers at me, squeezes my hand so hard it hurts, and tells me to shut up. We walk on until I'm exhausted. So many walled-up, hopeless faces, such contrast between the bleakness of ordinary lives and the gold leaf dripping off the palaces and museums. And no sign of the Merc or its occupants.

The *Fortuna* is due to sail just before six. Max and I stroll back and forth across my picture-book bridge till I see them starting to untie one of the gangways.

'Go,' he says. 'You can't do any more to help. I'll find her. There's only five million people after all.' He caresses my shoulder. 'You've cast a spell on me. I can visit you, if you'll let me. There's a thread between us that won't be broken.'

Earlier we discussed, in a bantering way, the possibility that he could get a visa; he carefully wrote down my address.

'I have to go back on board for a minute or two. Will you wait?'

'I'll be here till the ship sails.' He kisses me hard; a farewell kiss.

'Let me have one last try at persuading them to wait for Dee,' I say.

I trot back and forth between ship and shore, trying to get the bored officials to help me. The surly green-uniformed dame in the passport control shed with its stupid slanting mirror makes a three-act pantomime of gazing carefully at my passport photo, then at me, each time I pass. Madwoman! I want to club her over the head. Police are summoned, but they don't bother to take off their sunglasses, and the tour manager is still too nonchalant for his own good.

'We have a schedule to keep,' he says, 'and so does the port.'

My knee twitches with desire to make contact with his groin.

'You're not proposing to leave her behind?'

'She'll turn up. She has her passport with her. She can fly on and rejoin the ship at Tallinn.'

'She's been kidnapped, you moron!'

'What nonsense. We've been bringing tourists here for years and I've never heard of a single one having that sort of problem.'

Paolo Conti puts in an appearance, lays his hand on my shoulder in an avuncular way, and speaks to me as if I'm a naïve five-year-old, addressing me throughout as "Miss Stuart" (never got around to having my passport altered to either Fergus's name or the one I'd decided to use professionally). I want to tell him to piss off, but instead I smile enigmatically, make the purser cash the largest cheque I dare to write, pack a bag quickly with essentials, and totter down the last gangway, already half-untied. Men on the ship and the quayside yell and swear at me in a variety of languages.

Max grins and shakes his head when I reach him.

'Idiot,' he says. 'Incurable romantic, I thought you were sure to fall in the water. I'd have had to rescue you again. And I can't swim.'

'What do you mean you can't swim?'

'Some old witch — a fortune-teller — told my grandmother I'd die by drowning. So she wouldn't let me learn. "It'll be a quick, gentle death this way," she'd tell me. "It's the swimmers who drown slowly, in agony." '

What a silly idea! I make a mental note to teach him to swim. Not in a chlorinated pool though. I've never been able to stomach the smell.

I watch in relief as the last ropes are loosed, and the *Fortuna*'s bow-thrusters start to churn the dirty river water, as she steers out into the middle of the river. No time now to regret what I've done, or change my mind. Fait accompli. In any case, I'm still a little spooked by the Baltic after the *Estonia*.

Max's eyes are warm, and he hugs me so hard I know he's glad in his heart. We sit on the embankment wall, beside the over-optimistic fishermen. 'Do they actually eat fish out of there?' I ask dubiously, but Max says if you're hungry you eat anything. We watch the *Fortuna* get under way. Paolo's on the bridge, of course, and he doesn't so much as glance in my direction. "Captain": I used to find the term reassuring. A captain looks after you. The bastard doesn't look my way. Don't know what I expected from a divorced man who still wears his wedding ring. ('Security fence,' he told me, grinning.) He's playing a part. The company probably pays extra to get a handsome man, to keep the women passengers coming back for more. He'll be on commission from the on-board photographers.

'You said you had some cash?' mumbles Max. 'Let's eat.'

I make him take a handful of notes.

'For safe keeping,' I say, hating Russia for humiliating him.

He eats like a starved wolf, scarcely chewing the meat before he swallows it. Then he looks apologetic. It breaks my heart to see it. I have an urge to look after him I never experienced for Fergus.

I spend another night snuggled in Max's bed, and once again he seems content to cuddle rather than trying anything more. I'm a poor enough friend to fall asleep instead of lying awake worrying about Deirdre.

Nevsky Prospekt, 18th June, morning

'Are you absolutely certain Zhenya doesn't have a mobile phone?' I ask Max.

'I'm sure he doesn't. Costs too much. And too easy to trace.'

I don't find this reassuring.

'So how do we find him?'

'He'll get in touch, I promise you.'

'Dee has a mobile. I don't know why she hasn't tried to contact me.'

'I told you. Probably the battery's flat.'

'We need to go to the police.'

'You already saw how interested the police are.'

I don't find that reassuring either.

'Well, the British Consulate then.'

'Let's wait till this evening. If we still haven't found them, I'll take you to the Consulate.'

We spend another day sightseeing. We wander round the Hermitage – you could visit a dozen times and still not see everything worth seeing. It all melds into one: the paintings, the Fabergé eggs, the tapestries. The babushkas stationed in every room glare at us, and Max glares back. I can see he's not entirely at his ease in such a public place, so we leave after just over an hour.

We trade notes on parents. His lip curls when he mentions his mother.

'My mother never gave herself the slightest inconvenience. I daresay when I was born she took herself into an empty room, dropped me, hitched her skirt down and hailed a passing nurse. "Here – attend to this, will you?" '

Even at lowest ebb, I never felt quite so detached from Morag, though I understand where Max is coming from. I always reckoned my mother must have had the part of the brain where emotions reside neatly excised. Sounds as if his was exactly the same.

On our first evening together, I'd heard the story of his father, dead in car wreck when Max was still a student, the car spinning off a straight road with no obstructions, no ice. A stroke while he was at the wheel, or else he was so drunk he lost control: that was the official version. Max has never believed it. The body was too badly burnt to tell. 'The forces of evil,' he said. 'They're what killed him. Bad things happen to good people in this country, and no one cares.'

'My father was a genuine patriot,' he tells me now, as we stroll among the fountains and statues in the Summer Garden. 'He had a responsible job – an engineer – but my mother never let pass a chance to belittle him. He took it out on me, wouldn't let me start on the cello till I was too old. I'll never be as good as I could have been because I was late starting. It takes twenty years to train a cellist. Same with Nureyev. They didn't let him start to dance till he was well in his teens. His technique wasn't the best; I've heard dancers say so. I don't have his brilliance though, to compensate.'

Even on our brief acquaintance, I know better than to mutter platitudes. Instead, I tell him about Morag and her sister, about Balvaig, about our move to Glasgow the summer after I turned ten.

'And you have no brothers or sisters?'

'None. I have very few relatives. Just my aunt. There's a cousin too, but we never see her. She lives in Poland. And you?'

'I'm the same. Apart from my mother, no one. Tell me why you studied my language at school.'

'My father, Frank. He was besotted with your country. He idolised Yuri Gagarin, of all people.'

'Did he look like you?'

'Not at all. I take after my mother's side. He had reddish hair and brown eyes. And I can't pretend he was an engineer or anything clever. He was a newspaper printer. What they used to call a compositor. He'd been in the navy for a few years, straight from school, then he came out and served an apprenticeship. A real dyed-in-the-wool Communist party member, same as yours.' Much good it did him. They sacked him at the earliest opportunity. On principle he'd have set his mind against every single piece of new technology. 'And he was an alcoholic,' I add.

But he loved books and print, he said the smell of ink was like a drug to him, and he never ceased to marvel that the same letters could be used to typeset the Bible or *Lady*

Chatterley's Lover. The ultimate democracy, he'd say. He introduced me to literature most unsuitable for a primary school child – the Kinsey Report *(Read this,* he told me. *He was a clever man. Maybe if you read it, you won't end up like your mother. Though we have to make allowances for Morag. She was raised by your Grannie, after all…)* Even in conjunction with an ancient Black's Medical Dictionary, I couldn't make head nor tail of it. I think of my father when I find articles about Kinsey's alleged involvement with child abuse. Frank was so hot on exploitation you'd have thought he'd see through Kinsey.

'Same as mine,' Max says. 'Always swimming against the tide and always on the booze. I think our fathers were brave men.'

I never thought of it in that light. Always put it down as selfishness.

Frank gave me my love of words and my obsession with Russia. He also gave me my brief and heady spell of popularity at Hazelpark as the daughter of the man who said the c-word to the headmistress. I shouldn't have been there at all, because he disapproved of private education, but Morag had been hell bent on sending me; Peigi paid the fees. No compromise would satisfy him.

'You've got it in the prospectus,' he said to the Head, his tone still reasonable.

'Serena won't need the Higher to take it at university. They provide an intensive course in first year.' Her big mistake; the condescension in her voice.

'So what do you want her to take instead – German, I suppose? You've forgotten who was the ally, and who was the fucking enemy,

haven't you? What do you think we pay your extortionate soddin' fees for if the girl can't take the subjects she wants? She could take German at the local school without all the fucking expense.'

I tugged at his arm, hissing, 'Dad! Dad.' I was sure I'd be expelled the same afternoon.

'At least we shall do our best to discourage Serena from learning Anglo-Saxon, Mr Stuart,' yelled the Head, puce in the face.

But he was on a roll. *'Maybe you think we send our lassies here so they can wear your scummy uniform? Fetish-fodder for all the dirty old men in Glasgow, like the perverted cunt who followed Serena and her pal round Markies waving his dick at them?'* (Dee had told her parents; I'd never have mentioned it.) *'Making them wear these stupid wee kilts.'*

Frank prevailed over Higher Russian; the Head got her way on the rolling-over of our tartan skirts at the waistband and the lunchtime excursions to Marks and Spencer.

In the end I took English and History at university; the obsession with language had put down roots for I'd grown up with the books Frank left behind when he finally moved out, especially the poetry: Pushkin and Esenin and Akhmatova. He took the *Communist Manifesto* with him – no loss, for it was boring – and the unintelligible Kinsey.

'I was certainly on bad terms with my father at the time he died,' I tell Max.

Frank turned up at my graduation blootered out of his mind, so I was ashamed in case anyone suspected I was related to him. I wept quietly in the changing room. 'Why does he always let me down?' I asked Dee. 'At least he came,' she said, trying to cheer me up.

He was in hospital three weeks later. Not cirrhosis as

my mother had gleefully predicted; subdural haematoma. He'd fallen, hit his head, and been carted off to the Southern General to have a blood clot removed. He took himself home five days later, head still swathed in bandages, and managed to burn his flat down. '*I always said he'd kill himself; smoking when he was drunk,*' Morag said. '*Imagine. The whole place a heap of ashes, not a damn thing left that's saleable.*'

No chance of a damages claim due to negligence either, because he'd signed himself out of hospital, to spite my mother. And worst of all: the fire hadn't been quite hot enough. There was still a body for us to identify, and deal with.

'*What on earth can we do?*' said Morag. '*I suppose we have to have a funeral, and all the expense of a grave. I suppose we could have him cremated. Maybe they'd give us a discount, in the circumstances.*' And we giggled together. I'm hot with shame to think of it even now. In the end, my aunt paid for Frank's funeral.

'And your grandparents?' I ask Max.

'They were happy together, my father's parents. I never knew my mother's. My grandfather still thought of himself as Finnish. They used to have religious services in their own language. A priest who could speak it travelled out from Petersburg. They were old-fashioned people.'

A Finn! That explains the blond good looks.

'Your voice changes, when you speak about them.'

So do his eyes. They become dreamy and unfocused and gentle.

By evening, I'm tired enough to want to turn in early. I've resigned myself to not finding Dee any time soon; I'm still trying to reassure myself I'd have a sixth sense if anything bad has happened to her. We eat out in a cheap café, and lie down again together in his bed. Max settles at my back, his arm around my waist. I haven't had to explain to him – he knows instinctively. I think this is the man I've dreamt of finding all my adult life.

I fall asleep remembering my Aunt Peigi's stories about Twin Flames.

Baltiyskaya District, St Petersburg, 19th June

I wake, consumed with guilt for not losing more sleep over my friend. We spend the best part of the morning and afternoon wandering aimlessly round the city. I'm terrified of being stopped and asked for my ID, because I only have a limited tourist visa, but by dinnertime we've not been approached by anyone who looks remotely official.

We've just finished eating when I spot the car and its driver. I never thought I'd be pleased to see that oaf. But Zhenya is alone.

'Can't tear yourself away?' he asks me.

'What have you done with Deirdre? Because of you, we're stranded here. The ship sailed two days ago!'

'Because of me? Don't worry, she's safe enough.'

'Where is she?'

'My dacha at Pushkin. She was delighted to drive out there with me. Maybe she thought I lived in the palace.'

'Why on earth didn't you get in touch, to let us know where she is?'

He smiles at Max. 'Grishkin has no phone. Didn't he tell you I'd not let her come to harm?'

'Why didn't you bring her back into town with you just now? She'll have to catch a plane.'

'The state she's in they wouldn't let her near a plane yet. I'm buggered if I was having her in this car; I don't want her throwing up all over the seats. Get in.'

Max frowns and hesitates.

'Come on,' I say. 'It's not far, is it? We must collect Dee.'

He holds open the door and we clamber into the back.

Zhenya adjusts the driving mirror so he can look at me. 'So – Grishkin has kept you well entertained?'

'Where did you and Dee get to the other night?'

'We tried a couple of clubs. God in heaven, she can put away the drink, your friend.'

'So you've left her alone in the middle of nowhere for a few days while you swanned into town?'

'What do you take me for? When she sobered up on Tuesday, I took her to Vasilievsky, but the ship was gone, so we went sightseeing. She wanted to go clubbing again at night, and try more vodka. I left her within the last half hour. Anyway, Inna's with her. Poor Inna!'

Zhenya turns off the main road after half an hour, bumping a couple of hundred yards down a rutted track towards birch-woods. The house is disappointing. Not one of the quaint wooden ones you see in old picture books of Russia, but single-block construction with an ugly felt roof.

Inna appears in the doorway, glowering at me. 'You should have come sooner to mop up after your friend. It's not my job.'

Inside it's sparsely furnished but seems relatively clean. I breathe a sigh of relief. Then I spot Dee. I'm so relieved to see her, I fling my arms round her, but she's so out of it I don't think she recognises me at first. She can't even focus her eyes properly. No way she got in such a state through alcohol alone. At least it doesn't look as if he's mishandled her. Her clothes are grubby but all present and correct. Her tights aren't laddered, and I can't see any bruises.

'Are you all right? Did he hurt you?' I ask, but she just mumbles.

I grab her bag. Her wallet and her passport both appear to be intact. Her phone's there, but the screen's blank and it won't switch on.

'Take us back to town, Zhenya,' I say, taking charge. 'She's better now. She won't throw up.'

'Grishkin'll take you. There's not enough gas anyway.'

'You need to get some. I'll pay.'

'Go yourself.'

He chucks Max the keys over his shoulder without looking. Unerring aim. Everything about the man is scary. I've finally figured out what his eyes remind me of: photos of Rasputin in history books.

Max hesitates. 'I'm not keen to drive you around in that car any more than I have to. Will you wait here with your friend? Zhenya – you'll take care of both of them.'

'For God's sake, just go and get fuel,' I press money

into his hand as tactfully as I can. 'I have to get her away tonight.'

Max leaves hurriedly. His pal has vanished too. As soon as Zhenya reappears, I'm right in his face.

'And you! Why did you get Dee in this state, you bastard?'

He snatches me off my feet. I thump his chest as hard as I can, but it feels like hitting a brick wall.

'She's a big girl, I think she makes her own decisions. You learnt Russian at school?' His laughter sounds as if it comes from under a great depth of water. 'Progressive school! I prefer a woman who fights and curses. You and I can have fun together sweetheart. See the size of my butt? Takes a big hammer to drive a big nail. I daresay the cellist's rosined his bow?'

'Maksim's a gentleman.'

'Just as well I'm not. Don't worry – I'm not too keen to grease my axle anywhere I might catch a dose. I watch myself with the ones who have the front door open after a couple of drinks. I prefer the shy ones, like you, Serena. I'm all for safe sex. You have beautiful hair, haven't you, sweetheart? Lovely long thick hair. And eyes the colour of ice-flowers. We'd be good together. Calm down. I'm teasing you.'

He flops into a settee and draws me down beside him. His grip feels as if it's cracking my bones and he has a scar across the palm of his right hand; it cuts into me like a leather strap. Utterly foreign, he seems, in a way that Max could never be. I don't know what he's on, but I do know it isn't legal. I can't believe this is the level Dee has descended to.

'Why were you in Petersburg?' Kuzkuz's tone has changed. Friendlier.

'Holiday.'

'I'm not an imbecile. Why here – why not France or Spain or Italy or Greece? Those are where your breed pass their vacations. Why here?'

'Because Dee fancied it. I've been forever singing its praises. I love this country's history and culture – what it stood for.'

He yelps with laughter. 'It stands for fuck all now. Nobody has ideals any more. We just want cash, a job, a place to live.'

'You have your freedom now. Isn't that good?'

'Sure – we're free to beg.'

'I don't want to see kids and old folk begging any more than you. But your own people have caused it.'

'As long as they make money from parading us, nothing will change. You need a real fright, you lot.'

'Why don't you mug a few tourists? Soon scare off the rest.'

'You get muggings in any city now. Madrid, Paris, even London. I bet they warned you it'd happen to you here. You still got off the boat. The West forgets quickly. They've repaired the palaces and they serve food you could eat in the foreign restaurants. Our people stand in line to sell the clothes off their backs. But not in a spot the tourists might see. The police keep moving the poor bastards on. You think giving us Big Macs is enough to make us forget?'

His eyes are blazing again, spinning in his head. Dee seems to have fallen asleep, and there's no sound of Inna.

I'm peeping through a window that has been sealed up for many years, and any minute it will slam shut again.

'You have visited Kronstadt?' Zhenya sounds moderately sane again. 'I'll take you to see it tomorrow, sweetheart. Warships, hundreds of them, tied up and rotting. People went hungry so these could be built to protect us from the Americans, because the Americans could afford to buy the whole of east Europe; tell them we were their enemies. They didn't need bombs, the Americans. Hamburgers and dollars. So the ships can rust to buggery. No money for fuel for them anyway. No pay for the crews.'

'My father told me you were the good guys.'

'You're sweet,' coos Zhenya, 'the first decent Westerner I ever met. Don't you want to love me? I'm descended from royalty; my mother was a Tajik princess. I'm from an older civilisation than all this crap.' He waves his hand dismissively in the direction of the Catherine Palace.

The ring finger of his left hand is missing above the middle joint. Why haven't I noticed before? Clearly an old would – the stump is completely healed over. I begin to feel a little sorry for him; I prefer maudlin to violent, and right now I feel no more threatened by him than I do passing the knots of elderly winos on Edinburgh's Royal Mile. I still wish Max would hurry back.

'So you've fallen for little Grishkin?' he says. 'Your Max who's such a gentleman – and he is, Serena – if you've nothing, extortion's no crime. His father was a good man, strong principles, afraid of no one. We need men like that.

Yeltsin should have had a bullet in his gizzard long before this.'

'I thought people our age were all for Yeltsin? The tour guides think he's wonderful.'

'It's because they've bought into the system.' Now he's rambling again. 'Fucking Europe. They're so busy with their snouts in the trough they don't give a toss about anyone else. Look at Bosnia. Look at the whole mess; they'll let all the rest go to buggery while they worry over their eco-fucking-nomic union. All I ever wanted to do was fight for my country and earn my bread playing music. You want to see my guns? I have quite a collection.'

I hear car tyres scrunch on the track. Max bounds in, rubbing his hands.

'Let's get the girls back into town. They have to go home.'

'We could make us some cash, Grishkin. We could get their people to pay a modest finder's fee.'

'We could get ourselves killed. Are you driving?'

'Stay tonight. They can't travel anywhere at this hour,' says Zhenya. 'I have no intention of going out again.'

'Now.' I hiss at Max, 'you and me and Dee.'

Zhenya shrugs. 'You keep the car meantime.'

We manoeuvre Dee into the back, and I slide into the passenger seat, beside Max.

'Go, go, go! He's deranged, your pal. He's on drugs too, isn't he?'

Max grimaces as he starts the car. 'He saw enough things in the war to drive anyone out of their mind. His kid brother blown to pieces right in front of him. Can you imagine? Your brother's brains and guts spattered in your face? I have nightmares about it still. You kill one of theirs, and they'll find you. I used to wake up wondering if I was dead.'

'I presume that's how he lost his finger?'

'Hell, no. We both came through the army unscathed. Relatively. His wife did it, when she flipped.'

'Is Inna his wife then?

'No! He was married to a real bitch of a woman who tried to knife him while he was sleeping.'

'What happened to her?'

'He grabbed the knife by the blade, pushed her arm around, and cut her own throat with it. Afterwards, he called the police.'

This makes sense of the scar too.

'Why isn't he in prison?'

'No case against him. Self defence. Enough of their neighbours testified they'd seen her with the knife – it's not unusual you know, plenty similar cases here, women murdering their husbands. She had the knife, she started it, no one disputed the facts.'

'She cut off his finger?'

'Silly bugger wouldn't have it seen to. It turned septic and started to rot.'

He's driving faster and faster, but I'm not afraid. It puts the miles between us and Pushkin.

'And this paragon's your best friend?'

'Christ, Serena, I'm not condoning it, but the man lived for music. His hand was so badly damaged he can't play properly and it affected his mind. He had a great gift. Just coming into his prime.'

'You left me with a junkie who cuts up women?'

'You were safer with him than in a stolen car with me. He'd not have allowed anyone to come near you. If you want to worry, start worrying now. If Mayakovsky's sidekicks are around we'll see about getting cut up.'

'Zhenya needs treatment.'

'I know. The only treatment he'll get is a bullet in the back of the head.'

'Why do you associate with him, with these people? You seem different; you're not like them.'

'More alike than you think. I daresay I'm not much use to him.' He brakes abruptly. 'You can't know what it is to live in this country, Serena, with too little food, no real home, no one to help you. It's a wonder more of us aren't criminals; they're the only ones with money. The rich pay no taxes in Russia. Nothing new in corruption; every last Communist official was crooked, but not the ordinary people. Jesus, what I've done, merely to live.'

He lays his head on his hands on the wheel. I'm so taken aback I can't find the right words to say; I stroke his neck, and then, just as suddenly, he cheers up.

'Maybe I'll end up dead for stealing a Mercedes Benz. Excellent car. I prefer this to a BMW. Last time a mafia boss got blown away hundreds of these turned up at his funeral; downtown Petersburg was gridlocked with fancy cars, while the old women tried to sell the shoes off their feet on the pavements.'

This is something I've forgotten since 1985: the roller-coaster of the Slavic temperament.

We draw up at the entrance of the British consulate; I help Deirdre out of the back seat and point her in the direction of the doorway. I wait till I see the door open. She has promised to phone me as soon as she's home. She won't mind having to fly, and she always has plenty of slack on her credit cards.

'Serena, you've found your friend,' Max turns to me, 'it's time to go home now. I have to leave you here and dump the transport while I have the chance. I can send your things on from the flat. I have your address.'

'I don't want to say goodbye like this. I don't know when I'll see you again. Drive a little way so we can talk. Please, Max.'

He gazes at me, sighs, and drives towards the river. We stop in a secluded street. I need quiet to think. I need to tell him gently about the plans I've been shaping in my head since the second day I knew him.

'Max – suppose I stay on here?'

'How can you?'

'I have enough money to last for a few weeks. I could get a job teaching English. Maybe I can even get a job as a journalist. The BBC has people in Russia. I can apply for a visa to stay, for a few months at any rate.'

He slides his arm round my shoulders and laughs. 'If you stayed, where would you live?'

I try not to hesitate or show disappointment.

'I'll find my own flat.'

'Without me? Who'll protect you from mice?'

Tomorrow he can teach me to haggle for food in the market. There are supermarkets too, the same as home.

He's frowning again. 'I couldn't expect you to live this way. It's awful. I'm used to it, but you couldn't stand it. You'd be ill for weeks till you got used to the food and the water, then you'd go out of your mind trying to live in a place like my flat.'

He's right. I couldn't survive in a room where I don't know how you'd get out in a fire. But I refuse to become depressed.

'Well, we can find a better place together, if you'd like to.'

'If I could provide for you, I'd like nothing better. There's no future here for a girl like you, no opportunities for you to use your talents. You'd be wasted.' He groans. 'I'm not putting this well. We're not in a romantic movie. I can't conjure up a happy ending here for us, Serena. But go home, and before you know it, you'll get a call from Edinburgh airport to come and fetch me.'

'Max, stop trying to send me away.'

He looks into my eyes for what feels like a long time.

'I suppose I can get a job too.' He has cheered up enormously. 'I'll start looking tomorrow. Employment to bring in enough to keep us. Honest work,' he adds, seeing my frown. 'I've been foolish, wasting my life and all the training when I should have settled down to my métier. I should have joined an orchestra. Perhaps it's not too late. You can apply for a visa tomorrow.'

'If we're both working, it won't be so bad.' We'll make a new life together. Even here, it must be possible. 'It's settled – I'm staying for a while. Let's get rid of the car.'

He massages my shoulder absentmindedly.

They appear without warning from the twilight. It's the noise that frightens me most – harsh voices, shouted commands I only half understand, because they're speaking so quickly – total confusion. They're in uniform, but it's not one I recognise. They carry guns. I catch a glimpse of Max's face, sickly-white, before we're dragged from the car; separated.

I'm spread-eagled against a wall while a lout runs his hands all over my body, up between my legs, over my breasts. He takes his time about it. Then he starts going through my bag. He's disconcerted when he finds my passport and then my press card: all the years I've carried the damn thing, and never once had to show it. Nerves make me want to giggle. He allows me to stand up and I glance round, looking for Max.

They have him face down on the potholed roadway, his beautiful, fragile fingers laced behind his head; bones delicate as a bird's. Just one casual blow from a boot, and he could end up as damaged as his friend. One of them stands over him, a gun pointed casually at his back. I imagine bullets ripping into warm flesh, splintering bone, spurting blood; special bullets, crimped in six places along their edges. Lives still fall light as leaves in this place, even now. What am I thinking of? I wasn't Fergus Learmonth's wife for a year or two without learning a few survival tactics. I dig my elbow into the oaf's ribs so hard I bruise it.

'Is this the way you treat your city's guests?'

'Foreigners shouldn't be in this district at night. Who are you anyway? Why do you speak Russian?'

'I'm a journalist researching a documentary on your

tourist industry. That's why I was lent this car, and this driver. You'll surely get promoted for your contribution to encouraging visitors.'

He falters. No turning back now. 'You were lent this car?'

'Why else would I be in it? You think British journalists steal cars?'

They let Max stand up.

'Now,' I say, 'if you'll permit us to be on our way, we'll forget it. You made a mistake.'

I have fifty dollars loose in my blouse pocket. I press it into his hand, while I fantasise about spitting in his face. 'Thank you for your assistance.'

He half-salutes as we drive away. Max hasn't stopped trembling.

'Bastard,' he keeps repeating, 'I wanted to kill him for putting his filthy hands on you. Shit! I should have killed him. What the hell. I should have grabbed a weapon and let him have it. I'm a good shot. The Russian army gave me that at least.'

'It was no worse than I've had at airports. Don't dramatize.'

After a couple of blocks, Max stops the car again, and we get out. Still swearing under his breath, he goes to the boot and opens it. Inside, there are two green canvas sports bags, unzipped and stuffed with cash, notes spilling over the top; dollars, roubles, Deutschmarks, a numismatist's stockroom. There are taped-up plastic bags too; they could contain anything: drugs, body parts, trash. I want to throw up. We slam the boot shut. It doesn't occur to either of us to help ourselves. Max's face is a death mask.

'Let's get the hell out of this. Do you understand now why I say you shouldn't stay? We need to get you to the airport.'

'And you?'

'I'll lie low for a while till they forget about me.'

'Will you go to your mother's?'

'She has her own life. She'd be really happy to see me, especially if I'd a few thugs at my back. Mayakovsky won't hurt me, not much; amputate a finger or two. Serena!' he adds, forcing a smile. 'This is a large country, plenty of places to hide. I'll be all right. I'm a survivor.'

Another huge car swings round the corner towards us, and for a moment I think Max is going to pass out, he's so pale. The car slides by.

All the years of history, the stylish buildings, the bridges and canals. All gone the way of their literature and their sportsmen and their dancers and musicians, even their circuses, damn it. I'm not thinking straight. But it seems to me that by saving this man I can help save a species on the brink of extinction.

I don't know why I imagined it'd be easy – even possible – for me to find work in St Petersburg. Besides, I have to be able to go on paying my mortgage, and how can I find a tenant for my flat plus rehome a cat from here?

'Max,' I say, 'I have a plan. Let's go back to your flat now and collect our stuff.'

'Maybe not such a good idea to go there.'

'I'll go in. No one knows me.'

He stares at me for a few moments. 'If you're sure. I know you want to collect your bag.'

Clutching his keys, I climb the stairs two at a time, feeling my way against the wall, and manage to unlock the door without making too much of a racket. I empty the contents of my bag on the bed, and then chuck every item I don't absolutely need at Maria's door. I take as much from Max's cupboard as I can stuff into the space that's left: almost all he possesses. There's an old shoebox containing a few photos and letters. I tip the lot in.

'Ah, Katya, welcome home!'

Max's neighbour breezes in without knocking. I recognise her throaty voice.

'Oh! I'm sorry. I thought you were someone else.' She gives me a gap-toothed, knowing smile. 'I thought Katya had come back, when I heard Max had company. Excuse me.'

'I put some things outside your door,' I say. 'Clothes and skin cream. If you can use them, you're very welcome.'

Not a chance she'd get into any of my tops, but she can always pass them on.

'I want to travel light,' I add. 'This Katya – she lives with Max?'

Maria reddens. 'She visits from time to time. Not recently. In fact, I haven't seen her for many months.'

'Ah well. Goodbye. Nice to have met you.'

'Thank you for the clothes.'

She kisses me on both cheeks, then I sprint down the stairs and along the street to where Max is waiting.

'I shouldn't have allowed you to go there alone. Brave

as well as beautiful. I won't let you take any more risks. I'll get you to the airport and you'll be safe.'

'I'm not going near any airport. I loathe flying.'

'Well, the train station then.'

'Who is Katya?' I ask.

He jumps as if he's been electrocuted. 'Katya's there?'

'Maria spoke to me. She thought Katya had come back. Who is she?'

'Someone I used to know.'

'Where is she?'

He wriggles uncomfortably. 'Still at home in Odessa, I suppose.'

'She lives with you?'

'She has slept in the flat from time to time, yes.'

'So you have a woman you live with, expected back any day, apparently?'

'She may come back to Petersburg, but not to me. There's no sort of understanding between us. It's not important.'

'I don't enjoy finding I've slept in another woman's bed.'

'You haven't. You slept in mine. I'm glad you did.'

'What would you have done the last couple of nights if she'd turned up?'

'Slept in the middle, to avoid arguments. It would have been cosy, but we'd have needed to borrow another pillow.'

Frank could always make me laugh too when he was in the wrong. At least Max seems to have got over the worst of his nerves. We head for a bar, to plan our next move.

'Show me a picture of this Katya.' I open my bag and

hand him the photos I've brought.

'Why does it matter? I don't have one, truly. I think you find it difficult to understand the way life is here, for most of us. It affects relationships, families, love. She'll have met someone else many months ago. Sorry. I told you, I don't express myself well.'

'I suppose she's a musician too?'

'She's a violinist, yes. I know her from the days when we were students at the Conservatory.'

What does she holler in bed? *Allegretto ma non troppo – Ritenuto!*

'Why didn't you get married? Start a string section.'

He shrugs and tuts. 'I don't suppose anyone would want to marry me. I have little money, no prospects.'

A Ukrainian fiddler's reject.

'Anyway, I'm not good with commitment.' He grips my wrist across the table. 'If I'd brought you home because I was without a woman, you think I wouldn't have taken what I wanted? It's not what this has been about, and you know it.'

His use of the past tense makes up my mind. That and hearing my father's voice in my head. *No matter what your mother tries to tell you, no country, or its people, could be evil where books cost less than bread. It's a beacon to the rest of the world. If we still had decent men like John McLean, Scotland would have followed her lead long since.*

'I can't leave you in this mess. Why don't you come home with *me* now?'

'To Scotland?'

'To Scotland.'

He shuffles his feet awkwardly. 'I'd need a visa. I'm not properly registered here. I haven't got all the documents I should have, even for our own authorities. Your people know who my father was. He tried to get into Britain in '91 and was turned away. In any case, I swore when I got back from Chechnya I'd never board a plane again.'

'We'll go overland then. Finland isn't far, is it? We could work our way across Scandinavia to the UK from there.'

'You think they would let me in? Anywhere I went they'd stick me on the first plane back. Mayakovsky will send a welcome committee.'

I know he's right. I've seen too many documentaries about airports where hunched men and women with gaunt faces are herded down the long corridor to a sinister plane waiting on the tarmac, their passports stamped: "Deported". Not a chance of ever getting in again.

'They'd let you in if we were married.' The words fly out of my mouth like hornets, stinging him so he winces. Still too soon, Serena, too abrupt.

'I don't believe they would. Anyway, I can't marry. I can't support a wife.' He doesn't forget to be polite. He omits to say he doesn't like me enough. 'Suppose I managed to get out that way, where could I go?'

'Edinburgh. I have a house, with plenty of space for both of us. You can share with me.'

'I don't see how it's possible.'

'It's a way to get you to somewhere you can build a new life for yourself. For God's sake, you're an educated man, a trained musician; you speak two languages fluently.

You shouldn't be having to live like this.'

'But what happens until I can earn? I will not be a burden to you or take advantage of your generosity.' He studies my face. 'You'd really do this, to get me out?'

'It happens all the time,' I say casually. 'Marriages of convenience. It's not a huge deal, in this day and age.'

'So – if you want, we can end it when we get to Scotland? Divorce is as easy there as it is here, I'd think.'

Half a dozen terse lawyer's letters. An official document that should arrive any day now; probably lying waiting for me at home. Easy peasy.

'And till then we'd be husband and wife?' His eyes are glittering. 'We'll live together?'

'We've got on OK so far. I think we could manage to share a house for long enough to get round the authorities. I know you need as much paperwork to get married here as you do at home. You told me you can buy just about anything – could we buy a quick route to a marriage certificate?' I say.

'With enough money, possibly. We could try tomorrow. Tonight we'll stay with Edouard and Anna, friends I can trust, over beside the Finland Station. We'll be safe with them.'

Something's still troubling me.

'Max, how did you know there'd be something in the boot of that damn car?

He looks blank, shrugs. 'Just an impulse. I didn't know there'd be anything at all.'

The other matter chewing at my mind we can discuss in detail on the way home.

Vyborgskaya, St Petersburg, 24th June

We have spent five chaste and uncomfortable nights on his friends' floor, and I'm getting accustomed to living more frugally than I'd have believed possible. It feels like being a student again. This morning, I give Max as much as I dare of the cash I have left. He looks miserable.

'It's only bits of fancy paper,' I say. 'Use whatever you need. However much it takes, if it gets us *both* away to safety.'

As we approach the ZAGS office on Tavricheskaya St, I'm sure I'm going to throw up any minute.

Max will never be able to make me understand how he knew which one to bribe. They both look formidable to me; battleship women stuffed into navy blue suits two sizes too small. He walks confidently and casually up to one of them, while I dither in the background. They enter a long discussion. I don't see the cash change hands although I'm watching with the concentrated attention terror brings, because I should have documents from our government that take many weeks to get; I should also have a copy of the bit of paper which confirms I'm no longer married to Fergus (I haven't even seen it yet myself); my passport should have been stamped at the consulate. I expect to be arrested any minute. Max beckons me over.

'Lucky girl,' coos the official, 'marrying a wealthy man so desperate to have you. Ach, to be so much in love you can't wait.'

She looks rather pointedly at my belly, then pinches my cheek and flashes a mouthful of gold teeth, while Max writes Anna's address under my name on the form. I sign it

in my childish Russian handwriting, using Frank's old
Parker 51, the one he gave me when I was sitting my
Highers. He'd have liked to see me set down a Russian
name with his pen: Serena Lermontova. The first and last
time I've ever used Fergus's surname. It seems a good idea
as I do it; I almost immediately regret it and start to panic
even more. God knows what address Max gives. Not where
he's been living, anyway.

'Beautiful pen,' gold-teeth says bitterly.

Max takes it gently from my hand, and puts the cap on
it. He holds it out to her. 'Here. For you. A gift.'

I open my mouth to protest, but he glares at me so
eloquently I shut it again.

'I'll get you another,' he says once we're out of earshot.

'That's not the point.'

Max shrugs. 'She was going to start making problems
for us. You think she doesn't know what's what? She
wanted it, and I wanted to shut her up. It's only a pen,
Serena.'

He goes to a street-phone, and I nurse the fantasy that
he's phoning his mother. I can picture her; tall and elegant
like him – a strong personality, not much time for men; a
MacKenzie woman in disguise.

'Zhenya will come as our witness,' he says quietly.

So he *does* have a number for him? The sorcerer at the
feast. I resolve to be polite to him, because he's Max's
friend.

Wedding Palace, 25th June

Anna has lent me one of her dresses; rainbow-striped flimsy
cotton, with hundreds of tiny pleats. It's too wide, so she

pins it in at the back. They've also managed to borrow a suit; it almost fits the groom. Zhenya arrives, and buys me bunch of blue scabious from a street stall. He holds them up beside my face. 'They match your eyes,' he says. Pity they clash with the rest of the ensemble. He counts out the blooms carefully, throwing one away to leave an odd number, for luck. Superstitious people, even Max's generation.

Now our ill-assorted party is standing in a dank, magnificent, misnamed 'Wedding Palace' while I stumble through my answers. I still expect the police, or worse, to arrive at any moment.

Max slides Morag's ring – the one I've worn since she died – back on my right hand, and we sashay out, clutching the paper that says I'm Maksim Grigoriev's wife.

'They thought you were just nervous,' Max whispers as we leave. 'Weren't you? I was. It's not every day you get married.'

With borrowed clothes, and paperwork not quite on the level, like Ferdinand and Isabella.

'I'll buy you another ring, I swear it,' he murmurs against my hair as we trail onto the street. 'I'll work till I drop to get you a new one. Expensive wedding, all the same. And this was without a decent dress for you. We should have helped ourselves from Mayakovsky's savings. Perhaps it was his present. Never mind. We have the certificate.'

I have ten exposures left in the camera. Edouard fools around, pretending to be a photographer, then takes the film out carefully.

'Keep it in your bag for safety,' he says. 'For your children and your grandchildren. I can tell. You'll have half a dozen.'

Max has spun his friends some tale about how we've known each other for years as pen pals.

We all drink sweet, lukewarm Russian champagne, standing there in the dusty sunlight, and after a few glasses Max is misty-eyed over the farcical event. 'I'm a married man,' he keeps repeating. He takes my face between his hands and kisses me, but he's laughing, we all are. Play-acting; kids who've found the dressing-up box while the adults' backs are turned. I should have a net curtain for a veil and a ring out of a Christmas cracker.

'Now you have to lay your flowers at Peter's statue,' says Zhenya

But the symbolism of the custom's not lost on me. I still recall the nightmares I had when Frank read me Pushkin's *Bronze Horseman*. Even now, Peter gets the first flowers.

'That old lecher has as much chance of *droits de seigneur* with me as you have Kuzkuz,' I say. 'Anyway, the tourists take photos of the wedding parties. I thought you disliked the idea?'

Tourists from Morningside taking pictures of Serena MacKenzie as a Russian bride, with safety pins all down the back of her gown.

'They only take pictures of the ones in fancy white dresses,' says my new husband bitterly. 'Handsome couple, aren't we? Neither of us in clothes that fit.'

He was so happy a few moments ago, now he's

morose, his friend's arm around his shoulders.

Zhenya slides his hand into Max's pocket. 'I have to make you a gift.'

Wonder whose wallet the gift came out of? Perhaps Dee's. Although the last few days have been a miracle of budgeting, I know we'll need more cash. And I still haven't figured how we'll manage border checks. The two men move a few paces away from the rest of us, and are deep in conversation. They embrace.

'You'll look after him for me?' Now Zhenya hugs me tightly. 'You're a sweet girl. He's made the right choice this time.'

I become weepy. We've all drunk too much. 'I wish we could take you with us,' I say.

'Deirdre didn't get around to proposing. You must visit me one day. We'll go for a long journey into the forests, just the three of us, to look for the white cranes. We might see a pair of them dancing together, Serena, their courtship dance is such a good omen: we'd all live happily for the rest of our lives, we'd never run out of good luck.'

Then he's gone.

The others want to throw a party for us.

'You can't have a Russian wedding without a party,' says Anna. 'Afterwards, we'll move out till tomorrow. You want privacy on your wedding night.'

But Max recognises I'm not up for any further delay, and this isn't a wedding night as his friends imagine it. Another round of drinks and we're back into our everyday clothes, everything else packed in my bag and an old rucksack of Edouard's.

We lay down our pathetically inadequate luggage at the door, and we all sit silently with bowed heads. 'For luck, for an untroubled journey,' says Anna. We could be posing for a refugee relief poster.

They walk with us to the Finland Station to start our journey, because it's too risky by road, according to Edouard.

'Police?'

'Bandits,' says Max, 'long before we get to the border guards at Torfyanovka. We'll be safer in the forest.'

We get off the train at Vyborg, and walk out of the town into thick conifers stretching as far as the horizon.

Fifty metres in, and the forest is so thick it's already twilight. The sweet yeasty aroma of decayed vegetation is as fragrant as bread. The antique scent of woods fills me with nostalgia as well as the fear I've never fully faced up to or expressed.

> *In yon green-wood there is a waik,*
> *And in that waik there is a wene,*
> *And in that wene there is a maike,*
> *That neither has flesh, blood, nor bane;*
> *And down in yon green-wood he walks his lane.*

'You're not afraid?' asks Max. 'You're trembling.'
His fingers are strong and comforting round mine.
'Are there wolves?'

'Wolves, bears, snakes, and monsters. The forest is no fairy tale.' He laughs and shakes his head at me. 'I'll protect you. It's my duty now. My grandparents' home was only a few kilometres away. All this used to be Finland. We're safe.'

But for an accident of history he'd have been born in a different country. We'd never have met.

For the first few hours we walk on soft, mossy ground beneath a canopy of mixed birch and conifers. Not another human being do we meet, but I can feel animal eyes watching us from the undergrowth as we twig-crack our way across the deep silence of star-strewn clearings. I've not known such skies since I was a child.

'You can hardly see the stars properly at home any more,' I tell Max. 'There are only a few street lights on Soma – some in Balvaig, some in Portmore, that's the only town on the island – but even there it's enough to spoil the sky. As for Edinburgh – forget it.'

He looks up, vaguely. 'They're pretty.'

'Don't you get depressed thinking about how the stars are rushing away from us? One day people will look up, and it'll just be unrelieved black. Then we'll be sorry we didn't look lovingly enough while we had the chance. They'll all be gone.'

He squeezes my waist. 'Not in our time, Serena.'

Exhaustion catches up with me. 'I don't think I can walk any further tonight.'

In a clearing, Max gathers wood and builds a substantial fire.

'To frighten off the wolves,' he says, grinning. 'Our

midsummer bonfire. Hold my hand. I'll look after you, I swear it. The fire's my witness.'

There are worse animals in forests though; ones that do not wear fur, ones that look human, right down to their lack of sharp, pointy teeth.

Max makes a quick ring in the grass with his cigarette lighter, scorching a circle where we are to lie down.

'To stop bugs and ticks crawling in. My grandfather'd always do this,' he explains.

It'll shield us from anything more untoward too, because he made his circle sunwise; *deiseil.* In the old days, the Gaels would cast a ring of salt round a new-born baby to ward off the fairies, so they couldn't steal it away and leave a changeling in its place, but the important thing is to form the circle the correct direction. Merely stirring a pan of tinned soup, I have to stir it sunwise.

'We didn't buy chocolate,' he says. 'If you get hungry you'll just have to chew birch bark.'

'I won't be allowed to forget that, will I?'

'Of course not. Here. Let's eat an apple. It's better to peel them, but I didn't bring a knife.'

'I have one.'

He pulls a face at me. 'That's quite a beast. I didn't realise women in Scotland carry knives as weapons. I suppose it's better than a gun.'

I push away the vision of Donald John Munro, the one they called the Daftie, with his trousers round his ankles and the blood running down his thighs in Ollasdale wood; the knife in his hand, the guilt on mine.

'It's not a weapon,' I say. 'It's hardly even big enough

to peel fruit. You never know when a knife can be useful.'

'We'll plant the apple seeds,' Max says, 'then a whole grove of apple-trees will grow, and everyone who passes by will know two lovers spent their wedding-night here.'

Not exactly a propitious symbol where I come from. If Eve had left the apples alone, we'd still live in paradise. 'Tell me about that – is it from a folk-tale?'

He blushes slightly. 'I think they stand for fertility? Probably because one apple has lots of seeds.'

I sit on the woollen rug Anna gave us, leaning against the homely bulk of an old pine. My new husband sprawls beside me, his head in my lap.

I'm torn between a desperate need for sleep and the enervation that comes partly from release of tension, partly from feeling my father would be proud of me, and partly from knowing I've done something that'll make Fergus spectacularly angry – and could yet see me in a foreign prison.

'I knew something amazing would happen to me this year,' Max says, 'because of the lights in the sky in February. Everyone said it was UFOs. I knew it was a sign.'

Signs and portents! At last, someone who won't laugh at my belief in them.

My three-times-great-grandmother Sarah, the matriarch from Skye, apparently refused to get on a boat well over a century ago; the one the landlord had laid on to take them off Skye and off his land and off his conscience, all the way to Adelaide. She marched south to Glasgow instead, her four children at her heels, another in her belly, and her man and dozens more were dead of the smallpox and typhus before the *Hercules* reached Cork to pick up its next passengers. The story in the family is that she'd had a vision of a long procession of weeping women in widows' weeds.

I play with Max's hair, and tell him about the first time I was convinced I've inherited the Second Sight that's supposedly come down through the women on Sarah's side of our family (though my Grannie would have none of it, and more than once she belted me for even speaking of it).

'Fergus – my ex-husband – was researching a documentary about the vice bosses in Riga and Tallinn. He only took me with him to save on the cost of an interpreter. We'd got onto the *Estonia* for the return trip, but I panicked. Fergus wasn't best pleased.' While an interested audience of crewmen and passengers looked on, he'd yelled in my face: *It's because you're too hysterical to go on the sodding plane like a normal person we're on this tub to begin with. Bugger off. Walk home for all I care.* But by then he was spooked too, so he followed me down the gangway. We trailed back into town and had to take a room in the most expensive hotel because it was so late. 'We got off, and on the way to the airport next day we heard what had happened to the ferry.' The only time I knew Fergus to be speechless. 'I've never been convinced it was anything greater than coincidence, and I've always felt guilty.' If I hadn't been so willing to go quietly, more might have been saved, instead of lying curled like larvae, deep and dead in their cabins. 'Fergus said it meant I was a witch, but I know in my heart it was just the Sight, or my guardian angel. You believe in those things, don't you? You're not laughing at me.'

'I believe. You and I have more in common than we

think our parents did. Although we hardly know each other, I feel it,' says Max. 'Tell me more about your family. Your real family, not this *Fergus*.'

'My aunt's been more of a mother to me than her sister ever was, though she was away in Canada most of the time till I was ten. She just came home every summer. My mother and I didn't get on.' Morag's voice echoes in my head. *This is your fault, Peigi MacKenzie, all your primping and vanity, filing the child's nails, and putting ideas in her head about 'halved souls' and suchlike rubbish. You've taught her your filthy ways.*

'And your mother's passed away too? It's sad to part with a parent on ill terms. You and I now, we can learn from their mistakes. You must find me cowardly,' he adds suddenly, 'to flee from my country because life's difficult. I don't want to die young. I always felt I was put into the world to accomplish a worthwhile task, not merely to survive.'

'Not cowardly. Pragmatic. I think you're all pragmatists.' They've had to be. Look at Gagarin, my father's hero: dead at thirty-four in a clapped-out MiG-15. All the way out into space and back, the whole world watching and listening and cheering him on, and they set him to being a test pilot again. The best scientific minds available ploutering about among the dust of Chernobyl in the type of protective clothing you'd put on to sand your floor. Men sent to face German tanks with pitchforks.

Max sighs contentedly. 'The happiest times of my life I spent with my grandparents in a wood like this one. They were happy together, my father's parents. I never knew my mother's. They were old-fashioned people. I wish you could have seen their house – like one in a fairy tale, with carved wood all round the eaves and the most beautiful porch, shutters with hearts and flowers cut out of them. Surrounded by birch woods where you could gather mushrooms, and all sorts of berries, black ones, red ones, purple ones.'

'Blaeberries and cloudberries, perhaps. The climate's not so different at home.'

The forest trees are the same. This could almost be Ollasdale wood. Plenty of birch and hazel, plus conifers, and similar plants in the understorey. Brambles – my favourite taste of all, like eating the earth herself, and the smell of bonfires is the same as that taste, and the autumn mist's the colour smoke from the berries would be. I love to crack each seed individually between my teeth, and savour the sensation. Grannie used to say if I swallowed a plum stone it'd grow into a tree in my gut and burst my insides open. Perhaps a bramble seed slipped through, and what lies tangled in my innards is a briar patch.

> *Kilmeny, Kilmeny, where have you been?*
> *Lang hae we sought baith holt and den;*
> *By linn, by ford, and green-wood tree.*

I wish I could tell Maksim I loved my grandparents too. I have no memory of Frank's parents. I assume they were dead before I was born. Grannie was a figure of terror. They used to call her the Spanish Lady for her black, black hair and exotic looks. Forty-one years of Granda – you don't get such a long sentence for murder. And Granda himself; my strongest memory of him is fear, even before I was disgraced. Bog cotton for hair he had, and eyebrows so long they blew in the wind like a terrier's, for he was an old man by the time I remember him. He'd not married until he was forty, and it was another fifteen years before Morag was born. His eyes were the grey of a winter sea, and as merciless, and his frame had shrunk from the six-foot-four he was in his prime so that the skin hung on him like a rumpled candlewick bedspread.

'This autumn, maybe I can take you over to Balvaig,' I tell Max. 'We can gather as much fruit in the woods there as you want.'

He's silent for a while, but his eyes are sad.

'We could come back here some time too, if we're still in touch, Maksim. You could take me to see their house.'

He slides his hand over mine. 'Their house is gone anyway. The people who took it after my grandfather died burnt the old place down and built a concrete shack as ugly as the one Zhenya has.'

I wonder if he had the chance to say goodbye, either to the house or to them? Granda lingered a year after I killed him with the shame I'd drawn down on the family; more fearsome than ever with his hair whiter than the pillowcase, and his good eye roving maliciously while his mouth dribbled prayers and accusations. We assembled at the deathbed and I saw his soul drift up through the ceiling, blue-grey and insubstantial as peat-reek. No more Granda. No more prayers. No more hope of salvation. Doomed. We all need roots if we're not to end up as restless ghosts.

Max sits up suddenly. 'What do you mean, "If we're still in touch"?'

'Well – once we're in Scotland you'll want to make a life for yourself?'

'My life's to be with *you* isn't it, at least for a little time? Or do you want me to leave you as soon as we get there?'

I can hear scuttling and rustlings in the undergrowth, but I know it's only benign animals. Nothing can harm us in our charmed circle. He relaxes against my knees again.

'Of course I don't. I just chose my words badly.'

'Tell me the story of your husband.'

He changed the subject quickly when I mentioned Fergus earlier, but now he seems ready to hear.

I laugh, avoiding the question that's too hard to answer.

'You can't expect me not to wonder about how you met, why you parted,' he adds.

'I met him by accident, in the middle of Edinburgh. He works in TV. He's quite well-known, in Scotland.'

He sits up. 'You still work with this man?'

'I hardly ever see him. He was with the BBC.' Just a white lie. No need to tell him yet that Fergus had moved to Albion as their senior anchor-man before I met him.

Max doesn't lie down again, but sits cross-legged opposite me, studying my face.

'He found you this work?'

'Why would you think he did?'

'You told me you met him by chance. If you'd worked there, you'd have known him.'

'I got the job after I met him, but it was on my own merits, because I'm classed as a native Gaelic speaker. They couldn't throw enough cash at Gaelic broadcasting a few years ago – it wasn't hard to get a job in media. I've hardly done anything in Gaelic since I got there, though. They only need one newsreader, and they had one already.'

Reclaiming my inheritance. I used to believe it's what justifies my work, but I was misled. They would have hired a talking dog as long as it could manage *'Ciamar a tha thu?'*, and they could claim the subsidy. The word in the office is that Blair's government will cut the funding for it.

'I only asked.'

Stupid to be so snappy over it. 'Hardly anyone speaks Gaelic nowadays anyway,' I say. 'Like your Finnish church services, I should think. Granda used to preach in Gaelic.'

'Your grandfather was a priest?' Max's interest is rekindled. Thank God, it's taken his mind off Fergus.

'Not a real one. What they call a lay preacher, in the Free Presbyterian Church. Very much a minority movement.'

Damn all I could ever find free in it. No proper music, or rousing hymns like other churches, because it was sinful. The old ones hankered after the time they could get away with chaining up the kids' swings on a Sunday, and preventing folk going in bathing. You couldn't hang washing out, and when my mother was young the ones who considered themselves the spiritual elite refused to cook on the Lord's Day. Cold food every Sabbath in the depths of winter, to humble the spirit and crush out sin. And sin was everywhere. Even the old Gaelic rhymes they used to croon to bless the boats and the cattle were anathema to Granda because they'd the reek of papacy. Paganism it was;

reverence to fire and sun as well as Brice and Columba, but I didn't recognise that until I was grown up, and then I laughed to think it was the whiff of incense worried Peter MacKenzie more. He even disowned his brother because he'd married a Catholic.

'It wasn't a real church as you'd imagine one,' I tell Max. 'It was an uninsulated corrugated iron shed painted a dismal dark green, with no organ or any other instrument.'

It's what I hear in my head when I look at the sea though; Gaelic psalms sounding older than history, the precentor's voice spare, pure as salt-bleached bone, and lonely as a tern headed into the wind. I'd look in his face, and it was transfigured, like the faces of saints in paintings. The face of my people, judging the sinners.

'I have no time for organised religion,' says Max, 'though my grandmother had me baptised, secretly. My mother would have killed her. Our women get religion when they're old. The men just take to drink.'

'So you have a baptismal cross, and all the trimmings?' There was nothing of the sort among his possessions.

Earlier, he'd sifted through the papers I'd saved, and showed me his certificate from the Leningrad Conservatory. 'You're a precious angel, to have known this is important,' he said. I could see it was the only item that really mattered to him. He hasn't shown me the photographs.

'I suppose there must have been something of the sort. It's been lost.'

'Won't your mother have it?'

He throws up his hands and laughs.

At Kingdom there are boxes and drawers stuffed with

memories. My teething ring, my first real shoes, all my school reports, photos; my entire life wrapped in tissue paper. (Who saved these though? My mother or my aunt?). I resolve to build a store of mementoes for Maksim. Everything I'll treasure, starting with Edouard's pictures. I'll make it up to him that he has abandoned his history. I forgive him in my heart for the pen.

'All right,' he says, shaking me gently out of my reverie, 'so this husband, this Fergus, didn't get you your job. Why did you stop loving him?'

'I don't know I ever started.'

I used to believe I was the only woman in the land who got married because she couldn't think of anything better to do in our times of ultimate free choice, when I needn't have married at all. Impossible to own up to one of the more esoteric qualities I found attractive in Fergus: he looked the part for Balvaig. I'd pictured him standing down at the pier in the evenings, with the other menfolk, smoking a pipe and discussing the price of fish. I was a very shallow thinker in those days.

'I suppose I was flattered because a famous man – even if only in Scotland – wanted to marry me. He can be charming when he wants to be. It wasn't a wise move, but we both realised our mistake and so we split up.'

'You didn't have a child?'

'Of course not. Neither of us wanted children. I wasn't his first wife you know. He'd been married twice before and never had any, so I assume he never wanted them with me.'

'How long were you married?'

'A year or two. It took longer to get around to the stage

of a final divorce.'

Max moves closer and slips his arm round my shoulders. 'Poor Serena. And this Deirdre, this woman you call your friend?' He has made not the slightest attempt to conceal his contempt. 'How can she have been your friend since childhood? She's unworthy of you.'

'I've known her longer than any of my other pals. She rescued me when I was ten, and dumped from a tiny island village school into the posh one in Glasgow. She's almost a year older than me, and she stopped the other kids from bullying me. Her parents were kind to me too. Her mother'd buy me new clothes, then make flimsy excuses she'd got them for Dee and they didn't fit. Eva's a saint. Dee's just over-exuberant.'

And she still hasn't phoned me. I calculate the battery in my mobile may last one more day.

My compassionate new husband snorts, while it dawns on me that there are many things about Dee I've never liked much, in my heart. She believes the people begging in Princes Street should be grateful to live in Edinburgh. *They make plenty*, she says. *They're probably better off than a lot who work.*

We snuggle together, our jackets over us.

'You're not getting off the hook,' I say. 'What about you; do you think I'm not still curious about the woman you lived with?'

'Katya? I told you, I didn't live with her.'

'I want details.'

'Same age as me, about your height, a lot plumper, black hair, not nearly so long as yours. She's a violinist, not as gifted as Zhenya, by a long way. I haven't seen her for months, and I'll never see her again. End of story. Goodnight.'

'And the others? I'm sure you've had lots of women.'

'So many I can't remember. Lie down properly.'

He draws me against his body, spoon-fashion, tucking his arm round my waist; we could be Hansel and Gretel. That was always my favourite story: the brother who looks after the sister and risks his own life for her. Pure and innocent.

'I'm sorry,' says Max. 'I shouldn't have to ask you to lie down in such a place, on your wedding night. We should have had a room with a huge, comfortable bed.'

Better still, two of them. I'm right to be worried. He still hasn't quite understood.

'There are comfortable rooms and beds at home. I don't mind this.'

'Maybe it should have been in a church, our wedding,' he says. 'Perhaps you feel this wasn't good enough?'

'It doesn't matter where it was. What matters is the fact that now you can get to somewhere you'll be safe, and have the chance to make a better life for yourself eventually.'

He sighs.

'Max, I wish we could have seen the white cranes.'

'We will. One day.'

Forest close to Lappeenranta, Finland, 26th June, 11 00 am

I'm sure we must have been close to Finland's modern border before we lay down to sleep last night, for today the nature of the terrain has changed: everywhere you look, through the trees, you can see small lakes. Max has relaxed. The police – anyone in uniform, from a postman upwards – they obey the rules once you're over the border. Even the ones with guns don't point them at passers-by, or rake your crotch with stubby fingers.

Max whistles happily as we stride along; a sweet, pure, limpid sound that reminds me of my father. You rarely hear men whistle nowadays. Morag used to yell at Frank for whistling indoors; as unlucky as bringing in hawthorn blossom or peacock feathers. So I'd hear him whistling down the street, then the sound would stop, like a doodlebug bomb. Sometimes there'd be an explosion anyway, sometimes not.

I don't want this journey to end; I want to linger for years in the shadowy places with Max, but by afternoon the trees have thinned, and then stopped, and we catch sight of red roofed houses. Max grunts with relief.

'I was afraid I'd get us lost and we'd run out of food.'

He asks directions fluently.

'My grandfather never forgot it. He taught me.'

So little I know about him. Not his shoe-size (other than "huge"), or what his favourite foods are or which side of the bed he prefers. But I know he sleeps so silently I wake wondering if he has died, and his skin is always warm, even on a chilly night outdoors. I know he hated maths at school. (*I never gave a fuck what x equalled*, he said.) I am confident that what I've done is worthwhile.

To save money, we lie down in a barn to sleep, though I know Max is alert as a fox for a sound of anyone sharing our space. I'm still worried about getting across the other borders, even now we're inside Europe.

'Don't worry. I have Kuzkuz's wedding present,' says Max.

'You can't bribe officials here.'

He draws it from his pocket and holds it out for me to inspect: a perfectly ordinary-looking British passport, not a new one either. He flicks it open. Even the photo is obviously a few years old. The name hasn't been altered. David Henderson. Place of Birth: York. Height: 1m 89. Hair: Fair. Eyes: Hazel.

'He thought of everything,' Max says. 'He took the picture off an old student card of mine he had lying around. It's the only thing that doesn't look perfect because of the part over it. As long as they don't look too closely, or measure my height with a ruler, it's OK. If anyone starts to speak to me so I have to answer, walk on ahead. Then if I'm stopped you don't get into trouble. Otherwise, just remember to call me David.'

We plan our route. From Helsinki we'll travel across Sweden to Norway with no trouble, because we can stick to minor routes where no one seems to bother with ID checks.

Oslo, Norway, 28th June

We've been on buses and small ferries for what seems like weeks though it's less than three days. I haven't felt so happy and carefree since I was a student, backpacking round Europe.

'It'd have been quicker to fly,' I say. But they inspect

passports too meticulously at airports.

'Fly? Never. I told you, I hate flying.'

Fate. When you get to sharing irrational prejudices, it's proof.

I've already told Max about the Russian pilot who died in a plane crash near Balvaig. 'He was flying with the British air force; it was during the war, 1944. I'll take you to see his gravestone when we visit my aunt. It's interesting. I suppose it was the one of the first places I ever saw Cyrillic script. His name was Max too. I heard people say he was a White Russian, so I thought it must mean he had very blond hair, like yours.' And indeed, he had, though in the grainy black and white newsprint photograph, you can't tell what colour his eyes might have been. 'He was a prince. They say in the village that his people came for him after the war, and took his heart and buried it in Paris where they lived. I always thought it must be nonsense, how on earth could they find his heart after such passage of time? But right enough, when I visited the Russian cemetery at St Geneviève-des-Bois, I found his gravestone. It's near Nureyev's.'

But all Max replied was, 'It just proves flying's dangerous. And sorry to disappoint you, Serena, but I'm no prince!'

I'll show him the dog-eared copy of the newspaper article I have at home. Then he'll understand why I thought I recognised him as soon as I laid eyes on him.

We've completely run out of cash, and we still have to get to Bergen. I try Dee's home number again. Answering machine. Dee's parents, Hugh and Eva? I don't want to alarm them; perhaps Dee hasn't been in touch yet. They're not close these days.

In any case, maybe Eva still has her problems. I remember hearing Morag tell Peigi that the reason Hugh went through a secretary a year was that he was always knocking them off and knocking them up. My eleven-year-old's mind pictured Dee's father clouting his poor secretary across the head, sending her flying off the blue typist's chair in his outer office.

'We should have gone the other way round,' says Max. 'We could have visited your cousin and borrowed a little. You said she's rich?'

'I don't know her address.'

'I'm teasing you. You think the Poles love the Russians nowadays?'

I phone my aunt. I know how hurt she would have been if she'd got a card telling her I'd got married abroad. As bad as her pal Jean MacPherson's daughter who went on holiday to Rhodes with her boyfriend and sent an ordinary picture postcard: *Ross and I got married out here yesterday. See you soon. Love Nicola.* Any ruse to prevent her mother from attending.

Peigi deserves better. I decide the unexpurgated version can wait until I visit her. I tell her merely that a man I met in St Petersburg is coming home with me for a while, to be my new flatmate.

There's a resounding silence at the other end of the line.

'A Russian man? But you've known him longer than a few days, surely, if you're going to let him live in your house?'

I prevaricate. 'He plays the cello. Like Bonnie Prince Charlie. Only Maksim's good.' I think. And brave. He'd never flee and leave his followers to lift the tab…

'Serena – you've known him longer than a couple of days?'

'Circumstances weren't normal. You'll like him. Frank would have got on with him too. They could have spent the next few months talking about Communism. I can just imagine the pair of them sitting in the pub.'

'Can you indeed. Och, child, why can't you find yourself a nice Scots boy your own age?'

I know she doesn't mean it; she's thinking aloud.

She and Fergus hated each other on sight. *A cruel mouth, yon one had,* she said, the day the divorce papers were lodged. She'd come to Edinburgh to lend me moral support – not that I needed it. She took me to Jenners to buy me a bottle of Givenchy Organza, then to the Carlton Hotel for afternoon tea. *'These fleshy little lips pouting under his dirty big beard. And he liked to make it obvious he considered he'd married beneath himself. Well, Serena, I think it was you did that. Thank God there are no bairns to fight over.'* 'He tried to get custody of the cat,' I said; we laughed so raucously I thought the po-faced waiter would throw us out.

'Max is my own age, Peigi. In fact, he's a year younger. And he's single. But I'm just going to have him as a lodger for a wee while, till he finds his feet.'

I'm not going to ask her to send me money. One bank on the island supplies the entire district with coin and gossip. My friend Carla is in France with her father, and there's no way I'm asking her husband. I've always been a little ambivalent about him. In desperation, I call Fergus.

'Can you wire me a hundred and fifty quid? You'll get it back as soon as. Can't explain now. Have you heard anything of Dee? No – I'll explain when I get home, should be tomorrow.'

Newcastle, 29th June

The last ferry of the day is tremendously crowded. In no time at all, we're at Newcastle.

'Walk. Look normal,' I say. 'We have to stick together. I won't leave you. I won't let them separate us.' Too bloody nervous; they're trained to look for such signs.

Max doesn't look nervous at all. He strolls casually into the line for a female officer, and treats her to an endearing smile. *Shit. Big mistake. Wrong country.* But the nature of his smile makes anything seem permissible. He coughs, and puts his hand to his mouth.

'Excuse me.'

'Summer cold?' she asks sympathetically.

'Froat,' he croaks, gesticulating.

He's blown it. Any minute now: *If you could just step this way a moment, sir –*

'You want to get home to bed.'

He grins and nods, then winks at me.

It's my turn. She gives me a much harder time.

Once we're on the train to Edinburgh my head is splitting; I can't believe we've managed it. Max leans against my shoulder and dozes off, but I'm too keyed up to sleep. We're safe; I'll be home in a couple of hours.

I shake him awake at Haymarket. He automatically

lights a cigarette the minute we leave the station, while I try to bite my tongue. He finds it amusing that I believe it'll harm him.

'Russian men don't live long enough to worry about what they'll die of,' he says. 'The booze gets us long before the tobacco does. I don't mind. I don't want to live to be old and worn out. I'll go while I still have my faculties and my appetites intact. You've only another twenty years to put up with me, at most.'

'Don't joke. It's bad for you.'

'Life's bad for me at home.'

'This is home now. I wish you'd stop smoking.'

He kisses the top of my head.

'Soon. I promise. Let me get my nerves back.'

PART TWO: CAPRICCIOSO

Dunstaffnage Place, Stockbridge, Edinburgh, 29th June

The Stockbridge Colonies. Edinburgh's Chelsea. The house I've brought Max home to is an upper flat in a terrace built more than a hundred years ago. I suppose the half-dozen streets with their small strips of garden were the work of Victorian do-gooders. They started as working-class housing, but even by the '80s they'd become trendy. An upper one with converted attic – almost identical to mine – sold for over a hundred and twenty K just before I went on holiday.

Some of the streets have upper flats accessed by an external stair. In others, the stair's inside, off a postage-stamp hallway. My first sight of the house was when I was trotting hot-eyed through the dusk with Fergus Learmonth a few years ago; even then I remember thinking: *Ah, this is a cut above the other streets.*

The phone's ringing as I unlock the door, so I sprint upstairs in case it's important, leaving Max to follow me up. It's only Fergus himself, and he's deliciously angry.

'I'm going to have you sectioned,' he says. 'For your own safety and the public's.'

'I'm newly home. What's wrong with you?"

'Dee says you tried to throw yourself under a train in St Petersburg, like Anna Karenina. "Not Serena's style," I told her. "She'd pick something easy like pills." But now I hear it's merely social and professional suicide. You've brought some stray tomcat home, have you?'

Ah, yes, that Dee. I left a message on her answering machine when I tried to phone her from Oslo. I hadn't suspected these two speak to each other; they never used to.

'How is Dee? I've been trying to get hold of her for days. How did she get home?'

'I haven't the faintest idea. She's still in the clinic in Perthshire, as far as I know.'

'Clinic? What sort of clinic?'

'Och, Pitlochry Hydropathic establishment, or some such joint.'

'Idiot! Is she all right?'

'That rattled you, didn't it? As far as I know she is. I haven't had the pleasure of knowing the lady intimately.'

Dee and Fergus? As nauseating as the idea of picking up a stranger's gum from the pavement.

'Don't be childish.'

'So this stray's what you needed my sub for? Trifle pricey, was he? Love lance in good working order, I hope. Hate to think you'd been diddled. You stupid, stupid bitch. I suppose he hasn't any of the relevant papers? They take months. How do you know he doesn't have a notifiable disease? You're priceless, Serena. You're the one who was always so keen we keep our quarantine laws. Met his folks did you? Don't try to lie to me. You wouldn't buy a kitten under these circumstances.'

'I happen to be fond of him. I'm aware this concept won't make much sense to you.'

Max is standing in the doorway, looking awkward, too polite to barge in, though I'm trying to mouth: *Make yourself at home.*

'I have to go,' I tell Fergus.

'Knickers off and ready, is he? Well, don't let me detain you from sexual ecstasy – you remember what that is, do you? Buggered if I do. I'll have my money back, by the way. I'm not into subsidising illegals or gigolos. You know you'll lose your job over this, if not end up in the clink? Serve you right.'

'You'll get it as soon as I can get to the building society.'

'Jesus wept, he's waded through all you had in the bank has he?'

'Actually, Dee's brilliant holiday plans waved goodbye to all I had in the bank, and more.'

But open warfare's not a good tactic. I'm careful to maintain a civil tone as I bid him goodnight. Damn. Why is he being as negative as Peigi? Why can't anyone just be happy for me?

I start sifting through the mail I swept up from the mat on the way past. It's there right enough. I recognise the longer-than-usual legal envelope. Nothing else should matter at the moment. But it's all ruined.

I've been dreaming of letting the surprises unfold gradually, showing Max his new home, with its tiny garden burgeoning into its neighbours so that passers-by gawp at our small enclave with envy and lower their voices to whispers. I wanted him to savour the way summer twilight blurs the boundaries; the way the leafy green tunnel to the river melds into darkness until it expands to meet the stars, when you can see them. All the way across Scandinavia I've honed the mental image of our sanctuary snoozing in the hazy sunshine, the light slanting across the polished wooden floor – from the kitchen side in the morning, the sitting room in the afternoon. The cobalt blue and red Qashquai rug with its small woven-in mistakes to remind the faithful only God can make perfection. The cosy evenings Max and I will have beside the dark red Vermont woodburner I stubbornly retain in the centre of town, and feed with precious tit-bits of driftwood carried from Balvaig.

But Fergus's analogy has taken root in my head. Now all I can think about is how long I'll have to keep him shut in to make sure he won't run away, and whether I need to have him vaccinated and buy him a collar.

'Look at the dust!' I say. Edinburgh dust's like love. Golden and glittery as it falls, even in weak Northern sunshine; dead and grey as sloughed skin once it lands. 'Wouldn't you wonder where it comes from in an empty house, in a couple of weeks?'

Jesus, it really *has* been such a short time!

Max is high-stepping round the sitting room as if it's carpeted in broken glass. 'Such a huge house! I must be careful to keep it tidy. Your friend designed this for you?'

'Who – Dee? I couldn't afford her!'

The junk is Morag's, the result of welding atavistic memory of failed harvests to proximity to the Barrows, a burden I haven't got my head round how to lay down. Just as well he can't see the tiny attic. My Feng Shui book says the state of it shows why my head's cluttered. And if I had a basement... but a shed stuffed to the roof is even worse. Detachment.

'*Our* house,' I say. 'You live here too. You're my flatmate now.'

It sounds insincere. It would have been better left unsaid. Max gives the small irritable click of the tongue that's half gesture of impatience, half sigh.

He prowls softly from room to room, touching things in a tentative way, a small boy in a china shop. He examines my pictures quizzically enough to make me nervous. Dee disapproves of the print I brought back from Nice. To her the couple on horseback represents abduction or rape; I've always perceived it as rescue. Fergus says anything painted or composed this century doesn't merit the name of art. *Hang it on the stair, if you must*, he snapped, when I moved my few possessions from my own flat. *I suppose I have to thank Christ it's not Kandinsky.* But I had to live with his damn photographs of nude women who had bigger breasts than me.

'Chagall,' I tell Max shyly.

'I know.' He gives me the slow, sweet smile that twists my heart.

Now he's studying my print of Gustav Klimt's *Fulfilment*. (Acquired on a holiday in Vienna, years before Fergus.) It's not a particularly good example. In the original, the woman's hair is dark red, but in my print it looks black. 'I think this is you, wrapped in your bride's quilt!' he says.

I'm happy he's noticed. I've always believed she does resemble me.

'But who's the man? He has dark hair. You have to take this one down, or I'll be jealous.'

I have a good deal of explaining to do. I still haven't

succeeded in making him understand what this arrangement is about.

He looks at my smallest painting for a long time: a tiny pastel of a darkened hillside with three low white cottages. In the gable windows of two, the roseate glow of a lamp.

'Your island home?' he asks.

I know from the label on the back that it's Donegal, but to me it's always been Balvaig. I used to pray that the unlit window wouldn't be mine.

'I hope you'll be happy here, Maksim.' How I love to say his full name, roll it off my tongue.

He embraces me awkwardly. 'You've always lived here alone?'

'Yes. Since Fergus left.'

The smile freezes. 'It's your husband's house?'

'It was, before we married. I bought his half as part of the divorce.'

One of the few fair things Fergus has done. He gave me the confidence that I could cope with the mortgage and he asked only half of what he'd paid for it in 1986.

'I won't live in another man's house. Wasn't it you who argued about sleeping in Katya's bed?'

'It's all mine now. I've lived alone for ages, except for the cat.'

He recoils. 'There is a cat?'

Damn. Maybe he hates cats, the way Frank did. Russians aren't exactly noted as animal lovers, despite the penchant for keeping gigantic dogs that Dee remarked on in St Petersburg. One of my mother's first acts when Frank left was to bring a cat down from the croft, not because she wanted one, but to spite him. *See? I have a cat, and that's better than a man.* Fergus and I had stronger words over Gorby's future than over mine.

'Don't you care for cats, Max?'

'I never had one. Where is it?'

'My neighbour looks after him when I'm away. I'll fetch him tomorrow.'

His frown relaxes. No need to tread carefully for fear of a desiccated heap of fur and bone lurking behind a sofa.

'Fetch it now. I want to meet your cat.'

I complain that it's too late, but I know Ursula's still up; I can hear her moving about downstairs.

'You wait here then. I'll introduce you to my neighbour tomorrow.'

I carry the cat up, wriggling in my arms. He likes Ursula.

I've been contemplating some emergency re-naming, but Max thinks it's funny.

He ruffles the ginger splodge on top of the cat's white head. 'Gorbachev. Very apt.'

'You don't think it's disrespectful?'

'Only to the cat.'

'Aren't you tired? I'm terribly tired.'

'I don't suppose you've anything to drink?' he asks. 'Whisky? It's what Scots drink, isn't it? I have to learn to be a Scot.'

I leave him with a full glass and sprint upstairs to haul fresh sheets out of the cupboard. I carry the weight of my grandmother's superstitions as well as her commentary on Genesis. Leaving a house with the bed made up tempts the

Devil to sleep in it, and he can never resist temptation. I start to make up a bed for Max.

I mean it to be just for him, but at the same time it would be so nice to drift into sleep with his arm round me, his hand stroking my hair, nested together the way we've spent all our nights thus far. I decide to take the risk, and when he finishes his drink, we head for the stair together.

'You can have the bathroom first, then go up and unpack your bag,' I say.

I'm already in my nightie when I climb the stair to join him. He's lying in bed, the sheets drawn to his chin. I can't tell if he's wearing tee shirt and pants the way he did when we slept in his bed.

'You're wearing a dress?' he says.

'A nightdress.'

He grins, seems about to say more, then hesitates.

'Aren't you going to get in beside me?'

'I suppose so. At least we have a bit more space in this bed. And a pillow each.'

I slide gingerly under the sheet. Already I can sense this is not a good idea, but it's too late to change my mind without the whole thing descending into Victorian melodrama.

As soon as I'm beside him, Max reaches for me, draws me round to face him, almost roughly, and begins to kiss me in a different way, possessively. I'm suffocating, hyperventilating, my heart thumping so harshly it feels as if it's about to rupture; they must be able to hear it next door. I push him away and leap out of bed.

'What's wrong?' he cries, sitting up in alarm.

'I don't want to do that.' I try to conceal the nausea catching my throat.

'You're my wife. Husbands and wives make love.'

'I'm sorry, I thought you understood.'

'What do you want then? I don't know what use I am to you otherwise. How else can I repay you for all you've done for me? I thought it's why you wanted to marry me.'

'For sex?'

'Not only that. I know you meant to help me, but I didn't expect a white marriage, a pretend one. I misunderstood. You want to sleep in the same bed with me and not make love?'

He's angry now, but I know it's because he's confused and his pride's wounded. I've been too quick to forget he's a man, a flesh and blood one, not a character from a poem.

He sighs, flings himself down flat on his back, the covers pulled to his chin again, and glowers at the ceiling.

'We've slept in the same bed since we met. I thought you understood,' I say.

'I don't understand anything.'

'It was daft thinking I could sleep beside you tonight. This is to be your room. I have a bed in the room downstairs. I'll sleep there. We need to talk about this, tomorrow. We need to work out how we'll share this house.'

'This is your room,' he says coldly. 'I will go downstairs. I'm the intruder. In any case – I suppose this is the same bed you slept in with your husband?'

'I bought a new mattress. I didn't want to be reminded of it either. It's only the wood that's the same.' I practically had to make do with the bedding he'd shagged Katya on, complete with crud no doubt. 'Stay here, Maksim. The other bed's not big enough for you.'

I grab my clothes from the chair and flee. How Fergus would laugh.

My Grannie's voice is in my head. *God is watching you, Serena. He watches your every action, and he sees your wicked thoughts.*

Even when I'm asleep?

Even when you're asleep. God never sleeps.

Does he watch me when I go to the toilet?

She slaps me so hard I fall off my chair. *Dirty girl!*

Well, if He's watching me now, I hope He's pleased with his handiwork. I huddle in the cold sheets of my own narrow bed, and try to sleep. A euphemism for the grave, in the old ballads, a narrow bed.

Albion Studios, 30th June

Thank God we only had one morning to creep around each other in the flat, like hostile cats, because I've had to come back to work. Plan A: reunite Fergus and his cash. I don't have enough in any account to cover it until next payday. I decide to prevaricate. He has calmed down, and reverted to his old bantering, avuncular tone.

'You always were too soft-hearted. I suppose I'm lucky you didn't bring home a planeload of tramps. Darling witch, I can't bear to think of you with an uncouth stranger. What do you know about him?'

He's a lot less uncouth than you. But I recognise the nuances of Fergus's voice. It'd be entirely in keeping with his nature to have the immigration authorities on the doorstep within half an hour.

'You gave me the money to bring him into the country.'

'Only because you lied to me. Anyway, I didn't give, while we're on the subject. It was a loan.'

'You'll get it soon, don't worry. I didn't tell you why I needed it. Could have been to buy a load of crack cocaine for all you knew. Cash transfers are easy to trace.'

'Are you threatening me, Serena?'

'No more than you're threatening me.'

He laughs. 'Touché. He hasn't broken your spirit anyway. I prefer it when you give as good as you get, it's more interesting. Why couldn't you have been more like this when we were together? Did you get your bit of paper from the Court of Session, by the way? I cried when mine came. Real tears, Serena. We were so good together.'

He's at his most dangerous when he waxes lugubrious. It's a thin veneer over a viciousness more alarming than his anger.

'Just tell me you're not sleeping with this Russkie,' he says. 'I can take anything but that.'

I'm not proud of my reply.

'Really?' he crows. 'Daft wee lassie. What are you playing at? I hope you lock your door.'

He remembers perfectly well how much I'd have given to be able to fit a lock to the door; the jamb's too shallow. But Fergus's voice is silky and affectionate and unpredictable.

'And not a penny to his name. Priceless. You married

my bank account rather than me, didn't you? That and my house, so that you could paint it up to look like a Carl Larsson calendar. Jesus, what's between this man's legs? That doesn't cut much ice with you, does it? That's it. No cojones. Serena's found herself a eunuch at last.'

I escape into the newsroom and slam the door on him. I reckon he's had enough interest on the loan.

I try to put on a fresh-back-from-holiday face for my colleagues. I know I should be grateful to be here, because nearly everyone I know envies me. It's my own fault that I haven't taken to it; I lack the media mindset, as Fergus has never tired of telling me since we decided to part.

'Face up to it, why don't you, kitten,' he'll say, 'your days in this game are numbered. Speaking a language both outlandish and antiquated isn't enough. You're not cut out for it; have to be more assertive. Reading the weather or sitting on the sofa beside the real presenter, showing off the legs. Only suitable openings for tottie in this game. You need balls to be a broadcast journalist.'

As if it hadn't been his idea in the first place. And as if it's not the very worst analogy in the world for being able to take the hard knocks. Look at these ridiculous box things cricketers wear in their pants.

I find it boring. There, it's said. It's incestuous. Everyone chases the same stories, ourselves and the BBC and the papers, and then we drop them the next day. It's all beginnings and no endings. And when a juicy lump of genuine news drops in the pond, there's a feeding-frenzy; blood on the water. Nauseating, and dishonest too. As often as not we write the cue before we do the interview, so we know exactly what we want them to say. It's what makes Paxman a genius: he excels in situations when they won't co-operate, and it's going out live, and he doesn't have the luxury of ten shots at getting the sound bite.

I'm not particularly fond of the people I work beside either, except for Nick, and he's not typical. He's not into Feng Shui and he hasn't got an altar and he wouldn't dream of having his clutter professionally cleared. He is an expert falconer, and has a licence to keep Harris hawks and peregrines.

Drew, the other news reporter, is never in the office, and when he is, all he talks about is his damn kids. There's a cameraman too, Dennis. A poppet, but there's an unspoken caste system in the office. He doesn't get to share the journalists' coffee mugs. Sums up why I hate it.

Anita Forrest's my boss. I've never been able to work up much enthusiasm for Anita. A callous bitch, she seems to me, who doesn't care who gets trampled on, but Fergus maintains she's incomparable at her job. *She's focussed*, he says. *And she had the savvy to get onto the production side well before her sell-by date. Though she could have gone for radio instead. It wouldn't matter there whether you can count the rings on her neck. Best microphone voice I ever heard, though she's done her best to ruin it with smoking.*

Roger Braithwaite, who manages Albion's entire operation, is a distant figure. I seldom see him, speak to him even more rarely. This arrangement suits both of us.

Katie-Mary MacDonald I'd like to kill, if I could find an undetectable method. A genuine native speaker from Benbecula. Until she contracts a terminal illness or is horribly disfigured in a car-crash, not another soul has a chance of reading the Gaelic news, and apart from that their only specialised use for me is the odd documentary.

'The Board have no more intention of implementing their minority-language obligations than stuffing raw chillies up their arses,' Fergus never tires of telling me. 'The chillies have it. No contest.'

'Wait till we get our own Parliament.'

'In the unlikely event we do, these buggers'll keep awfully quiet on the subject of the Gaelic in case they're expected to learn it.'

I spend my first morning back clearing my inbox and writing the script for a piece on the latest radioactive hot-spots on the beach beside Dounreay. I need someone who'll be on my side, so in the afternoon I tell Nick about Max – though not the wedding part. I know he'll understand, after what happened to his sister, Ruth. She got involved with an Armenian man the year before last, and overnight he disappeared. The builders who'd been hiring him as a labourer got cold feet when awkward questions were asked over a work permit.

Ruth had been away in London on business. She called him to check what had happened the minute she got back. She'd been with him the night before she left and they'd been making plans to get married. She phoned, and day after day it just rang out. There was no reply when she rang his doorbell. She became frantic and made his landlord let her in. Some of his stuff was still in the drawers and cupboards. Of Hagop himself, not a sign. Then his phone was cut off. The irritating mechanical voice repeated over and over: this number is not available. Ruth tried the operator, got a human being, got the run-around, and the set pieces implying you must have an ulterior motive for asking, that you're a stalker, intent on sexual harassment. She knew so much of the fine detail, all his endearing and irritating quirks; the way he whimpered like a puppy and brushed away imaginary flies in his sleep, the crescent-shaped mole above the cheek of his left buttock. None of it helped. He'd vanished, and though she believes he's still in this country, she's given up looking. He left less trace than snow that's melted.

'She's begun to blame herself,' Nick said at the time. 'She keeps asking what she did to drive him away. It's harrowing, because no matter what we tell her, she doesn't believe it. She doesn't know if he's dead or alive. It'd be easier for her if she knew he was dead. And of course there's no point trying the "official channels". These buggers won't tell you anything. Mind you, Claire and I thought privately that it suited her, in some ways, after the tourist visa ran out. It gave her the whip hand. But I'm sure it didn't really make a difference to the outcome.'

'Well, good for you,' Nick says when I tell him about my new flatmate. 'I hope you have more luck than Ruth. I wouldn't worry about the visa. I always felt Hagop would have been better without one from the start. Then they wouldn't have known to come looking for him.'

'It's a secret for now, Nick. And he *is* just a flatmate. You won't tell the others?'

Dear, kind, Nick, who resembles his falcons so closely, with his clever eyes and sharp beaky nose. I used to wonder how it would all have turned out if I'd gone to Albion straight from university, and found him first.

Albion Studios, 1ˢᵗ July, morning

When I reach the newsroom Anita starts whistling the Soviet national anthem under her breath.

'Hear you brought home something more exciting than a painted egg,' she says. 'Most people make do with a rabbit-fur hat with earflaps. You certainly don't believe in letting the bed get cold. When do we meet him? Does he speak any English? Does he have a schlong eighteen inches long?'

Will there never, ever be a man who doesn't let me down?

Dunstaffnage Place, 2ⁿᵈ July, evening

Next on the to-do list: make peace with Ursula. I couldn't dream of a better neighbour; she's kind, cultured, sophisticated, urbane. Fergus refers to her as The-Dyke-Downstairs. I've always felt she's one of those women who are just completely asexual. I'm secretly in awe of her. I used to envy women like Ursula, and my aunt, who can be so complete on their own. But not enough to want to be like them.

'He's sweet,' she says, when Max has wandered back upstairs after the introductions, 'but Serena, he's so thin. Maybe he brings out the mothering instinct in you.'

'No one's ever accused me of that before!'

She does a particularly irritating line in knowing little smiles.

'How brave of you to bring home a man you've newly met. Love at first sight. How romantic. But you can scarcely know him?'

'Don't get the wrong idea – we're only sharing the house, Ursula. It's why you'll have heard me downstairs, in the guest room.'

'You used to sleep in the downstairs room anyway, when Fergus was still in residence.'

I moved out of Learmonth's bed soon after we got back from Tallinn. He didn't object at that stage; I believe he was a little in awe of me. 'You're a witch right enough,' he said.

'Fergus snores so,' I mumble.

'Not much deadening between the floors in these old houses.' Ursula lays a tentative hand on my arm. 'I used to worry over it and wonder whether I should come up to see if you were all right. I'm not a brave person. Och – don't cry. It'll be fine now, won't it? And in the circumstances, it couldn't be too difficult to get rid of Max, I mean, if he's just a lodger?'

'Wheesht!' I wonder how much you *can* hear from upstairs. 'I had to really work on persuading him to come with me, he was in a terrible fix.'

Shit! Her eyebrows vanish under her fringe, and back comes the cynical smile.

Nothing for it but to phone Dee.

'Are you OK?' I say.

'No thanks to you.'

'Balls. It was your own fault entirely.'

'And you've brought mega-creep's pal back with you? Bit extreme. He was quite cute – but there's a limit. How did you smuggle him in anyway?'

'Wasn't difficult.'

'Bloody hell. No wonder this country's in the state it is. Gross. You must be crazier than I thought. You already tried it once, and it doesn't work for you. Nice warm man on tap when you want it. I'd buy that. However, if the cap fits why use a condom, as they say. You'd sampled it, and it didn't suit you, so why the hell are you trying again?'

As if living together was something everyone should have a bash at just once, like sky-diving or bungee-jumping or evening classes in pottery.

'He's sharing the house with me, Dee. I'm not like you, I don't have to leap into bed with anything that has a dick.'

She snorts. 'Sez you. Oh well, we'll see how long your resolve lasts.'

'Meet me for lunch tomorrow?'

She agrees, with an ill grace.

Dunstaffnage Place, 10th July

I lie awake in my narrow bed each night listening to Max tossing and turning in the room above. I sob silently into my pillow so he won't hear – for him, for myself.

I bundle his sheets into the machine without looking at them, and then I lean my brow against the cool glass of the window-pane and remember how I'd sit through Granda's sermons, puzzling over Onan who sinned because he spilt his seed on the ground, for I knew all the farmers in the land did that, it was the only way you could get anything to grow. Granda did it himself: he tore the corner off the neat wee square foil packages and dribbled seed through his cupped hand into the drills where he wanted carrots and neeps to appear. I had more sense than to take it up with him. Just another mystery to make our beautiful island an unconsecrated desert, brimming over with sin, sin, sin. Sin also lies in communism, cremation, divorce, artificial insemination, homosexuality, Scottish nationalism, British Summer Time, Sunday buses, the cinema, female preachers, use of tobacco, women in trousers, and anyone who believes in the Second Sight.

Max continues to do a strong line in puzzled-Labrador expressions. He also loses his temper with me. He tells me he's not asking for anything unusual.

'I don't want to wear your underwear, or chain you to the bed,' he said peevishly this morning. 'We got married. I didn't realise you meant me to be on my own every night. I'm a man. I have needs. Any other man would have made you quit this caper the minute we got back here.'

Don't preach at me about Any Other Man. I lived with him for two years, and no, he didn't put up with it, but what could I do? If I'd tried to bring a marital rape case against Fergus Learmonth I'd never have worked again anywhere in the Scottish media.

I hear Max get up in the night, for I wake from my half-sleep hyperventilating, remembering another, heavier tread on the steps. I hear him enter the bathroom or the kitchen. I think: *now he's outside my door.* And I stop breathing until I hear him climb the stair again.

A hundred years ago, even up to my Grannie's generation, I could have got away with being like this. Now, when anything's possible, I'm a freak, an embarrassment, an apology for a woman. I remember Frank calling Morag those names. But now she's gone, I'm the only one in the world who's been left behind. As much of a dinosaur as ever my father was. But I'm sick of being labelled. I don't need anyone else to tell me I'm from a dysfunctional family, or that I suffer from sexual dysfunction. I'm me. This is the way *I* function. No one can fix me until I find a way to fix myself.

I used to believe it would get better as I got older; easier each time. The opposite has turned out to be true. I know it's because I'm more in my own head, and it's the part of my anatomy where the problems start. I didn't need some high-paid shrink to tell me the score. And I *was* getting better. But ever since Anita forced me to cover the damn baby rape case three years ago, memories spring up again, as vivid as any TV drama, when I least expect them. My muscles clamp down on the fear, just as they did when I was ten.

Dunstaffnage Place, 18th July

By now, Max and I are hardly speaking to each other. I have tried to explain to him what has made me the way I am, but he doesn't seem to listen. It's about a lot more than sex. How softly the arguments have escalated, and the friendship faded, so soft and slow I've scarcely noticed. Why won't he make an effort? It's as irritating as grit in my shoe. He feels it too. Our mutual politeness becomes more studied by the day. It was a mistake to expect solidity in a relationship welded together by chocolate.

Sandringham Terrace, West End, Edinburgh, 19th July

It's been too long since I saw my friend Carla, and I know she'll get on with Max, because she's a musician too.

I met her at Giverny, six weeks before I was due to become Mrs Fergus Learmonth III. She flitted past me like an exotic butterfly – scarlet sunhat, conker-coloured hair, turquoise top, jade and peacock skirt – trailing a wake of *Opium* and a dazzling smile. The elderly bearded man walking several paces behind her gave me an odd look.

'Striking colour-scheme,' I said, leaving him to choose whether or not to think I meant the nasturtiums.

'My wife's from Chile,' he said. 'I'm almost accustomed to it after two decades.'

We grinned at each other in mutual recognition; two dowdy Scottish moths blinking in the sunshine.

They invited me to eat with them in Vernon, and after a single evening in Carla's company I was under her spell. I basked in the attention she drew from every man who passed, and in the smoky warmth of her voice. She insisted that I accompany them to her parents' house in Brittany for the rest of my holiday. *So I can make sure you don't do anything daft*, she said.

Had I obeyed, I'd never have married Fergus. She hated him already, sight unseen.

Every component of Carla is flamboyant; her tawny skin, her hair, her laugh, her dress sense. She can wear fuchsia and russet and royal blue all together and look magnificent. Her dark copper hair's always artfully tousled, but she has a dancer's controlled grace, swaying her hips so her progress is syncopated by the tintinnabulation of bracelets, necklaces, ear-rings – a perambulating ethnic crafts shop, but on her it never looks crass. Her voice is rich and dangerous; she's retained an exotic, sexy accent despite twenty years as a respectable Edinburgh housewife. I envy her the effortless way she can be a woman without thinking about it.

She's a more than competent violinist, and she can play the piano to professional standard too. She teaches music at St Angela's Ladies College and I've no idea what they make of her; an enormous orange cactus-flower burgeoning in a funeral bouquet.

'Why do you bother to teach if you can afford not to?' I asked her, once I knew her well enough to understand just how wealthy her family is.

'It amuses me,' she said. 'I never do anything unless it amuses me.'

Dougal, on the other hand, is a predictable type – he has a doppelgänger in every traditional University department. He's high in the pecking order in Moral Philosophy, but he'll never make it to Professor now, so he doesn't care whom he annoys. He's heavily bearded, pot-bellied, terribly clever and witty, entertaining company, a hell of a boozer. When he was drunk and I was in the post-Fergus doldrums, he'd grope me given half the chance. Possibly he pitied me and intended to cheer me up. It's impossible to imagine him in bed with Carla. He'd bounce off her pneumatic breasts like a melon on a trampoline.

I adore their house; a slice of Bohemia in a West End drawing room flat with enormous rooms, ornate plasterwork, and skirting boards half a metre high. The whole end of the drawing room's taken up with Carla's Steinway, nothing less than a full concert grand. I expect its entry was straight from an Ealing comedy: a crane, a precarious rope sling, the entire window removed. Their bedroom could serve as the set for Victorian erotic photographs – enormous, ornate bed, heavy fabrics, sensual colours: burgundy and deep peacock blue and dark green velvet. An intensely feminine brand of decadence.

Carla and Dougal have never married, though he refers to her as his wife. He had one of those before, and didn't bother with a divorce.

'Doesn't it worry you?' I asked her once, on a day of mortgage-induced depression. 'If anything happened to Dougal you might lose your home.'

She shrugged with the insouciance that makes me want to slap her.

'Then I'd get another.'

If I had to name one failing, it would be her inability to imagine not being able to ask Papa for another pot of cash. Papa lives in France or New York as the mood takes him, with his fourth wife, who's considerably younger than her stepdaughter.

I was afraid Max would detest her. I quickly learnt that he despises loud, pushy women in the Anita mould. He loathes blatant use of make-up, and has forbidden me to wear perfume at home because he claims it makes him sneeze.

But he adores Carla, from the minute they meet, and close encounters don't have him reaching for the tissues. There was an immediate bond; they can laugh at the Brits. Max can't contain his delight when he finds she's a musician too.

They talk of nothing except music. I watch miserably as Max – who has told me it doesn't matter that I'm a musical incompetent – blossoms again in her company, and goes back to being the funny, tender man I met in St Petersburg.

'Dougal will grow jealous, Carla,' I say.

'He only needs me to keep him warm at night.' She pinches my cheek patronisingly. 'All the while I speak to Max, he's watching you. It's a way of passing the time for him, till he can take you home to bed. You're a stunningly handsome couple. You both have physical beauty but it doesn't compete. You complement each other. No wonder people stare at you.'

I normally find it easy to be frank with Carla, but I do nothing to disabuse her of her immediate assumption that my flatmate and I are lovers. It would seem disloyal to him, somehow.

Max plays on Carla's precious Steinway, more than passably. Because I can't read music fast enough to turn the pages for him she does it, leaning across his shoulder.

Why didn't I pay more attention at school? Too much time wasted sniggering over the words that sounded dirty. *Rubato. Con fuoco. Smortzando.* That's what Dee said you felt after a *poco troppo vigoroso.* Maybe music teachers were formed after the common mould was broken. Ours was the youngest in the school, wore short skirts and was newly married. She looked harassed most mornings. 'A *poco prestissimo* before she came out,' Dee would whisper. 'She's worried it's going to run down her leg when she reaches up to write on the board.'

'Well,' I ask Max as we head home, 'what do you think of Carla?'

'She's great. A very competent musician. Though I don't like her house.'

He was given the full guided tour.

'Their bedroom's like a whore's waiting-room,' Max adds.

I shouldn't laugh. She's my friend. When did he become such a connoisseur anyway?

Dunstaffnage Place, 24th July

While I contemplate exactly how long it will be until it's safe to turn him loose in Edinburgh on his own, Max and I grow ever more distant.

He laughs spitefully at my minuscule Japanese garden with its cut-leaf maple in a blue pot, the square metre of raked gravel, the pebble fountain, the mossy rock from Ollasdale, the woven reed panel to screen the shed, the small, luxuriant clump of bamboo, and the single metal chair. My friends and neighbours have praised it as a miracle of planning. I've always intended to buy another chair, but I can't afford a duplicate, so it will have to wait. I'm not about to spoil the entire effect by getting one that doesn't match.

'It doesn't go with the house,' Max says.

'Well, I'd need to have either a Swedish garden or a Japanese interior. Don't know enough about one, can't afford the other.'

I'd hoped he'd smile, at least, but nothing lifts his frown.

'What's it for?' he asks.

For him, function determines form; use confers meaning.

I've been trying to learn to meditate for the past year. On our way home across Scandinavia, I pictured him sitting on the ground beside me here, his head against my knees, closing his eyes and letting the calm seep into his brain too.

'It's a place of tranquillity,' I say, 'designed to soothe the mind. And I happen to enjoy the sound of running water. It's restful.'

He glowers at the fountain. I try to see it through his eyes: it is ridiculous, after all.

'This is a civilised country. I suppose you want me to plant a St Petersburg garden, to make you feel at home? Fine. I'll chuck out this lot and plant weeds for you to empty your bladder on, and fetch in some broken junk.'

'Not far to bring it,' he says. 'Just open your shed door and stand back.'

We glare loathing at each other across the three-foot abyss.

'Russians wouldn't have crap like this,' he snarls. 'Why don't you grow vegetables? You can't eat stones.'

'I can get vegetables in the shop. Anyway – there's no room.'

In the midst of my anger and disappointment I know

he's right. It is a waste. Along with all his training, which he never mentions, all these skills mouldering away. I'm becoming increasingly obsessed with waste, but I hold my corner over the garden. There's more amiss than a row of cabbages would fix.

I pull out my antidote for the need to raise my voice.

'I'm going for a walk.'

'I'll come with you. We'll walk in your *civilised* country.'

'Only if you don't talk.'

My legacy from Morag – beyond the earrings and the apple-boxes crammed with matching pairs of ornaments and the knowledge that men are dirty creatures – is the urge to walk, fast and aimlessly, when I'm upset. Not for pleasure she walked once we'd moved to Glasgow, but to exhaust herself, lay ghosts, be excused from feeling. Like a demented gypsy she'd stride out, with me in tow, along the grey hard pavements, to Riddrie and beyond, walking, walking, walking.

We held no conversation on these frenetic pilgrimages to streets where the tenements had run out and there were proper houses, with small gardens and green-painted gates and rows of gladioli or chrysanths: funeral flowers. At twilight we'd set out, after her work, when the house lights were being switched on. Looking into the rooms was like watching a silent film.

That's what drew her, the uncurtained windows where we could observe a family around a table or beside a fire watching TV. We spied on other people's cosy and contained existences; we were hungry ghosts. It wasn't unusual for one of the group to rise suddenly and draw the curtains, as if the intensity of Morag's stare had entered the room: a sudden draught of cold air on the back of a neck. I still can't catch the damp-earth, suffocating scent of chrysanths without re-living the panic of imagining a gesticulating man, an Alsatian dog released to chase us.

'Nuts,' Frank would say. 'Your mother's flipped. Gaga. Country folk don't go walks for the hell of it. A real townie's trick.'

She was still beautiful in those days, coming in out of the mirk like a dark flame, before her face took on the petted, embittered look that marred it long before the cancer. She lived her entire life through trashy novels and TV and other peoples' windows, and I know less about her past than I do about the characters in her soap operas, for she hadn't such a well-written script. My mother's life has come down to me in snippets from her sister.

We were all great readers, but my mother read only for herself. There she'd sit hunched over her Mills & Boon, eyes glazed, strands of long, black hair sticking to her hot face, her lips moving slightly. I daresay it's where she found the name she branded me with: Serena. How was I supposed to know what a "Serena" should be like when there had never been another, either among the MacKenzies, or on the island of Soma? Greta Garbo and Catherine Deneuve – they could easily be a "Serena". But she wouldn't let me change it; she didn't care whether I loathed my name, because she didn't like hers either.

Morag; the name you might give a pet sheep.

So Morag named me, though it was her sister who taught me to believe in fairies and princes and soul-mates.

I regret not making more effort to understand her. I've often wondered if she still walked after I'd left home, all alone down darkening crescents and avenues and drives. Did the houses know the final time she passed? There'll be streets I've walked – the back alleys of Funchal; the palm-shaded paths inside the Kasbah of Rabat, a tranquil side-street in the Musicians' Quarter of Nice, the Nevsky Prospekt – and have already passed down for the last time; people I've said goodbye to casually, without realising the finality.

'Max,' I whisper, drawing him close, 'I'm sorry. Please, let's not fight any more.'

St Edmund Avenue, The Grange, Edinburgh, 25th July

It was purely by chance I noticed the cello this morning, discreetly sandwiched between Dalmatian puppies and upholstery cleaning services in the *Scotsman* classifieds. I always assumed superior instruments changed hands exclusively through dealers. I've already asked timidly at one of those, and blanched at the figure mentioned. *You did say a professional instrument, madam*? The advert didn't specify price, merely a maker's name, which is meaningless to me.

I called from work and hated Marjorie Adam at first hearing. She suffers from what people recognise as a "Morningside accent"; it conjures up coffee mornings and bridge. The type to have a lap dog and chintz-covered furniture, and a little woman who comes in to "do" for her.

'You're not another dealer?' she asked frostily. The cello was her brother's. He's been dead for two years and she has finally accepted he's not coming back to collect it.

'An instrument of this calibre needs to be played,' she added.

I cleared my throat. 'I'm not the musician. It's my – my husband. We can't afford commercial prices.' I expected her to hang up.

'Your husband is a young musician, starting out?'

'Quite young. He has no work at all at the moment. And no instrument.'

'He's properly trained?'

Open College of the Arts, a whole year on the postal course.

'He studied at the Leningrad – St Petersburg – Conservatory.'

'Ah, he's Russian?' The lift in her voice pruned at least thirty years off her age. Reassuring to know I'm not the only obsessive in Scotland, all the same.

'Why don't you bring him here to see it?'

Let her see him, to be more accurate, but perhaps there's no harm in it. The address confirmed my suspicions. Posh retirement flats, that part of the Grange – snobs' paradise.

Even so, I'm unprepared for the reality. I didn't realise any of the original houses remain inviolate. Max hasn't been in Edinburgh long enough to lose his innocence, so he's unfazed by the drawing room the size of a tennis court, the plethora of Chinese porcelain, the paintings.

But my prejudices concerning the woman herself were

not entirely accurate. Tall and dapper, with what you'd call a military bearing; white hair cut in a severe bob, blindingly smart trouser suit. Deaf enough to need a hearing aid, too bloody-minded to wear one. Just as long as everyone can hear her. Once upon a time, she was Reader in the School of Oriental Studies at London University.

Marjorie takes to Max from the moment they meet. He has eyes for nothing but the cello. It leans primly against its stand, unmarred by speck of dust or finger-mark. He gazes at it adoringly.

'A Ruggieri. I've never seen such a beautiful instrument. As for playing one... It must be worth...' He rolls his eyes sideways; I recognise he's mentally converting roubles to sterling. 'Holy God!'

I feel the room spin.

'The bow too,' he says. 'It's so beautiful I want to weep.'

Right enough, I can see the tears glittering under his lashes, but Marjorie doesn't avert her eyes tactfully. Perhaps she's used to foreign temperaments where nothing intrudes between a feeling and its expression.

'I'm sorry, we're wasting your time, Miss Adam,' I say.

She ignores me. 'Please – will you play a little for me?'

He adjusts the spike, draws the instrument into his arms and runs the bow over the strings.

'I'm afraid it's quite out of tune,' Marjorie Adam says.

'And I'm quite out of practice. I haven't played for a year.'

He turns pegs deftly, tries a few arpeggios before beginning to play in earnest. I don't recognise the music, other than: probably Russian and probably twentieth-century. Not something you could *whistle*, but beautiful. I'm sure I'm dreaming: the opulent house, my Maksim turning out to be a magician as well as a prince. It is, after all, a clump of horsehair applied to a grotesquely expensive wooden box. Pandora's box. The last item left in that was hope.

He looks up at me triumphantly from beneath damp lashes. He wants to please me, though I know I should probably be lying on the floor, kissing his feet. But after a few moments he stops, swears at himself. 'Ach, never have I needed practice so much!'

It has been a mistake after all. Now Marjorie Adam is studying me curiously; I force the corners of my mouth up, but she isn't fooled.

'He plays well. As skilfully as I've heard in long enough, if it's true he's a little rusty.'

'So he should be able to find work?'

'As easily as any other classically trained musician nowadays. Not that it's much consolation. Of course, my brother was a banker. He didn't play professionally.'

She and Max launch into a discussion of composers I haven't heard of, and I've never seen him so animated. Tcherepnin: a fellow-graduate and a fellow-countryman who escaped in the opposite direction from most and went native in China for a time. Marjorie produces a file of sheet music. 'Bright Sheng', she says. What's that? Fifty-second hexagram in the I Ching? Apparently not. A very young, very new Chinese composer who uses a lot of traditional material. Why have I smuggled a Russian all the way to

Edinburgh to have him learn Chinese fiddle tunes transposed for the cello? I suspect Marjorie is the type who collects obscure composers the way her grandmother might have collected butterflies, but I'm wrong. Her great and abiding god turns out to be Bach – and not even CPE, but JS.

'I'm sorry. I'm afraid we're wasting your time,' I repeat. 'We can't afford to buy the cello.'

'Stockbridge isn't far,' she says, studying Max's face. 'If I were to lend it to you, would you come here to play for me?'

He looks at me pleadingly. My mind is still running on the bloated state of my overdraft. I can't take in what this woman is offering.

'It would be payment enough to hear it played again,' Marjorie Adam whispers to Max. 'Tell your wife not to worry.'

At least one of us is managing to appear sufficiently grateful.

'You could have sounded more enthusiastic,' Max hisses as we leave. 'And why did you tell her I'm Russian?'

'Sorry – should I have told her you're a Glaswegian with a speech defect?'

'You know what I mean. At least you told her we're married. I don't think you've told anyone else, have you?'

Glad he isn't pressing me on *why* I told her, because I have not the faintest idea.

'Anyway, what harm can it do if I play this lovely instrument?'

'I'm not delirious about the idea of you traipsing back

and forth manhandling a cello worth as much as some people pay for a house.'

'I won't lose it.'

'It makes you a little conspicuous.'

Getting it into the back of my Peugeot 205 makes both of us conspicuous.

'You could put a cat-collar on me with my name on it. If I stray off you can put an advert in the paper. "Lost, between Grange and Stockbridge mid-July, tall thin man, answers to Max, may be timid." Would you offer a reward, Serena?'

'I bet the immigration people offer a reward.' Bite my tongue.

'In this case, we have to sort it out, so I can find work. The worst they can do is lock me up for a while. Better now than later. Get it over with, so we can go on with our lives. It can't be so bad as we've imagined. This isn't Russia. Please God I haven't got you into trouble too.'

'But what if they send you back after all?'

'You'll come with me. God put us in each other's paths to be together. If it comes to it, we'll go to my mother in Kiev, start a new life.'

Too many mentions of God for an atheist. I can't decide if I prefer maudlin to angry.

'It's not been long enough yet. Leave it another few weeks, so they can't say you only married to come here.'

And so that I can figure out what game this is I'm playing. When Marjorie Adam said 'Your husband,' I felt a jolt of emotion I can't correctly identify.

Dunstaffnage Place, 27th July

I have mixed feelings about the cello from the start. A Věstonice Venus, with its etiolated neck and generous childbearing hips.

It's a man's instrument. I always thought women shouldn't play them. I'll avert my eyes from TV footage of female cellists, with their skirts hitched up and their knees spread in anticipation of sexual congress with a hippopotamus. It possesses the player.

It was meant to be the balm, his music, and half of the time it seems to be working as I'd hoped.

'When I play,' Max says, his eyes glittering like a lover's, 'my hands are filled with fire. I can see them glowing, and all the veins picked out the way they are when you shine a torch against the palm – like a Kirlian photograph. The music beats in my blood. I am filled with ecstasy.'

Then, just as suddenly, before I have the chance to tell him I think he's full of bullshit, he'll be swearing with frustration at his ineptitude. He has practised until the fingertips of his left hand are almost raw.

'Harpists used to draw a red-hot poker across to callous the skin,' he says. 'I can understand why.'

My flesh creeps at the idea. 'Don't you dare try any fancy tricks with pokers while I'm out.'

I dab his fingers with surgical spirit, while he winces and complains that it stings. Red-hot pokers indeed. *Surgical Spirit for the Soul.* I'd buy a copy.

I try harder than ever to understand his world of composers I haven't heard of, without success. I can't get my ear round these as *tunes.* My own pedestrian tastes in music give me guilt-pangs; I hid my CDs as soon as he was in the house. What turns out to be my saving grace – in his eyes, never in Fergus's – is my penchant for modern jazz. Even then, there's nothing clever or educated in my interest. I love the mystery of it rather than the virtuosity: the musician as shaman. I grow optimistic: Jan Garbarek could save *this* marriage. Max could have been a jazz player. It would suit his temperament.

'It was the only one of Stalin's purges that didn't succeed,' he tells me, 'he couldn't kill jazz, because it speaks to the soul. Even Gulag commandants have souls.'

Sandringham Terrace, 2nd August

Max and Carla binge on playing Ravel sonatas while I sit swallowing bile and wondering how to keep the vitriol from showing. Carla glows like a de Vianne lamp; her fingernails exude a tawny luminescence as she flashes her eyes in gypsy-in-silent-film mode and hollers and whoops as if she's having an orgasm. The way the sounds of violin and cello blend is so sexy I can scarcely bear it.

This evening, she's roped in a perjink Welsh pianist called Felix she picked up at the Usher Hall. Three's less intimate. I smirk to myself all evening. I know Max's prejudices better than I know his history.

Ravel leaves me cold. I prefer cool and orderly northern themes, like the piece they practise over and over, music as delicate as frost forming on a windowpane, twisting a knife in my guts.

'What's that?' I ask Max huskily.

'*Spiegel im Spiegel*,' he answers eagerly. 'It pleases you?

Arvo Pärt, an Estonian composer. It's the last thing he composed before he left to live in the West. His was forbidden music when I was young. He's familiar with exile and homesickness.'

'Because of your lot, presumably?'

He gives a wry smile. 'Because of my lot.'

Uncalled for. He played it for me.

'Are you so very homesick, Maksim?' I ask him on the way home.

'At times. Don't look hurt. It's inevitable I should miss it. I'd scarcely been out of Petersburg in my life.'

As we were crossing Finland, he said we'd bring our children to St Petersburg, to see where he grew up, but he's stopped mentioning either the trip or the children. At first, I was grateful. Now I find myself wishing he'd say it again.

A generation earlier and he could have been sent to the Gulag for playing the music he loves so much or for trying to buy the score. And yet Maksim is nostalgic for it; he prefers his homesick music to Bach. Nostalgie de boue. He's started sniffing the air like a deer, and saying, *The summer's growing colder.* I wonder if his Finnish ancestors had eight seasons, like the Sami? And I know he's dreaming of a townscape of exquisite, shabby, pastel-coloured buildings, with rain cascading over the pavements from drainpipes that end half a metre up, mud everywhere, buses and trams and trains reeking of damp clothing and hot bodies and houses with too few washing facilities. Perhaps if you don't have to struggle to live, the spirit is sapped. Max finds Edinburgh wanting.

'The people here have no sensibilities,' he announces.

'How many of them ever actually looked at a tree? They see any scrap of ground as a building-plot. Look at all the gardens sold to put houses in. Don't they want to have growing things? And look at the houses they put up. They're not homes. This is the only reason you love your house, Serena, because it's worth more than you paid for it.'

We have no culture either, apparently. I took him to Glasgow, to see where *I* grew up and where I was educated. The underground stations failed to please. And no point in trying to tell him there's anywhere in Edinburgh that counts as a museum.

'I'm lucky,' he says. 'My grandparents were peasants, but they had more culture than this. And they were wise, spiritual people. I didn't grow up believing in nothing. Not like my mother, or your Scottish people who don't trouble to speak their own language correctly. "I should have went there," they say. Why am I worrying? What can you expect in a country where books cost more than people can afford? It's as bad at home now. Maybe if I stay here I'll forget my native tongue.'

He bows his head.

I put my arms round him. 'Let's speak Russian all the time at home then. We'll make believe, like the ones who ended up in Paris and Nice, terribly patriotic and nostalgic and Bohemian. We'll get a samovar.'

Max pretends to laugh, but he keeps his face buried in my hair. 'It is my homeland,' he says. 'Even the chaos that's Russia now, I feel the loss.'

'You preferred Communism?' I need to understand, even if it means Frank Stuart was right.

'Jesus, no. But what's here is no better, or what's at home now. There must be another way. We just want freedom to tell all the politicians to go fuck their mothers. It wasn't as bad as they say, you know, the old system. We had education, a health service; yours isn't such hot shit, I can tell you. I see it on TV. People had work at least, even cellists. I'd have been found a job, wouldn't need to have tried myself. But our problems won't be settled until they bury Lenin. Imagine. A nation where they still queue up to see a stuffed corpse, as if it was a saint's relic.'

'You'd have hated it, not having your freedom.'

'When did Russians ever have freedom? But it was a game with rules, like chess, except they kept changing while the game was on, so you had to be a skilful player. It was exciting. When I was ten I was more street-wise than the adults here. And our spirit was always free. Even in the camps. What use is freedom without the means to live? It's poisoned my blood and left me twisted. You're wrong to trust me, Serena. You're wrong to believe you even understand me.'

Without rancour he says it; I put it down to guilt for having left. He watches TV reports on Russia with the same fascination people here had for the Gulf War. Zhenya was right – we huffed and we puffed and we blew their house down and left them to the wolves.

'Maybe Russia will never be the same again,' I say, without thinking. 'Everyone who can is leaving now, all the ones who can afford it.' Paris, Nice, Monte Carlo, all the places they fled to in 1917; they're filling up again with the ones who have cash.

'Russia is immortal. She will always rise once more from her own ashes, like the firebird.'

I wish I had this degree of faith. My country will have a political identity again, perhaps, but never a gender.

'Rats,' Max continues. 'They bleed the place dry then leave the sinking ship. Same as I did. And there are thousands more who bide their time, dreaming of finding a new Stalin.'

'He was a mass murderer. My father thought he was a saint.'

'At least he got the country up off its knees. Perhaps it's another Stalin we need after all. Another revolution. My country still has its hell to walk through. People used to have beliefs. Why didn't you tell Carla we got married?' he adds suddenly.

'I did – didn't I?'

'Don't lie. Maybe it's easy for you to forget. Perhaps you want me to do the same. Is that what you want? Fine. Plenty of other women, if I choose to forget.'

'Oh God, stop going on about it. I'm sure I told her. I'll call her tomorrow and make sure I did.'

Dunstaffnage Place, 5th August

The Colonies were built for sociable people. Outdoors there's a communality of living, and Max has settled into it as effortlessly as a cat on cushions. He knows more people than I ever did before he arrived; he has a fan club. He'll sit at the front gate, peeling potatoes for our meal, and people greet him by name as they pass. I press my face to the glass, so I can marvel at his blond head, bent so earnestly over his work. He works equally meticulously on everything he does, in total concentration. I envy him the facility in reaching the Zen state; I've not mastered it, ever. He's the gannet; I'm the petrel, skimming the tops.

I have become jealous of the cello though. Max adores the damn creature immoderately. It sneers at me. It says 'See how he changes as soon as he takes me in his arms?' I've reached the stage where I can scarcely abide watching Maksim in its company. It's as painful as imagining him enjoying another woman. Secretly I've christened it Katya-Two.

He takes Katya-Two outside occasionally to practise, and the whole neighbourhood listens, creeping out silently as elves; he doesn't resent it in the same way as when I ask him to play for my friends.

He's making a special effort to avoid fighting with me. I feel suspicion growing on me like a second skin.

'You're so lucky,' the pretty red-haired girl from the next street along said to me today, dreamy-eyed. I know her by sight, never to speak to before. She sounds Irish; she's the only person I've ever seen with truly green eyes. Emerald green. What a cliché. I don't know her name. She has a small child, still in a pushchair.

'Maksim's so talented.' She pronounces his name carefully and correctly and wistfully. 'My husband can't do anything clever like playing an instrument.'

I wince. No other woman is allowed to call him by his full name. It's my privilege alone. To anyone else, he should be just Max. And doubtless he knows her name, and her husband's, if there truly is a husband, and her child's.

Max is always aware when I'll be at home; he keeps a careful note of my shifts. Perhaps on the other days he doesn't stop at the door when he lifts the pushchair up the steps for her? She's beautiful, in a soft blowsy way, with her tousled hair and her creamy skin, and she makes no attempt to conceal her admiration for my husband.

I'm beginning to feel the cold more than usual. The nights are surely getting longer. I can't banish it from my imagination: Max with other women.

'The woman in the house with the yellow door – the red-haired girl – what's her child called?'

'The little boy? Charles. She's very particular about it. Not Charlie. Charles.'

'What does her husband do?'

'He works in the butcher's on the main street. You must know this. They've lived here five years, since they married.'

'I recognised her as a neighbour. I was talking to her earlier today.' I watch him carefully for any signs of alarm. 'What's her name?'

'Bernadette. But she gets called Bernie. I think it's why she's so touchy with the child's name. You hadn't spoken to her before? She knows you.'

'I suppose I never see these people, with being out all day.'

'I would be out all day too if I could work at a proper job, I wouldn't have time to gossip to our neighbours. Then I'd be the same as you, I wouldn't have a life.'

The edge to his voice should obviate the need of a knife for the tatties.

'I wasn't getting at you.'

'Always, always the tone you use, you're getting at me. I'm doing my best, Serena,' he says sadly. 'Isn't this good enough? I want to find work, so I stop being a burden to you. You told me I could make a better life for myself here.'

'Soon. We need to make sure that we do everything properly. It'll take a little while longer.'

He's not indulging in self-pity. I never knew anyone so little in thrall to that vice. But he's watching too much TV for his own good. There's a Moslem spokesman on tonight, demanding separate schools, maintaining they've a right to run their own areas according to their own laws, a state within a state.

'Listen to him,' Max says. 'I don't want to alter this country. I don't want to look different or make my own rules. All I want is to blend in and be the same as everyone else. How come they get to stay? They can shout on TV demanding their rights. I have to hide; we have to pretend I don't exist. This isn't fair.' His voice shakes with emotion.

I can't argue. No point in telling him again that he'll get sympathy because he looks more archetypically English than anyone else I know – Rupert Brooke rather than Rudolf Nureyev.

'Your people still love to hate us. James Bond, the hero, always fighting the wicked Russians who want to destroy the world.'

'Och, it's just films. People don't think like that in real life.'

Not a few of my shipmates were afraid to disembark in St Petersburg unless it was straight onto a bus.

'You'd be surprised. Anyway, everyone blames us for Chernobyl.'

'You were on our side in the war.'

'No one remembers the war. Not that one, anyway. The war people remember is the Russian demons battering hell out of Chechnya and Eastern Europe. All nations loathe us. You ever hear a Finn or a Pole on the subject, any of the Baltic nationals? The Georgians and Armenians as well, damn it. They blame us for the earthquakes. Even my mother's people in Ukraine hate the Russians.'

I remember the tour guide in Helsinki during the cruise. She practically spat venom every time she mentioned Russia. Her face contorted with loathing, she told us to relish the last time we'd be able to leave our jackets safely on the bus. *You won't be able to do that in St Petersburg. Nor eat the food nor drink the water.*

Max lays his head in his hands, then rubs his eyes hard and sits up again.

'Compassionate nation, yours. They love it when someone spends a fortune bringing home a stray animal. It was on TV. Some soldier brought back a dog from Bosnia. Probably give him a medal. He's a hero. I don't know why I believed anything would be easier for me in this country.'

Evenings like this, Max sits slumped in front of the set, watching in an indiscriminate torpor. Anything, just as long as it isn't a historical documentary. Those he classes with soap operas.

'History!' he sneers. 'Who wants to hear more lies they've made up about the past?'

American cop dramas hold a special fascination for

him; he classifies them as science fiction.

'They pretend there are poor people in America. What nonsense. You've only to see the audience on the Jerry Springer show. Like Christmas geese. No poor people.'

'As many as there are anywhere else.'

'As many as Russia? I don't think so. Even your commercials aren't for poor people. It's all expensive cars and confectionery. I have seen no adverts for things you need to live.'

'How can you watch such trash?' I ask him, angry when he sits watching soft porn late at night. 'There's no plot, no acting, only bare backsides and silicon implants heaving in the air. Nothing remotely artistic or even sexy about it.'

And you get to see the women full frontal and a lot more and a lot longer than you get to see the men; material made for male consumption.

Max's eyes glitter, and he chews his beautiful nails, spoiling them. 'I like to remember what I'm missing. You grudge me this? You should watch too. You might get the hang of being a woman.'

The first time Fergus brought home one of these videos, I thought he'd done it for a joke. I know some women like porn, but I could never take it seriously enough to find it arousing. I was more caught up in the technicalities, wondering how they got *that* camera angle without getting splattered, how the actors held their concentration with a lens so close. He made it plain he expected me to join in, there and then, in the middle of the sitting-room floor. It's when I started taking the bread-knife to bed with me. He agreed to the divorce when he found out.

'It doesn't help,' I tell Max. 'I know you've probably been researching this, and you've read that it does. Maybe for some women with my problem. Not me. It makes it worse for me. It's not sexy, it just gives me nightmares.'

But I can see from his angry, puzzled face that he still doesn't understand.

'What problem do you have? What's sexy for you anyway? A man with all his clothes on? You love nothing better than to get my cock hard, but the minute my hand goes anywhere near my zip, you freak out. As for you undoing my pants! You'd sooner die, wouldn't you, though you know it'd really turn me on. You'd sooner die than make the first move on a man.'

Until I was ten years old, I wanted nothing more than to be like "Bonnie Kilmeny". I wanted to walk up the glen, and find fairyland, and a boyfriend who was neither flesh nor blood nor bone, but was pure as myself, and never have to go home.

So when Donald John Munro told me he knew where the entrance to the Good People's kingdom was, I begged him to take me there, even though he was thirty-four, and I knew in my heart men that age have no truck with fairies. When he had led me a few hundred metres into the trees, he stopped, and unzipped his trousers.

'I know what that is,' I said. I'd heard my aunt say it to my mother: "You believed the entrance to fairyland was through a man's flies, did you?" but I knew Peigi was lying, because of what the kids at school called it. A snake, that's what it was. Probably the same snake that tempted Eve.

He asked me if I wanted to touch it. It's what flipped me over the edge. When he gripped my arm and forced my hand down and wouldn't let me run away, I remembered what I had in the pocket of my cardigan…

I know the important thing for both of us is to get the whole mess of Max's legal status sorted out, but I'm at a loss on where to begin. We've had a Labour government since May, and this should be a positive thing, but the media mill is full of rumours that Blair's nose is already so firmly up the backside of the US Presidency he might as well be wearing blinkers. And the Americans still distrust the Russians, no matter how far past the McCarthy era we are.

Every time I decide today's the day to start the process, I chicken out. Leave it another week. It's always better to leave it. The business of a visa for Max. The visit to yet another shrink. Making up my mind what to do about Fergus. Buying new shoes. Really, the list of things better left for another time is without end.

Henderson's Salad Bar, Edinburgh, 12th August

I've gone on seeing Dee in secret, because Max hates her so much.

'He'd have been better off with you,' I tell her wistfully.

'No thanks. Why?'

Indecently large, self-regulated income. An enormous flat with high ceilinged rooms and good acoustics. A well-stocked liquor cabinet. An accommodating body and a clutch of eggs awaiting reprieve from the freezer.

'You like sex.'

'Mmmm. He certainly has bedroom eyes. So what's the problem? You have a bedroom, I recall, and Fergus's orgy-sized bed?'

'We have a bedroom each.'

It takes her a moment to cotton on. 'Jesus H, Serena – you're not still singing from that hymn-sheet? I thought Fergus made you go to a shrink to get fixed?'

When we were teenagers, she just got annoyed when I spoiled my half of a double date. But she's grown up a lot since those days. Become quite the psychoanalyst.

'In the unconscious everything's supposed to turn to its opposite,' she says. 'You should be an insatiable nympho. I thought it's why you made such an effort to get into Captain Conti's pants. Trust you to be different. You just lead them on then kick up a fuss. Have you not read Eric Berne? "*Rapo*" personified, you are.'

'Stick to your own trade,' I say. 'Crooked walls are your province, not twisted minds, even if you have read a book.'

'Sex and design have a lot in common. The fusion of opposites to bring harmony. Shall I go on? Och, I don't know what you can do, Serena, but you need to do something. See a better shrink.'

The consultant I saw while I was still with Learmonth produced a name for it, triumphantly, ticking another one off on the list. 'More common than you'd think,' she said. 'You're not alone, I can assure you.' I fully expected her to give me a sorority badge. Something along the lines of the Isle of Man emblem, but with three pairs of crossed legs. I know I should have been glad to have a name for it, at last – other than 'frigid bitch', which was Fergus's name for it.

'Been there,' I say. 'Got the tee shirt.'

The policewoman who gave me a bath after the doctor was finished with me was an attractive blonde. She washed my hair, and let me use some of her rose-scented skin cream, because I'd scratched my face on branches, then found an enormous tee shirt for me to wear. They needed to keep my clothes. She fastened a thin leather belt round my waist, and said, 'Aren't you smart! Wish I was as slim as you. Some chance.'

And I wanted to put my arms round her neck and plead with her not to send me back to my Grannie's house, but to have me adopted instead, because I'd get into such trouble. For hadn't Grannie told me over and over: men are there to take, always take, so women are made to give, but the woman who gives without being forced is no better than a whore? 'Just asking for it,' she'd mutter in satisfaction, reading reports of a rape in the Daily Record.

'In any case,' says Dee, 'if you can tear your mind away from your own problems for five minutes, I've something to tell you.'

Suitable sperm donor at last?

'I've sold the business,' she adds casually. 'I'm moving to London.'

'London? You can't. You can't leave me.'

'Come with me then. There's plenty of work for journalists there. I won't miss this dump. I'm bored. Edinburgh's not the place it once was. It's too small. There are no new people worth knowing.'

'But it'll be better once we have the parliament.'

She chortles. 'That's what worries me. There seems to be a risk the referendum might get a "yes" this time. It pisses me off more than the lack of decent shoe-shops. I'm a tax payer. I'm a capitalist. I don't want to spend the rest of my life under the thumb of the Strathclyde Soviet Republic paying for bolshie dustmen who think they should earn the same as I do.'

'Crap. Soon Edinburgh will be all snobs like you. Men in suits.'

'If I wanted Communism, I'd have shacked up with a red. No, I'm off to be one of King Tony's loyal subjects. I'm going to embrace the values of Middle England. Farewell knees-up's tomorrow. Bring Stalin, if you must.'

'But when are you going?'

'Next week.'

'So you've done all this – fait accompli? And you never said anything to me.'

'You're so wrapped up in your own troubles no one tells you anything. But what's the point in all the worrying? Just *do* something. You'd feel so much better if you'd only act instead of analysing all the time.'

Maybe she's right. The past few years – since long before I met Fergus – I've let my life drift. Bringing Max home felt like a suitably decisive move, yet here I am, as undecided and unfocused as ever. Dee has shown me that there's no point in leaving your life on hold and hoping something better will turn up. You move on, or you might as well be dead.

Dunstaffnage Place, 16th August

I have finally accepted the fact that Max needs to be allowed to go out on his own. He has quickly eased into a pattern of spending a couple of nights a week in a pub called Colquhoun's down in Leith. Katya-Two can't keep him at home either. He comes back smelling of whisky, full of artificial love, and tries to pull me close, to make me notice him at last. It works. I slap him as hard as I can. He derives satisfaction from it, because he's won. He's made me do it. After, he'll either laugh or weep, and how am I to cope with either?

'When life's too much, drinking's the only honest act,' he'll say.

I open my eyes to the fact Max is a willing drunk. I can't claim it's a surprise. It's why they chose Christianity over Islam after all, because they couldn't do without it. Distilling was just another Western import, like VD and Big Macs. When the alcohol possesses him, he's not Max any more. He's a bumbling idiot, full of false bonhomie, grinning inanely. He's turned into my father. Max won't drink in Stockbridge either, even if I offer to go with him. Frank was just the same – didn't appreciate seeing a woman drinking. Boozing is men's business, same as leaving the house like a shit-heap. It's why Max would rather walk to Leith, alone.

'To drink with real people,' he says. 'Real men with real lives and rough hands. Not the beautiful people who work in the media, or in advertising, or in selling houses to other fools like themselves. Posers with their brains in their back pockets. Arse-holes with mobile phones – good, isn't it?'

He has the trick of farting on demand, as competently as any school-kid. He'll let one go, then pretend he's answering it. It's hysterical. It makes me sore to hold in the laughter, but I won't give him the satisfaction.

Sometimes a Russian ship is docked at Leith and he comes home reeking of foreign tobacco. I start in on him again until I know he's wishing he'd stayed on board and sailed all the way to Archangel. Does he guess that more than once I wished it too, in my heart?

Tonight, I make the mistake of taking Max to one of Anita's parties. Whatever her shortcomings, she's knowledgeable about real music, his type of music. He's on edge the entire evening. He sips expensive white wine as if it's hemlock, and throws a tantrum on the way home.

'They despise me. I felt humiliated. Why should I associate with people like these? They all talk to me slowly and carefully as if I don't fucking well understand English.'

'Oh nonsense, they're being polite, trying to make conversation. More than you do.'

'They treat me as if I'm something dangerous and smelly that needs to be kept on a leash. I'll give them fucking animal. I'll show them I can bite.'

It wasn't their fault. Stress is contagious.

'You're so false when you're with them,' he adds, 'your voice changes, your accent. I hate it. I keep looking to see where the camera is. Why can't you be yourself? The way you were in Russia. Spontaneous and loving. The person I thought I was running away with, not some actress who only cares about impressing pricks like these. You changed the minute you stepped on the train back to this place. You turned into my mother. Why did you stop being sweet and feminine? I liked you better when we were travelling through the forest together.'

I preferred me then too.

' "In Russia" was about three days. You've changed too. You've stopped being brave and independent. You're a spoilt, wheenging child.'

I feel real fear at moments like this. I know I have to let him have his turn first. That's manners. But, oh God, when we both start –

'Go to their parties on your own,' yells Max. 'The tall man, the English one, the one with a laugh like Founder's Day in the mental home – he's in love with you anyway. He doesn't want me there.'

'Nick? Don't be daft. He's happily married. You met his wife. They have a young baby.'

'Babies you get from screwing at the wrong time of month. Happy doesn't come into it. What is it he calls her – "Cleh"? What name's it supposed to be?'

'Claire.'

'Right. The 'r' is silent, as in asshole. He's in love with you. Doesn't trouble to hide it when he looks at you. You think he says this too – "Don't be foolish, Cleh, Serena's a happily married woman?" '

No. He thinks I'm a happily divorced one with a live-in lover. 'You make it bloody impossible for me to work with them,' I yell back. 'As if it wasn't bad enough already. I need my job.'

'Oh yes, married to a shiftless lout like me, who can't support you.'

It's been easier to control what happens if I invite a few of them to our house, but no more fun; social evenings as relaxing as walking barefoot on broken glass. The first time, I made the mistake of asking him to play for them. He wouldn't embarrass me by refusing though I swear I could hear his teeth grinding above the sound of the cello. And he let me have it afterwards. I never met a performance artist who so loathes having an audience.

Other evenings he'll have me in stitches after they've all left, for he's a superlative mimic, especially of bullshitters. He can produce a very convincing version of me. A squeaky voice and a wee bum-wiggle: Serena-on-her-high-horse. I bet he's popular with his drinking pals.

Dunstaffnage Place, 18th August

I'm less than overjoyed when I find Max is not always such a coy performer. He admits he's been out busking with three other musicians at the top of the Mound, with Marjorie Adam's zillion-pound mega-fiddle.

'It's brilliant. You should have heard the audience. Didn't want to let us stop. They say now the Festival's started, we could be on the sound stage in the Princes Street gardens.'

And I yell and nag and swear and won't let myself be the tiniest bit pleased for him.

'At least they're friendly. I can jingle my coins in my pocket. My pocket money. Big joke, eh? Not Serena's money. They treat me like a man. They don't know I'm the lodger in Serena's wonderful fucking loveless house and I get to sleep alone in her husband's bed.'

The guilt is too painful, so I nag him over trivialities instead. I nag him over leaving his clothes lying about, and burning food in the frying pan, making all the clean washing smell of burnt grease. I nag him over the size of his feet.

'For Christ's sake, Max must you leave your shoes cluttering up the floor?'

There's so little space in our hallway at the foot of the

stairs, and you can't tuck size elevens in a corner. He doesn't do it to annoy me. Ever since he could walk, ever since he's worn shoes, he's taken them off as soon as he enters a house. Dreadfully bad manners to do otherwise. He condemns the Scots as filthy people.

'You know I don't like to wear my outdoor shoes in the house.'

'Do you think I want this to be the first part of my home people lay eyes on, your bloody shoes?'

'The streets of Edinburgh aren't exactly clean, Serena. Maybe you prefer me to tramp dog-mess through the house?'

'You could watch where you walk, or wipe your feet.'

'I'm hot for you,' he hisses, 'I desire you, I want to make babies with you, I want to have you squirm with pleasure in my arms. I'm prepared to wait till you feel ready. But all you care about is where I put my fucking shoes.' He hurls them up the stairs so hard he takes a chunk out of the plaster.

'Your habits are disgusting. You pee with the bathroom door open – when you bother to do it indoors. You think I want to watch that performance?'

'I am like some pet you bought on impulse,' he says. 'Oh dear, it's so difficult to house-train it, too much effort. And it costs so much to feed. You could take me back for a refund. Pity the receipt's in Russian.'

'No, with a pet there's always the Cat and Dog Home as a last resort.'

❖

At lunchtime, I buy a small wooden shoe rack to fit on the wall. Max smiles to himself when he sees it, and immediately fetches rawlplugs, a hammer, screws. It's set to become a standing joke with anyone who visits us. 'Serena's mosque,' they'll say. 'Where do we perform our ablutions?'

But it's like having a mouth ulcer you can't keep your tongue off. 'It'd help if you'd just try to be tidy. And clean the toilet once in a blue moon,' I tell him.

'Why should I do women's work?' He tosses his head in the petulant way he has. 'The hell with it. I'm the man in the house. I shouldn't have to take orders, put your shoes there, don't light your disgusting cigarettes here. You told me this is my house. In my house I do what I want.'

He picks a hazelnut from the bowl and deliberately and loudly cracks it with his teeth, to see if I'll rise to the bait the way I did initially, screeching at him: *Use the nutcrackers.*

What did God give us teeth for?

He cracks more and more, specifically to annoy me now. He'll take crown tops off beer bottles the same way. 'You want me to thank you? I came with you, didn't I? You thank me. Come on, bitch, tell me how ungrateful I am. How you rescued me from starving in the gutter.'

'I've never said that. But you weren't far off it, were you? Starving. I could tell from looking you never had enough to eat.'

'I wasn't like all your lot. You can tell from looking at the people in the streets of Edinburgh they've had too much to eat.'

'Well at least here you don't normally see a doctor's child wandering round with a wee sign on his forehead saying "feed me".'

'Look at our literature, our art, our music. Nothing you have here can hold a candle to it. You are the paupers. I am proud to be Russian.'

These are the spine-tingling moments when I think he means to thump me. But he pulls his irritating trick of becoming calm.

'We're too much in each others' company. You need some woman-friend you can let this all out with.'

'I used to have some of those, before you scared some off with your abuse, and seduced the others. And you've been using my deodorant again. You always leave the top off and your disgusting hairs stuck to it.'

Oh hell, hell, hell. I brought him home to be kind to him and look after him. When did Act Two begin? I haven't read *Mars and Venus*. I always made the mistake of trying to follow him when he flees to the cave. 'I don't mean to go on at you. But it's not really quarrelling, is it? Squabbling. It's all about small things. We see eye to eye on the big issues.'

'Couples get divorced over how they squeeze the toothpaste, Serena, not over their philosophy of life.'

Dunstaffnage Place, 26th August

Our Colonies gardens are beautiful in the twilight, when the sky's sucked the colour from the flowers because it's jealous; an arty soft-focus sepia-tint, rose-fragranced vignette. I've left the windows open to let the last breaths of summer warmth come in. Dougal cried off; new students to be processed. Maksim and Carla are lingering outside.

When I left they were dismembering Bartok and half of me wants to strain to hear if the topic is still the rudiments and theory of music.

I'm desperate with loneliness, because by now I'm afraid of Carla's fondness for Max. She's a sexy woman, and Dougal's not a sexy man – but *my* man is. The body chemistry between them is tangible. (Fergus maintains chemistry doesn't come into it. 'Physics,' he says, 'volume, friction, generation of heat. Biology too. You're all searching for the one with the biggest antlers in the hope he'll have an enormous cock and a high sperm-count.')

They've lowered their voices, and from my bedroom it sounds like the murmur of doves. They're laughing too much. Carla's laugh always sounds as if she's been told a particularly filthy joke. I can't think of an excuse to intrude in my own garden, but the temptation to look is irresistible; I stand well to the side of the window, in case they see me. Always the same, the wee girl with her nose pressed against the glass, burning with envy. I despise myself. I thought I'd be the one lingering in the velvety dim light with him, giggling and licking scented raindrops off the neighbour's rose-petals, or sipping wine and sharing secrets.

They're not touching, though they are sitting close, still drinking. I don't know what I'd do if they'd been in a clinch, or if I hadn't been able to see them at all. I pad aimlessly into the kitchen, away from the sound of their sexy giggling.

'Serena? Carla's leaving now. Aren't you going to say cheerio?' Max prances into the room, bright-eyed, his face flushed from the wine.

'I'd gone to bed.'

'Why – aren't you feeling well?' He goes to the sink and begins rinsing glasses.

'Not particularly, as a matter of fact.'

Carla strides in. She doesn't knock. 'You deserted me, left me with only this boy to entertain me. Max, what are you thinking of? Serena's all ready for bed, it's rude to keep a lady waiting.'

'He seemed to be doing all right. I could hear the pair of you braying like jackals.'

She pulls a face and lays a cool, heavily ringed hand on my forehead, a slender unshod foot on top of my bare one. 'You have a slight temperature but your feet are like iceblocks. Max, take her upstairs at once and comfort her.'

'Don't get too close in case I'm coming down with something right enough.'

'Off you go then, and warm the sheets for your man while he drives my car backwards up this damn street.'

I experience a strong but fleeting urge to ring the politzei and report her as a drunk driver.

Maksim places his hands on my shoulders when he comes in. 'Are you really feeling ill?'

'What were you talking about?' I can't prevent the catch in my voice. I want a cuddle to make me warm, but he gives me a quick peck on the cheek, and then holds me at arm's length.

I turn away and start to dry the glasses, mechanically. She used to be my friend. This too you've stolen.

'Didn't you want me to keep her outside?'

'I don't know why you had to canoodle in the dark with her.'

'Canoodle! What kind of word is this? You think I was screwing her? You claimed you had work to do. I thought you wouldn't want to be disturbed. You said you wanted peace and quiet.'

'That was Dougal.'

'My God, I believe you're jealous.'

'You love it, don't you, the way she leans across you shaking her maracas in your face.'

'The only thrill I get. You never do that do you? Of course, I don't see what you get up to with the men at work.' He pokes around the fruit bowl and selects an apple. 'Or your husband.'

One of the five survivors from my set of Edinburgh Crystal Thistle wine goblets (a wedding present from a cousin of Learmonth's) shatters on the floor.

'Careful!' says Max.

He sets down his apple, grasps me round the waist and lifts me clear of the glittering debris.

'You'll cut your feet. That looked as if it was expensive.'

He starts sweeping up the shards. He can't possibly know. It's not as if anything has *happened* with Fergus. Max has just struck lucky with a multi-purpose throwaway accusation.

'We're seeing far too much of Dougal and Carla,' I say. 'Too dependant.' Co-dependants. Willing victims. Collaborators.

'All right, so we'll see more people. It's because you don't invite others.'

'I'm fed up with being the only one who provides

friends for company. It's like having to continually think what other people want to eat.'

He shrugs and goes on eating his apple. 'Hardly my fault. If we'd stayed in Russia it would be the same. You'd be complaining that it was always my friends.'

I'm shivering. It's not only the night air. You expel your devils, you expel your angels too.

Dunstaffnage Place, 27th August

I'm spying on Max more and more. I ogle him from behind the curtain, like a dirty old woman. I watch his bare back as he sets up two chairs as a makeshift sawhorse in the garden and begins to saw the wood to make new shelves for the bathroom. His back is the most beautiful, erotic object conceivable. It gives me a stomach cramp to see how the muscles ripple beneath the skin as smoothly as an animal's. He's been training hard, since he found he could use the community centre gym for three pounds a session. He says musicians have to be as well-honed as dancers.

He's the fittest man I've known, and the cleanest. Because Max can't go to the sauna every week, he scrubs himself all over with rough salt, and rinses it off in a cold shower. Afterwards I can feel the heat of his body across the room and his skin is immaculate; good enough to eat.

He's found an old carpenter's belt in the shed. I've no idea where it came from, for Fergus never messed with wood and nails. Max labours with utter concentration. He'd never find it demeaning to work with his hands, whether he's sawing and shaping wood or playing Bach. The belt is too big; it has slipped down over his hip-bone at one side, the worn leather obscenely sexy against the creamy skin at the other. I know exactly what he's up to. The effect on me isn't uncalculated.

I used to while away the hours of Peter MacKenzie's sermons day-dreaming about Jesus, and in my imagination, this is how he looked. I never understood why the school bibles showed him as another wimp in a girl's nightie. He must have looked the way Max does now, as he worked alongside Joseph and James, sawing and planing and shaping timber, his hair tied back, his elegant, narrow, Byzantine-icon face beaded with sweat, a fine film of dust lying across his arms and shoulders. A handsome, muscular, sexy working man, with sticky resin on his fingers, and the sharp, hot scent of fresh-cut wood on his skin.

He'd a temper too; flinging the money-changers out of the temple, and all their gear after them. I bet he swore at them. He knocked around with a bunch of fishermen after all. Not noted for their delicate language. A hard edge to him.

Zinging with life, he'd have been, to attract the attention of a woman like Mary Magdalene. She was no cheap tart, she was seriously stylish, and she'd not have wasted her time or her ointment on a lesser man. He had beautiful feet, I daresay, long-toed and elegant Giotto painted them, just like Max's; and the Magdalene would have massaged the oils into them languorously, bending her head so that her lips and her breast and her arms were drowned in her long, sultry hair. And he'd have sent the disciples away as she began to kiss his toes, and drawn her head up to look in her eyes. 'Mary, Mary, Mary! What are you doing?'

And the tree he was nailed to still growing green in a wood like Ollasdale.

Ursula's at my side, steadying me. I've forgotten I'd invited her for coffee.

'Are you ill? You turned quite faint. You're very flushed. Sit down.'

I can see what she's thinking. I'm almost ready to laugh at the ridiculousness of it. A former nurse should know pregnant women stopped falling in a swoon while Victoria was still on the throne anyway. I realize I'm merely losing my mind. Peter MacKenzie's flesh and blood, keeling over from having erotic thoughts about Jesus.

'Your inner thermostat's faulty,' Max told me calmly this morning. 'You start to get hot, then alarm bells ring and the freezer kicks in. This is not how it's supposed to work. You need to come to the boil, let it happen, and cool down slowly, slowly, slowly. It's exquisite. You have to get this fixed. For yourself. I'm not asking you to change only for me.'

I pushed him away. 'The Australian chakra woman I went to said my second chakra's blocked. About as useful an image as yours. If I knew how to unblock my sodding chakras, do you think I wouldn't?'

'Do you think sex is shameful? Maybe it's because your grandfather was a religious freak.'

It stands to reason that I did *know why Donald John took me to the woods late in an afternoon in July.*

God is always watching me, and knows all the secrets of my heart.

If he hadn't frightened me so much, I might have kept my thoughts clear and my hand in my pocket. I wanted to confess to the police doctor, because she was kind to me, and gentle. But I was afraid she'd tell, even though she made Grannie wait outside the room (Where was my mother? Not with me, anyway).

And when she spoke to her afterwards, in a quiet voice, Grannie raised hers to say, 'He hadn't interfered with her then? The Lord be praised!' and turned to me to tell me I'd been lucky.

The doctor said sternly, 'Can I have a word with you in private, Mrs MacKenzie?'

But I knew there'd be no gentleness waiting for me at home.

'You have to love me first,' I say.

Max sighs. 'It doesn't happen that way. Love's not like a thunderbolt. It's like a potato. You have to plant it carefully and tend the shoots and wait patiently to see what harvest you get.'

'Not a very romantic image.'

'I'm not romantic. I'm a pragmatist. And I'm a man. I have urges, and I need an outlet for them.'

'It's good for you. Freud would have said it's what makes you creative. You can sublimate it all in your music. You should be thanking me. Women have the raw deal. We don't have semen to conserve. If we had, we wouldn't waste it and spill it around indiscriminately.'

'Fuck Freud. What did he know? I never went without it for so long in my life. It's fucking bad for me.'

Albion Studios, 28th August

Max watches wistfully as I drive off to work. He loves driving as much as I hate it, and he's a good driver:

insouciant, skilful, and precise. But he doesn't have a valid licence, not even a Russian one to show; he'd have to fill in forms. So, although I let him back the Peugeot up the street out of gridlock hell, when we have to travel together he sits hunched beside me like a sullen child. 'You're the boss,' he'll say in the petted tone that pronounces me guilty. 'You can drive your car.'

As if this makes it all right. As if any of us extract any benefit other than money from our work at Albion. We pretend we lead interesting, glamorous lives, but they're as hollow and prickly and desolate as the sea urchin shells on my mantelpiece. Nick with his falcons, Anita with her flute; their lives are plays they act in. Peigi says it's the same in any workplace, but I know it's never as bad elsewhere. The people I work with have a higher-than-average need to believe in their own importance. Main reason why they're there.

Long ago, I realised they stop talking when I come into the room. In an imperceptible way I've been found wanting: not their type. Some days it makes me angry. More often I have to blink back the tears and fight the urge to run away, drive in the other direction and keep going, and have no more times when Anita can ignore me when someone important is being shown around and introduced. It used to amaze me to read reports of journalists locked away, tortured, or killed for resisting authoritarian regimes. In Albion you'd be trampled in the rush to volunteer as informers.

But I'm trapped like a moth in a lampshade. Maksim has a life, and I haven't. He wastes little time on self-pity.

He shops for our food, and is amazed because he rarely has to stand in queues. He tries to cook for me. He tries – unsuccessfully – to keep the place as clean as I claim to like. He glowers at the tiny patch of earth that was to have kept us in vegetables. He displays unhealthy interest in the winos on the Royal Mile.

'They drink meths?'

'Presumably not, these days.'

'Meths, perfume, boot polish on bread. Gorbachev made us experimental. And you can distil vodka from anything.'

Dunstaffnage Place, 28th August

We're both losing hope, though I forbid myself to think it'd be a relief to come home and find Max vanished, departed, deported, whatever. I banish the thought it'd have been better if I'd never got off the bloody *Fortuna*.

'Play me records of some of your Gaelic music,' he says sadly. 'I want to hear some new tunes. I want to understand your culture. It has to be mine now too.'

I put on the CD of Karen Matheson singing *Am Buachaille Bàn*, and watch his face. Without prompting, he latches onto it. 'Don't explain to me what the words mean,' he says. 'I want to have the melody pure in my head.'

Perhaps, for him, I might have sung it again one day. How strange. Nearly half a lifetime ago, the set piece that won me my medal at the Gaelic Mod was the ultimate love-song for a fair-haired man.

'I wish I could play an instrument,' I say. 'It'd be good to share an interest together.'

'A musician needs an audience. It's what you can do best for me, be my audience. I play only for you, no one else in the world, because you're the one who can hear me properly.'

'We'd understand each other better.'

'It'll come. I need you to listen to me, as much as I need to play.'

However, I've begun to regret not getting rid of my old piano before he had the chance to tune it. No sanctuary even in my own home.

'You don't mind if I play music with Carla?' he asks, casually. The pair of them have had the front off the instrument and twiddled pegs and got it more or less in tune. 'Carla'. It's a love-word in his husky, throaty voice that is not unlike hers, the rolled 'r' and the rich vowel-sounds. 'Carla'. A caress. Tigers purring after mating.

I try to smile.

He puts his arms round me. 'It's so pleasant to work with another musician again. She's good, it'll help me improve.'

And it gives him the excuse to spend half the evening with his face down another woman's cleavage. He holds me for a few moments, but he doesn't try to kiss me.

He smiles to himself. 'It's OK,' he says. 'I still want you. But it's amazing what will-power can achieve.'

'I think Carla wants you.'

'She has Dougal to console her.' He strolls over to the window and gazes out into the darkness.

'I don't know why Carla puts up with him,' I say. 'She's so attractive – she could have any man.'

He turns back to me, with a sigh. 'People stay together for strange reasons. I'm not terribly highly-sexed, by the way.'

He opens his arms to me again, and I hold him tight to avoid the pain in his eyes. We still have to face down demons worse than the immigration authorities.

'Let's go away this weekend,' he says, his mouth against my neck. 'I have somewhere I have to go on Saturday, but afterwards let's go somewhere, just the two of us. You have a tent in the shed – did you even know you had it? We could go to the seaside, camp out.'

'I'd love that. But let's wait till next weekend, when we have both days off. And it'll be cold at night in a tent, even at this time of year.'

'We'll keep each other warm. We have to make this work,' he says. 'We must make an effort.'

Perhaps he's right, though I've felt so defeated my thoughts have been tending in the opposite direction recently. One of the things that's held me back is the thought of admitting Fergus was right.

Central Edinburgh, 30th August

'Come with me,' Max says, after we finish our Saturday expedition to the supermarket.

He has to meet someone at an address in the Old Town. There's a map sketched on the back of an envelope.

'You'll easily find it without me,' I say.

'This is a big moment for me; I want you to be there. Aren't you interested?'

'Tell me what it is you're doing.'

'Playing music. This place is supposed to be a recording studio. I have a friend who works in the music industry. He's set this up.'

'Which friend?'

'Johnser. John Seaton. You'll meet him today.'

It's through a pend in one of the un-gentrified segments of the Canongate, where the steep sunlight of late August's too harsh for the lean streets. The acrid smell of horseshit always seems to hang in the air, though there have been no horses here for years. The smell is trapped with all the other phantoms in the dead stones; all the little lost drummer boys in the Ghost Tour guides' scary stories.

But it's not so bad once we're inside. Johnser sits me down beside him at the mixing-desks, and then Max and Katya-Two are tucked into a small glass booth; it's a crush!

The tune; so familiar, and yet so unfamiliar.

'He's brilliant, isn't he?' says Johnser. 'It sounds genuine. Traditional, like. Sounds as if it should have words.'

It takes me a minute to compose myself. 'It does,' I say. 'It's a Gaelic love song. It's about a fair-haired man.'

'Could be about Max?'

I hope not. The one in the song buggers off and leaves her.

> *What a deadly sickness is love*
> *There's none who suffers it*
> *But feels every day is a week*

'What's this for?' I ask Johnser.

'A whisky commercial. Did he not tell you? *Dunsmore Glen*. Likely he wanted to keep it as a surprise. Good, isn't it? Appropriate. I thought all the Russians drank was vodka, but he's real fond of a dram is Maxie.'

I'm angry, as if he's stolen something special from me. But it's my own fault. I haven't explained the significance of the song, and I think my heart's about to burst with the beauty of it. It's a brief session, not much more than fifteen minutes, because Max clearly spent the whole of yesterday practising. Johnser is beside himself.

'He'll have so much work he won't know what to do with himself. It's a waste to have him playing nothing but stuff written by dead people.'

'Arvo Pärt's not dead,' I say glibly.

Max grins at me as we walk back to the car. 'That'll bring in fourteen hundred. What did you think of it anyway? It's like a miracle. The inspiration only arrived in the last hours before I was due to produce the goods.'

'Fourteen hundred what?'

'Pounds. Cash. It's what I've earned.'

'Shit! That's impossible.'

'It's my share for arranging and playing. Johnser says I can make far more once I get known. He says the sky's the limit.'

'You get too well-known, friend, and you'll find yourself in Saughton.'

'Stop fretting. I have to be able to work, and drive a car, and be a real person. If it means I have to spend a while locked up, too bad.'

'They'll put you in prison, like a criminal.'

'It's what I am. It's not legal to travel with a forged passport. Didn't you enjoy my music?'

'It was wonderful. You're exceptionally gifted. You deserve to make money, but...'

He nudges my arm. 'Don't get depressed. Thank you for coming with me. I hardly see you the rest of the week, with your important work. I want to look at you. Best friends?'

'Anyway, it's marvellous you earned so much.' Too late, as usual with my appreciation.

'Not quite Maksim Vengorov, but I'll get there. It's not only the money either – this is what I love to do more than anything; to be able to get the tunes in my head out there for you to hear.'

Dunstaffnage Place, 1st September

Diana 'Queen of Hearts' is dead, and I haven't seen home all day. Some luvvie from Albion's mother station is yelling down the phone at me, 'What are you fucking Jocks playing at? Don't you know there are little children weeping in the streets down here?' We've been tardy in cancelling a football match, apparently. The Scots can't be trusted to grieve properly.

The studio is overrun by geeks with orange hair and attitude and "Souf' London" accents. The boss man himself arrives, and I'm sent downstairs to collect him. Anita meets us on the stairs and practically puts my eye out with her elbow as she rushes to gush, ignoring me completely.

'Rude, self-centred cow,' I yell after her, but she's in full flow by then. Doesn't even notice.

I walk home weeping with rage, and have to restrain myself from taking a hammer to the TV set. All these stacks of rotting flowers. Grown men blubbering like babies for the cameras. Teddy bears, for Christ's sake.

Max is glued to the screen.

'What the hell are you watching this for?'

'Trying to figure out what makes the British the way they are.'

I snort. 'Your lot and the French had the right idea about what to do with royal families. I bet you'd never heard of her before this.'

'Nonsense. All the Russian magazines wrote about her. They said she was very fashionable and beautiful. I didn't find her attractive. Too much like a calf on its way to be slaughtered, the way she rolled her eyes up.'

'I suppose they'll make her a saint now.'

'The way we did ours?'

We end the evening in truce, united by our scorn for making saints out of over-privileged people who excelled in nothing but self-pity.

North Berwick, 7th September

I've earned my time off. We drove to the seaside yesterday, to walk bent double against the wind, and eat fish and chips off the paper. We have slept stiffly side by side in sleeping bags in our inadequate tent, and pretended to enjoy ourselves. Not strictly true; Max thinks it's fine. At least we've been spared having to watch the State Funeral over and over on TV.

'You told me you loved the sea,' he says accusingly.

'Not this one. It's too open. I like the beach, but the open sea frightens me. I like to see land on the other side.' Only the North Sea's chilly, nacreous skies can I appreciate.

'I thought you said your island is far out to the west?'

'It is. But Balvaig's on the side where you can see other islands.'

I'm not from a race which built on hilltops to see the enemy coming. My inheritance is of caves and woodland to hide in, though, occasionally, we'd turn on our own and smoke them out or roast them.

'You're comfortable with wide horizons,' I say. 'That's the difference.'

We watch a couple throw sticks into the sea for a black lab.

'I'd like to have a dog,' says Max. 'A very big one. Something like a Rottweiler.'

'We can't have a big dog in town. Dee and I couldn't believe the number of enormous dogs we saw in St Petersburg.'

He looks wistful. 'You could reach St Petersburg, if you sail long enough.'

'You can see it in your head, can't you?'

'Always. Don't let's be sad today, Serena.'

I try to cheer up for his sake, and to stay happy when he suddenly heads for the water, shedding clothes, plunging naked into the waves and splashing around. I gather up the trail of garments, and stand at the edge like his nanny, racking my brains to think how he'll get dry. He sprawls in the shallow water on his back, kicking his legs so that small droplets land on my skin.

'Take off your clothes and come in. You said you'd teach me to swim.'

'It's freezing.'

'It's good for you.'

Then he's out, and in my arms while I try to rub him dry with my cardigan, slippery as a fish, his skin so hot it burns my fingers. Fire and water. He puts his arms round me, and I think maybe I will have to go in to cool down. He picks me up, still butt-naked, and runs into the water with me, pretending to drop me, clothes and all.

He wolfs down our cheap café meal with a better will than I've seen for weeks. It makes me smile. No chance of converting him to vegetarianism – he doesn't consider it a meal unless there's meat. The sea air and the exercise have put colour in his face; he could be a Scandinavian peasant farmer at his dinner, or a Dutch painting, with plenty of vermilion on the palette. Every few moments he makes me blush with a glance both bold and secret.

When he came out of the waves, disconcertingly masculine, and snuggled in my arms, and looked in my face lovingly, the way he did the early days, I found myself contemplating how it would feel to walk into the water and keep walking, until my feet couldn't find the bottom, take in my death by the mouthful and the lungful rather than wake to another day when there's hostility in his eyes.

'Maksim,' I say, 'when I die don't let them burn me. I want to be put in the ground. Or laid on a mountain for the birds to pick my bones. And I don't want dirges. I want a jazz band, and huge black men in white top hats.'

'What a time to think of dying, when things are looking

up. We'll both be put in the ground in a very long time, in a single grave. They can open my coffin and lay you in my arms. "And I will love thee still, my dear, while the sands o' life shall run", ' he adds suddenly.

And now he's reciting the whole of *My love is like a red, red rose* from memory; he has it word-perfect, and it's so beautiful in his sexy accent, I'm having to wipe my eyes.

'I didn't know Burns was still popular in Russia?'

'My father taught me. He loved poetry, all poetry.'

And yet, he didn't want his son to be a musician?

'Talk to me about your island. When will you take me there?'

All the way back to town, I tell him about the subtle colours of Soma's landscape. If I'd been born an artist, it's the palette I'd favour over the harsh, clear colours of the South. Grey on grey and no two shades of it the same. It makes you pay attention to texture and elusive shadows, to which surfaces hurl the light back in your eyes and which swallow it greedily. And the complicated Art Deco sunsets in peach, terra-cotta, lemon, amaranth, pistachio, with the sea a bolt of silk.

'It's a geography sculpted by ice as clearly as any in the Baltic or Scandinavia,' I say. 'The mountains are damson and slate coloured in summer and autumn, whiter than the wings of gulls in winter. There's a small bay – Ollasdale Bay – just below my aunt's house. Even a child can fish safely from a rowing boat there and catch mackerel. There's a scutter of islands, most of them no more than rocks. The village – Balvaig – is built in a basin of fertile land, so it's surrounded by crofts.'

And the sea, eternally present to the eyes, the ears, the nose.

Over on the mainland, there's the lushness of Inverewe and its eucalypts. I prefer the severe lineaments of Balvaig's face – a pine branch swaying against the full moon, waterfalls, small clear pools; cormorants on the rocks, wings stiffly extended, waiting for their deodorant to dry; peaceful, deserted beaches, shell-strewn and melancholy; moss in the woods, snow in the high corries on the three Beinns, bog cotton on the moor. Voluptuous touches too: wild orchids among the rushes, and the shameless swollen-lipped shells the sea would dump on the very doorstep of the kirk, like foundlings, to remind us of our sin. A sensual place, though the God of my people abhors sensuality. Having created this harsh, fragile beauty he abandoned it to folk with stones for souls.

'I hope you won't be disappointed with it,' I tell Max. 'There's not so much as a full-time shop in the village now. Just a sort of pub. The school's likely to close any year now. Most of the people are retired.'

They glean a little cash from the tourists; bed and breakfast, boat hire – few more personal services. The good-lifers arrive to make pottery and driftwood picture frames. Three times out of five they return from whence they came after a year or two, complaining of the shiftless and xenophobic islanders.

A grim and tenacious people, mine, like Max's. Survivors, frontiersmen. They know in their hearts you cannot buy and sell the land any more than you can own the right to look at the moon, and the odds are loaded against life being good. But what's the point of thinking of the past? The landowners cleared better places than Balvaig, and they'll do it again if it suits them. They've retained a preference for folk who think like sheep. The place is ruined. System-built bungalows spoil the view wherever you look, and there's more chance of Colchester or Coatbridge than Celt in the voices. The shops in Portmore sell crap as bad as any you'll find on the Royal Mile, and you can't get a decent cup of tea. Balvaig's less of a community now than the Stockbridge Colonies. But there's still the Balvaig Inn.

'There's an ugly fish farm there now, right in front of the village,' I tell Max. 'And the rain! It comes like stair-rods down your neck more than three hundred days of the year, from out of a sky as heavy as a mucky fleece. Most days you can't see the scenery for mist. When it's not raining, midges like zeppelins come out to firebomb the tender skin under your eyes.'

'Sounds good!' he says. 'In Karelia it's mosquitoes. You think I mind rain?'

I need him to love it all as I do, irrationally and completely. As I fear I'm beginning to love him.

Dunstaffnage Place, 7th September

Max opens a bottle of vodka when we get home, switches on the two dimmest lamps in the sitting room, and puts LeAnn Rimes *Blue* in the CD player – the music Fergus despises; country kitsch.

'I'm glad you came with me to the sea. I wanted to make amends. Forgive me?' He pulls me into his arms. 'Relax,' he whispers. 'We're only dancing close.'

I let myself lean against him and wind my arms around his neck.

'See? It's easy when you relax.'

Fergus used to yell that exhortation at me. *Relax, you stupid cow, how the hell do you expect to enjoy it if you don't relax?*

The tension returns.

I can feel Max's heartbeat. I want to have his blood beat in my veins, feel with his feelings, see the earth the way he sees it, experience me the way he seems to just now; desirable, not the broken, damaged freak I am. Have all his swaying, seductive rhythm inside me.

He begins to kiss me. Soon he's stopped pretending what we're doing is dancing. And I want it to happen, want to feel how reassuringly easy it is still for me to get him in this state.

He flops onto the sofa and draws me onto his lap.

'It's time, Serena,' he whispers. 'Everything has its time, and this is ours.'

And his hands are all over me, pulling at my clothing. I sit up abruptly, suddenly sober.

'Don't rush me.'

'Come up to bed then. Our big bed, rather than your narrow one.'

And now Max is drawing me gently up the stair, while I'm struggling with an imagination full of the narrow and unwelcoming bed Van Gogh painted in *La Chambre de Vincent*. And I'm wondering how a man who was surely a cold fish in his dealings with women used such hot honey-dripping colours, and painted stars looking like spermatozoa. And never a single one sold. What drove him to keep going? And what was in his deepest mind as he walked to the whorehouse, jingling his coins in his pocket? The Dutch used to be like us, repressed and buttoned down by religion, and now there's Amsterdam. They put Vincent in the madhouse too. Mad, mad, mad, and the blood running down the side of his face from where the ear should have been, and it was her fault, Rachel the whore made him do it…

and the blood's still running down Donald John's legs, the knife-blade is red and sticky on the grass, the glutinous, swimming-pool-smell mess on my hair and my dress.

'Max, I'm not ready,' I say. But he's past the point where the brakes work. His eyes are opaque and bleary as he tumbles me onto the bed, tugging impatiently at his own clothes and mine.

I'm losing control of my lungs, I'm struggling for air, I'm sure I'm having a heart attack. Max doesn't seem to notice. 'Wait!' I croak.

'I've waited so long,' he says. 'We've been married for a quarter of a year.'

He lunges at me. I shriek and roll off the edge of the bed, crawl to the doorway and flee to the sanctuary of my own room. I ram a chair-back under the handle and huddle under my duvet.

I hear Max's feet on the stair before my head's properly on the pillow.

'Let me in.'

When I don't reply, he puts his shoulder to the door, sending the chair skittering across the room. I roll myself into a ball, waiting.

'I didn't mean to hurt you. You're my wife. Husbands and wives make love.' He sounds utterly confused and lost.

He switches on the lamp and stretches out on the covers beside me, sliding a protective arm around my waist, warm and strong and comforting. 'Serena – do you find my body repulsive?'

'It's not that!'

'What then?'

'I can't. It hurts too much.'

'We didn't even try.'

'But I know it'll hurt. So I can't.'

'You were married, Serena. You must have been OK with it then.'

'I wasn't. But Fergus didn't care. He forced me. It's why we got divorced.'

Max lies for a while in silence.

'You have to get help with this. I know you wanted it too. You have to see a specialist.'

'I already saw specialists. They said there's nothing physically wrong with me.'

'But you can get treatment.'

'I don't want treatment. I'm me. This is the way I am. I didn't ever tell you that we'd have sex.'

'No, but we got married. I assumed we would. We should have spoken more about this before I left Russia. Let me lie under the cover with you, the way we did the first night we spent together. Serena, I thought you wanted me that night? I thought you were just shy.'

'And I thought you were the type not to hassle me about it all the time.'

'All the time? We've been together for months. We're supposed to be man and wife. I've been very patient.'

'I suppose you're sorry you didn't stay with Katya.'

'She didn't treat me as if I'm a leper.'

I push him away, as far as I can.

'I'm still here, aren't I?' His voice is desperate. 'Doesn't it hold any meaning for you? Who are you crying for?'

I try to slide my arms round him.

'Don't pretend to love me. You want to get me hot for you, and then you push me away. You call this love?'

'I don't want to be this way. But you think of nothing else these days.'

'I never thought about it two days running in my life before. Living in this house with you. I have to see you walking around in your underwear, hear you bathing, imagine you lying in your bed. It's driving me crazy. It interferes with practising my music, getting on with my life. I have to lie upstairs alone thinking of it. You never think about it?'

'Occasionally. Not the same way as you.'

'The way most people think about getting knifed.'

'So you've never done without, ever? Must have had an inexhaustible supply of women, if Katya was away so much. How many were there, Maksim?'

'Stop it.'

'Tell me.'

'Jesus, I don't know.'

'How many. Ten? Twenty? Thirty? Hundreds?'

He swears under his breath. 'Do I ask you this question?'

'You know you don't have to.'

'I have told you over and over: there was never anyone special for me. There's not one woman in the world you have to be jealous of. And no – I certainly haven't been with hundreds. I'm choosy you know, fastidious. You are jealous of Katya because you think I loved her? I don't say these words lightly to a woman, Serena, though I think you've said it to plenty of men. I don't want to know how many. I don't want to know if you told that bastard you loved him. Katya and I were friends, but all there was between us in bed was sex, not love. She didn't have this need you have to be reassured all the time.'

I can feel his heartbeat, strong and steady; he can choose to be calm when he decides to, damn him. Mine's fluttering like a trapped moth. I want to snuggle in the warm circle of his arm and make the words stay down too.

'I'm desperate for us to be friends. That's why I'm jealous. You were so close to her. I suppose she's extremely beautiful.'

'Is this why you always wanted to see a picture of her? She's nothing to look at, compared to you. You're the most beautiful woman I've ever been with. I can't understand why this matters so much to you.'

I sob uncontrollably again. 'So it wasn't only physical. Katya was your soul-mate?'

'Tell me what you really want, Serena. What do you want out of life?'

'I don't want to have to spend my life worrying over money and sex and all the rest.' I don't want to be a dried-up sexless object like my mother.

'I'm trying to find out what you *do* want.'

'This. Closeness, warmth, trust, companionship.' But I can't ask for it, because Grannie was forever telling me: *I want doesn't get.*

It would have been a different wish list three months ago. Higher salary, a speedy and terminal illness for Katie-Mary so I can be Serena Stuart MacKenzie, the face of Gaeldom at ten past six Monday to Friday. A bigger house. Designer clothes. Furniture that isn't from Ikea. Bigger tits. A Jack Vettriano original – probably *After the Thrill is Gone* (even though she has a fag in her hand).

'You want what I want, in your heart,' Max says. 'A normal life, a couple of kids, a home, not merely a house. It's safe to let yourself love. I won't let you fall.'

I know he's right. I recognise the nostalgia I used to feel when I read the gravestones in Balvaig Burial Ground. *Gus am bris an là...* Until the day breaks... Such long, long lives and long, long marriages.

He lies under the covers beside me.

Max's anger is a thunderstorm; afterwards, the air's so calm and sweet. He holds me close and kisses me the way he did in St Petersburg, friendly loving kisses, not sexy ones, the best kisses I've ever experienced.

'I want to have your babies,' I snivel.

'You will, sweetheart. We won't risk starting anything of the sort before you get your problem fixed. Don't cry any more. We'll find a doctor who can work magic on you. Now you have to answer me,' he adds. 'Who has damaged you so badly? Was it Fergus? He went on with it, although he knew he was hurting you?'

'I can make myself go numb. It's the first few seconds

that are worst.'

Max holds me so tight I can scarcely breathe, squeezing all the resentment and fear out of me.

'Tomorrow I'm breaking up the damn bed upstairs for firewood. It's brought us bad luck. I'll buy timber and build a new one, only for us. Your bride's bed. No one else'll ever sleep in it, except our children.'

'We could sell it. It was expensive.'

'Burn every last piece. Cleanse the evil.'

We're both awake a long time. I know he's in the place I've been so often; the long white corridor where you can't see the end, and all the doors are closed, and all the handles on the inside. He buries his face against my neck, and sleeps. We haven't been apart a whole day since we met, and this is the only night we've spent together skin-to-skin.

Dunstaffnage Place, 8th September

By the time I've had my shower, Max has made the bed, and is cooking breakfast. All trace of last night obliterated, as if I'd dreamt it.

'It's better if we sleep apart till you're ready right enough, Serena,' he says. 'I'll miss you, but it'd just be a repeat performance of last night. I haven't as much self-control as I imagined I had, and it's not fair on you. I know you brought me here because you were sorry for me. I had imagined you felt something more. But it's OK. I can wait till you do.'

'I do feel more, Max. But I still can't cope with *that*.'

In the evening, I help him push pieces of Fergus's bed into the stove.

Granda maintained the purpose of Hell is to burn up everything bad in the world.

'You'll burn in hell,' he announced when Grannie brought me back from the police station in Oban. He thrust his contorted features close to mine so flecks of spittle struck my face when he shouted. 'Jezebel! Accusing a man from a godly family. One of the Lord's innocents. You wanted to corrupt him, and look what's happened, the poor lad'll likely be shut up with raving lunatics for the rest of his days. You'll burn in hell.' Then his face turned purple, and the veins on his forehead stood out like ropes, and he fell over backwards. Grannie rushed towards us, wailing, 'Oh, Peter, Peter!'

Then she turned on me. 'Wicked girl — now you've gone and killed your grandfather.'

Next day, the doctor gone and Granda quiet in his bed in the Portmore hospital, we heard about Donald John's father. Nobody needed to tell me I was responsible for all of it. I remember thinking how clever it was of old Mr Munro, to think of pressing the trigger with his big toe, and that it was as well he'd locked himself in the byre, so Donald John's mother wouldn't have to clean his brains off her kitchen walls.

Max holds my hand tightly as the flames lick the stove's glass door. Burn up the evil. Lock my imagination in the cold, dark shed.

Dunstaffnage Place, 11th September

When I get in from work, I find Max has carried wood home from B&Q, and built a passable bedstead. We enter an amicable truce that lasts for the best part of a week, even though the advertising agency pays by cheque, and we have all the palaver of making sure they use the correct spelling of "Stuart".

'You couldn't have believed they'd pay you in used banknotes,' I say defensively.

But Max just smiles. 'I want you to have it anyway. It means I can begin to pay you back for everything. I still owe you for the meal on our first date.'

I have failed, and I don't know how to run this script in reverse.

'Go and vote,' he says suddenly.

'What?'

'It's your referendum, isn't it? Today. You still have time. Go and vote.'

'I already did, on my way to work.'

'You voted for independence?'

'I did, but that's not what it's about. It's just for our own parliament.'

'It'll make no difference anyway,' says Max.

'It must make a difference. We'll be able to decide more things for ourselves.'

'No difference. Not unless Scotland finds a new solution. Capitalism doesn't work.'

'Nor does Communism. You should know that.'

'But what do you think will be different? As long as money talks loudest, things won't change, except for the worse.'

I grunt something about needing to hope.

St Edmund Avenue, 16th September

Marjorie Adam has been hell-bent on organising a private recital now the Festival is well and truly over, 'to show the organisers how it should be done,' she says. With the double doors flung open, the drawing room is the size of a small concert hall. Superb acoustics. Max will be at his best. He's trying to look calm, but I know he's taut as an over-stretched string.

Marjorie has ordered a special little dais; it's not nearly big enough. By the time the piano has been heaved onto it along with the chair for the woman who is to turn the music for the pianist, Max will be squeezed in right at the front, and will have to turn for himself.

I sit very primly, watching my husband as if he's a stranger. He's had his hair cut very short. I didn't approve of it at first; too redolent of a Hitler Youth recruiting poster. But tactile, I discovered; crisp and sensual and electric, like running my hand against the cat's fur the wrong way.

He looks delectable in the suit he's hired. Marjorie obviously gave him some cash in advance. It fits him to perfection (the one he was married in left yards of wrist and sock exposed). I've never seen him dressed to kill; Max has his vanities too. He'd have nothing to do with the sort of bow tie that comes ready-made. He demanded a proper one, and did it up perfectly, no hesitation, without so much as glancing in a mirror.

The taut, stubborn set of the jaw, the haughty expression he has when he deigns to look at his audience, tells me he's in a bad mood: seething underneath the calm exterior. Marjorie has chosen the programme. Heated words were exchanged over the Bach Sonata in G major. 'I can't do it,' Max moaned. 'It doesn't move me. Bach doesn't speak to me. I'll never be able to do it.'

I haven't been sympathetic. I told him he's supposed to be a professional musician, so he'd better get on with it.

Marjorie has parked me on an elegant gilt and brocade sofa right at the front. I'm not deliriously happy about being so much on display either. I hate my dress. For some reason I haven't fathomed, Max was determined I should look the part for her damn recital. I wanted him to help me choose my new frock in my lunch-break yesterday, the way a real husband might. He was late. I stood in Jenners' doorway, out of the rain, and contemplated the people in the street, thinking how ugly most of them were compared to my fine-featured man. When he arrived, he was distracted and bored. I bought the first dress that fitted, hardly even looking at it.

Plummy-voiced dames are sizing him up like a piece of meat. 'A younger version of Nureyev,' I overhear one say. I store up this particular idiocy to make him laugh later, once he can relax. They can only look and dream; I get to take him home, in the back of a taxi. I'll snuggle against him and undo the top buttons of the immaculate pin-tucked shirt, slide my hand against the skin of his chest (which is almost as innocent of hair as an adolescent's), tease him, pretend he's some Lothario I've picked up.

Carla is there, smiling radiantly at me as she catches my eye, saluting me with her wine glass. He must have set up the invitation personally, and only when he looks at her does his expression relax. Perhaps she's thinking the same as I am, that he should lighten up the proceedings, start with his version of Dvořák's *Songs my Mother Taught Me*, which he can perform dead-pan, with a pained expression and just a smidgen off-key; he'd have his audience helpless.

He gazes into my eyes, a serious, long, quizzical look, before he begins to play. Once he starts, he'll forget everything else, he'd forget me no matter if we'd come hot from an all-day sex session. The tension in his jaw will soften, his eyes close; his head will be thrown back, his lips faintly parted.

I don't recognise the pianist who's accompanying him, though he obviously does. Big-boned and flat-chested, with mousey hair dragged into a migraine-inducing bun. She and Max eye each other with mutual loathing. Doesn't look promising for collaboration; more like confrontation. She glares at his back as he fidgets with the music, fidgets with the spike, fidgets with the bow, before turning to nod at her over his shoulder. 'OK. Now.' Once, between the second and third movements of the Bach he mutters something to her, and I think for a moment she's going to stand up, chuck her music on the floor and tell him to fucking well play by himself – either that or shove him over the edge. He faffs around, retuning for what feels like half an hour. When it's over, he leaves the platform first, as is his due (this much I've learned), and comes back to take his bow, while the pianist, fuming, almost trips over her too-long skirt. I can see this descending into farce.

But the evening is a success. They love him.

'Circulate, socialise,' he told me earlier. 'Enthuse over how wonderful I am!'

I try my best, though I'm terrified of being lured into a treacherous conversation where I'll drown. If anyone asks me if I enjoyed the Bach, an honest answer would place me around the middle of a Likert scale: 'neither liked not disliked'. I veer between feeling invisible and enormous, like a huge, pulsating purple zit. Carla is still flitting about as brightly as a disembodied flame, glass in hand, her hair gleaming like a beacon, her sexy laughter floating above the rumble of voices, doing a brilliant job on my husband's PR. When I first knew her, I remember thinking: This is what I want to be. This confident, this aware, this *normal.*

The young Nureyev catches my eye from across the room. Marjorie is wheeling him around, while he bares his teeth at old women of both sexes; he looks as comfortable as a Jewish vegetarian in a pork butcher's.

I'm barely aware of what he plays in the second half.

As soon as we're in the taxi to go home, Max loosens his tie. It gives him the air of a dissolute nobleman, but he's distant and distracted, and sits with his arms wrapped round Katya-Two's case. I don't dare touch him. He looks so tired. Poor Max – he puts everything into the music. Once we're home, I'll massage his shoulders and his neck (where he stores all the tension), and I'll caress each inch of his spine (even his bones are exquisite, he could stretch out on a table and be used as a model to demonstrate anatomy to medical students).

But he stalks so sternly and purposefully to the stair, I don't have the courage to follow him up. I sit in the kitchen in my ridiculous dress, waiting for him to come back and wish me goodnight, at least. When I eventually creep up to his room it's in darkness.

'What do you want?' He doesn't trouble to disguise the hostile tone.

I perch on the edge of his bed. 'You didn't say

goodnight.'

'I'm very tired. Goodnight.'

'Why are you angry with me?' I say.

He sits up and switches on the lamp. 'Why did you bring me here? You knew how it'd be, that I'd have to smile and scrape and pretend to be grateful. I hate the West and all you people stand for. The old witch throws me crumbs and expects me to sing for my supper.'

'Hardly fair. She paid you for tonight.'

'Why does she ask me to play for pricks?'

'Because you claim to be a musician and she's been generous enough to allow you carte blanche with a valuable antique instrument.' Which he loves more than he loves me. No need to ponder which of us he'd save in a fire.

He punches the pillow viciously. 'Musician! I don't know who I am any more. Jesus, I was terrible tonight. I should never have agreed to it. Vile bitch of a pianist! You didn't notice? She played the Bach about twice the proper tempo. It was terrible. Made me sound like an amateur, an idiot.'

'It sounded fine to me.'

'You! What do you know? This old woman, this Marjorie, thinks she can buy me. She told me I can stay over when I want. My own room's all ready.'

'Why would you want to sleep at Marjorie's house?'

'To get away from you.' He rolls to the far side of the bed.

'You told that old bisom you want to get away from me?'

'No, she can see for herself.'

'She thinks you're a married man, and she asked you to sleep in her house?'

'The invitation included you. But why fight in a stranger's home when you can fight in your own?' He switches off the lamp, turns his back to me, and draws the covers over his head. As I stumble downstairs my ears are singing the way they do when a train passes in the subway.

Dunstaffnage Place, 17th September

Max brings me breakfast in bed, and cradles me in his arms, nuzzling my ear.

'I was vile to you. I was hideously nervous. Too many people. And I hadn't practised enough. When I play badly I'm in deepest hell – can you understand? I know – it's no excuse.'

'Then why let yourself get so stressed-out? You're always telling me to stay calm.'

'I need it. I need to get the adrenalin running.'

Great. 'Why should I have to bear the brunt of it? You managed to shake off the stage fright when you decided to play in the street like a beggar. I hadn't done anything to deserve the way you spoke to me.'

'You say you love me. You have to love me when I'm a selfish bastard too.'

I don't smile for him. "Love is not love which alters when it alteration finds." I want what I imagined he was, the gentle, tender, funny man I ate chocolate in bed with. He's still there, somewhere.

Dunstaffnage Place, 20th September

A Maelstrom of tidying follows our quarrel. Max is clearing out the shed. He has long since discovered that the only safe way to open its door is with the foot extended to catch the junk that falls out.

Boxes of Morag's possessions and assorted detritus now litter my tiny garden.

'You're like my mother,' he says, 'always hoarding rubbish. What good will it do you? When the disaster comes, what use will any of it be?'

He lifts down a small cardboard box from the top shelf and opens it before I can stop him. He sits on the ground, the hideous red plush album in his lap.

'I'm so sorry,' I say. 'I wouldn't have wanted you to find these. I'd forgotten they were there.'

He flashes a dazzling smile. 'But I'm glad to have seen them. They're beautiful. You look like an angel in your white dress. A very expensive photographer, I'd think.'

A pal of Learmonth's. He probably did it as a favour.

'And you were married properly, in a church? You didn't tell me.'

Fergus presumably managed to bribe the minister. Two previous divorces isn't exactly an exemplary track record. I know Max has tears in his eyes, and I want to lie. I can't think of a glib enough explanation for the picture where the colours of a stained glass window spill over the white satin and velvet of my dress.

'This is especially lovely,' Max says.

Fergus took this one himself, with the big Wista eight-by-ten field camera, and he won a competition with it. I used to get goose bumps recalling how he looked at me after he pressed the shutter release, it made me blush so much I had to go out into the fresh air, while Dee teased me about hot flushes. Really, I should have given it back to him when we split up. He'd see it as a work of art, not the dross of a failed marriage.

'I'll put them in the bin,' I say.

'Is this your father?'

'It's Dee's father. Please – I want to throw them all away.'

He shrugs and hands me the album. Max has no time for sentiment, but I've realised this too late. What I perceived as deprivation was simply the way he chose to live. He's all hard edges. Even Fergus gets dewy-eyed over mementoes.

'Look,' I say, unfolding the dog-eared copy of the photo from the September 1945 edition of the *Herald*. 'It's the Russian airman I told you about. Don't you think he looked very like you?'

He barely glances at it. 'Perhaps. But why do you keep a picture of a dead man you never knew?'

Why indeed. Max hasn't let me hang up the enlargements I had made of Edouard's photos.

'Put them away in a drawer,' he said. 'I don't want to be reminded.'

'You don't want to be reminded we got married?'

'I don't want to remember I couldn't even do that much right for you.'

I sneak out a few of the photos I like best before I dump the gold-embossed album in the bin. It's incredibly vulgar: *"Our Wedding"* in fancy gilded script. We let Morag choose it, humouring her because that's what you do for the dying.

I was carrying a potted chrysanth to my mother in hospital when I met Fergus. I knew she was in the final stages of her illness and I was relieved and guilty; I'd feared I'd have to take her into my own tiny flat in the Old Town to nurse her. There simply wasn't space, and I was teaching full-time. I've never been good at coping with illness in any case, the smells and textures of it. It was a blessing that she was in hospital in Edinburgh, close enough to visit.

I'd got grit in my eye, and I was huddled against the wind-swept parapet of the North Bridge like a reluctant suicide, eyes streaming, nose dribbling, trying to avoid being trampled by the tide of folk bearing their Christmas shopping home, while I scrubbed my face with a disintegrating tissue. A heavily built man stopped beside me.

'Let me look at your eye,' he said, producing an immaculate hankie – a linen one, and ironed too. He drew me into the nearest pool of light. At the very instant, the street-lamp exploded, showering us with glass. The bearded stranger snatched me into his arms and shielded me with his own body. When the glass finished falling he inspected my hair and clothing and the potted plant for stray shards.

'Disgraceful. The council will hear more than a little about this. Are you all right, my dear? I'd asked you to look up. My God, if it had happened a moment earlier, I shudder to think…I wonder if I should take you straight to hospital, in case there's a speck of glass?'

'It feels fine now, honestly. But you've cut your hand!'

He brushed aside my concern. It was at that point I realised why he looked familiar.

'Come along,' he said. 'My house isn't far away. You can bathe your lovely eyes and I'll put antiseptic on this cut. You're safe with me. I'm Fergus Learmonth, by the way.'

'Yes, I'd recognised you.'

He raised his arm and a cruising taxi appeared from nowhere, wheeled around and was beside us at once. I was seriously impressed.

I agreed to go home with him principally because I knew it was my fault he was bleeding, and only partly because he was on TV. His name comforted me too. The name you'd give a loyal and dependable West Highland Terrier.

'Promise me you won't ever go home with anyone you don't know,' he said, settling me safely in my seat. 'You're too gorgeous to be out on your own.'

In his immaculate bathroom Fergus bathed my eye with Optrex from the cupboard, and a Bristol blue glass eye bath, none of your plastic rubbish.

'You have the most fucking amazing eyes,' he said. I shivered with delight over the nonchalant way he could make the ugliest of words complimentary. 'They're the colour of gentians. And it's not contacts, is it?'

'Certainly not,' I said primly. I expect I wrinkled my nose a little.

'Potassium bromide,' he said. 'It gives better contrast in black and white prints. I use this as a darkroom. Look.'

He pulled down the blind, blanking out every chink of light. I felt his breath warm against my cheek as he leant past me to reach the cord.

'Perhaps you'd pose for me sometime? I do colour too. I can just picture you draped in deep blue velvet, with your black hair and pale skin. I do quite a lot of portraits, for competitions.'

Then he made me tea, and fussed over me, while I basked in the pleasurable sensation of surrendering to fate. I'd decided he was handsome, and burly rather than fat. I was spellbound by the sheer *power* of the man. Stoat and rabbit.

'A teacher?' he said in disbelief, as we sipped our Lapsang Souchong. 'What a waste. You don't like children, do you? You don't strike me as a girl who'd want any of her own.'

Therein lay the enchantment. From the outset Fergus gave the impression he knew me much better than I knew myself. 'I'm a magician,' he said. 'And I can tell you're a witch. I'm going to transform your life with a single tiny flick of my wand.'

Afterwards, he drove me to the hospital, waited outside while I performed my daughterly duty, then dropped me at home, glaring in disapproval at the tatty close with bins outside it.

He courted me with flowers and flattery and a gleam in his eye proclaiming I was the only one he'd ever looked at *that* way. When he photographed me in those days, it was always fully clothed.

Three months and four days after we met on the North Bridge, I was working for Albion Media Group. Morag survived long enough to attend my wedding, though she was kitten-weak by then. She clearly shared Fergus's view that I was moving up a rung or three. Eva McCulloch it was, Dee's mother, who said it as she helped dress me for the charade of her husband giving me away – 'I haven't anything blue,' I was thinking. And out of the blue Eva said, as the white-ribboned cars were arriving, 'Serena – if you're not sure, it's still not too late'. But it had all seemed so official – Hugh in his best suit, the flowers, the three-tiered cake, the guests waiting in their new hats, my mother telling death itself to hang on a minute. How could I have gone in to work the next day as if nothing had happened?

Albion Studios, 22nd September

Fergus has always had a sixth sense regarding my moods. He perches on the edge of my desk, swinging a stylishly shod foot. I take the board-backed envelope out of my bag.

'Here. I found I still had this. I thought you might want it. You were always pleased with how it'd turned out.'

He studies the photo for a long time. 'Come for a drink with me.'

'Certainly not.'

'For old times' sake. Bugger it, witch, you know I'm jealous. I've never admitted any such thing to a woman before. I know you told me you're not with him in the way that matters, but still, he's in the house with you. I can't bear to think of it.'

'You can't bear to think of me being happy.'

'But you're not, are you? This gangly girlish-looking blond boy's not looking after you properly. And I bet he's not paying his way. I'm worried.' He lays his hand on my shoulder.

'How do you know what he looks like?' A moment afterwards, too late, I think: I should have struck him for implying Maksim looks in the least effeminate.

Even Fergus can be embarrassed. 'I popped round one evening to make my peace. I could hear the two of you from outside, well into the yelling stage of an argument. "It's around now she gets to throwing dishes," I said to myself. "Not a politic time." So I didn't knock. Then he came storming out of the house. I was torn between being tactful and wanting to check you were all right.'

I start to put on my jacket. 'How typical of you to skulk around.'

'What's wrong? All couples argue. We did. I didn't tell anyone. I'd have been mortified if some old boyfriend of yours had turned up while we were bawling abuse at each other.'

'You think the fact you were spying on me is likely to persuade me to come for a drink with you?'

'Don't be cruel. You still belong to me. Emotionally, at any rate.'

Where the hell have all my co-workers disappeared to? Never an audience when I need one.

'I never belonged to you. Especially not emotionally.'

I switch off my computer and head for the stair. Fergus falls into step beside me.

'Darling kitten, I know you were sorry for your Russian. But this is taking charity too far. It's been a dreadful mistake, hasn't it?'

'I wasn't sorry for him. He's a very independent person, a survivor. I'm extremely fond of him.'

'You were extremely fond of me once, or so you claimed. According to you, it doesn't last.'

'Fergus, we got divorced, remember? After you'd paraded our sex life in public.'

'The lawyer wasn't public. He's very discreet. Handles all my business.'

'I suppose you're on commission, after all your divorces. He's a salacious old pig. He was loving every moment of it.'

'Witch, a divorce is just a meaningless bit of paper. What matters is this: I care about you. I can see you're not happy. He'd be better back where he came from. We can make sure he doesn't arrive home penniless. I don't mind contributing. If we send him off with a couple of thousand dollars he's a rich man.'

I should be flattered to know Fergus sets my value so high.

'He wants to stay here.'

We've reached the street. I'm cursing myself for not having the Peugeot with me today; no simple or graceful getaway.

'It might be possible to arrange,' says Fergus. 'Political asylum. There've been a couple of cases lately where they pulled it off by saying the Mafia was after them.'

'I want him to stay with me.'

'You never understood how much you hurt me. Losing you was the worst catastrophe of my life, much worse than my other divorces. Let's be pals, the way we were before he was here. Let's work it out.'

He slides his arm through mine. His voice has the silky tone I remember so well; it means he's plotting. He could snatch away my career, quite casually, and my home with it, without feeling he's dirtied his hands.

I go to the pub with him because I'm a coward, and because of the lethargy numbing me like nerve gas. We end up in the place where we hung out when we were first together, and I spend three hours chattering, laughing at his jokes, and remembering why I married him. He lights one of his horrid, sexy cigars, narrowing his eyes against the smoke in the way that gives him an air of Bogart. If we could have lived our lives at parties and in pubs, and never had to go home to bed, I'd still be his wife.

'I'll walk you home,' he says.

'I'll take a taxi.'

'As you wish.'

And he kisses me full on the lips as we stand on the greasy pavement under the fake antique streetlight. He kisses me passionately. It's soothing and I've had too many drinks, so I kiss him back. I wrap my arms around his neck, and feel how warm and safe he is; the dubious comfort of a familiar body. I let him kiss me with his sexy mouth and his leg pressed between my thighs until he's hot and gasping with desire. I'm flattered and exhilarated to find that at least I can still turn him on.

'Come home with me,' he murmurs gruffly.

He bought a flat not far from Dougal and Carla's when we split up, even more glamorous than theirs. I've visited his new home, never his new bed.

'Don't be daft. You know I can't. That's all finished, Fergus.'

'It'll never be finished for us, witch. I need you. Come home with me, I promise I'll be kind to you, I'll only do what you like, I'll give you such exquisite loving you'll forget everyone else.' His stubby fingers are unfastening the buttons of my jacket.

I push him off. 'Stop it!'

'What does it matter? Christ, Serena, you're my wife.'

I'm so angry I can't bite my tongue hard enough.

'No I'm not. I'm Maksim's. I married him in Russia.'

'You couldn't have. The divorce wasn't final.'

'It was. The papers were there when I got home. It's all perfectly legal.'

'But you were only there for a day or two. There's no way it can be done so quickly.'

'They manage things differently there.'

'Do they indeed? We'll see about that.'

I've come home to my cold, empty house, showered then had a bath. I'm sitting up to yell at Max when he comes in.

Albion Studios, 26th September

Anita holds her hand over the mouthpiece of the phone, face full of concern. 'It's your Russian chap.'

I panic even before I hear Max's voice. He never rings me on the newsroom number, always on my mobile – and only in a crisis. I glance at it. Blank. I forgot to switch it back on after my last interview. House burnt down? Gorby run over? Immigration officers. He's at the airport, on the point of being deported. Unlikely. The haar is so thick they've stopped flying.

'I had a small accident, Serena,' he says apologetically. 'I tried to get you on your own number. I didn't know what else to do.'

'What kind of accident?'

'A car hit me. Not hard. But I'm too sore to walk home.'

The sob in his voice frightens me far more than the images I'm conjuring up. 'Jesus – where are you?'

I can hear traffic in the background. His voice sounds weak and far away. 'There's a church beside me – it's not a church now, I think, it's closed up. There's a traffic roundabout. I hadn't enough for a taxi. I'm sorry. I didn't want them to take me to the hospital, but I don't think I could make it home from here. Let me look at the street sign… East London, I think.'

'It's OK. I know where you are. Phoebe Traquair's church. Stay put. I'll only be five minutes.'

'Can I –?' asks Anita.

I shake my head. 'I'll come back as soon as I can.'

'Don't worry about it. We can cover for you.'

❖

Max is balancing himself on the low wall, leaning against the railings, face the colour of damp putty; it looks worse under the tan and freckles. He makes no effort to stand up.

'You were knocked down? Where's the car? He just drove off?'

'It happened up there.' He waves his hand in the direction of Leith Walk. 'It was my own fault. I know you've tried to teach me to cross properly. The driver waved me to go ahead, and I didn't go. He was still stopped, so I walked, but he started again at the same time. He was very upset. He thought I was drunk. Someone wanted to call the police. "No police," I said. They tried to get an ambulance – Christ, there were twenty people by then, I don't know where they came from. I told them I was all right and walked away as fast as I could.'

He's learnt the other survival tactics easily enough. Only the first time I asked him to post a letter for me did he waste hours hunting for a blue box. He's learnt that whatever the size of the shop you put the groceries in your basket before you pay for them. He knows that if you take a parcel to the post office you wrap it beforehand, at home. He has accepted the idea that Ursula's not risking robbery or rape because she doesn't have bars on her windows. He's got the hang of it that a bus breaking down is a talking point, and the trains run late by minutes, not days. But he can't get his head around the concept of courteous drivers. 'At home they'd be lining you up for a direct hit,' he'll say pathetically.

I sit on the wall beside him. 'Do you remember how we met?'

He starts to laugh, then clutches at his side.

'What were you doing over here anyway?'

'I was lost. I was trying to get home. In the fog it all looks different.'

He begins to sob, loudly and without control. It's terrifying. Passers-by are staring.

'Is it worse, Maksim? Oh, sweetheart, does it hurt more?'

'It's not that. I'm such a fool, useless, useless fool.'

'We have to get you to hospital.'

'No hospital, Serena. Just take me home.'

I have to support most of his weight to manoeuvre him into the car, and out again at the other end. He struggles to climb the stair. I undress him as far as I can and help him onto the sofa. The bruise on his right side, from his chest to his thigh, is already darkening and swollen. I prod as gently as I can. He winces and yelps. I can't quiet my mind enough to work out how much of a risk it'd be to take him to the Infirmary.

Ursula. She used to be a nurse. She's at home. She comes upstairs with me at a gallop.

'You must take him at once. He needs to be X-rayed.'

'I'm frightened to. Ursula – he's not here legally. He didn't have a visa. I'm sure they'll have umpteen forms to fill in. I'm so afraid if they find out he'll be taken away by the immigration people. Can't you look at him, see what you think?'

She examines him coolly and professionally. 'I don't think you've broken any bones. But really, I can't be sure. You might have an internal injury. You must go to hospital.'

Max sits up, grimacing. 'No chance. You get sick in those places. I'll heal myself. I'm not badly injured.'

'How would I know if it was serious?' I ask her in the hall.

'More pain. Acute pain. Vomiting. Loss of consciousness. He's certain he didn't hit his head?' She purses her lips. 'Keep an eye on him. Put ice on the bruise. Call me if you're in the least worried. I'll come with you. We'll cook up some story.'

I go back to Max and try to soothe the bruised part without hurting it, placing bags of frozen peas wrapped in tea towels. I'm terrified that he'll start throwing up as the shock hits him, or suddenly bleed profusely. I'm not sure I could nurse even this man, though I know I've fallen in love with him. But he's already more like his usual self.

'Kiss it better,' he says, with something close to the old grin. 'Lay your hands on me and heal me, woman. Pray over me, or something. I'm starting to feel better.'

'You've put on some weight since you came here.'

'I never had so much to eat before in my life. My skin feels different here. I have Scottish skin now. No more shabby clothes. You couldn't understand what a luxury it is for me to be able to put on a clean shirt when I want one. I'm so sorry to cause you trouble when you've been so good to me. Darling Serena.'

Russians and west coast Scots. We're both hopeless at love-words, because when we say them out loud they sound like bullshit. I leave him to fall asleep, while I curl up on the floor beside him.

He's so much better by morning it's obvious he'll be fine. In his sleep, he murmured my name, without resentment. He remembers to thank me for coming to rescue him. Again.

Arthur's Seat, Edinburgh, 11th October

Max is as fit as ever and we've resumed our wordless rambles; the slender thread holding us together. He's the only man I know who doesn't feel obliged to spoil a walk with the sound of his voice. Until I found *The Living Mountain* in Thin's second-hand department, I believed that we silent walkers were freaks. Now I know better. It's the purest form of companionship in existence.

In the early days Max would twine his fingers round mine; he soon stopped, but still, if my foot slips on a stone or if – as happened once at Cramond – we pass a stranger who gives me bad vibes, his hand is there at once to steady me. And he doesn't always let go immediately the moment passes. We're more aware of each other than at any other time on these wordless expeditions.

Today, we stand at the summit of Arthur's Seat, drinking in the view, and after a few minutes he sits down against a rock in the sun, his eyes shut. I know as surely as if I could see behind his lids that he's visualising another river. I perch beside him and slide my arm around him. His fingers close over mine, and we sit like this for an hour.

He hasn't been going out in the evenings. He plays the cello at home for the two of us alone. I sit on the landing, nursing my emotions. I can't be in the same room – it's too much like watching him make love to another woman. Katya-Two nestles between his legs, a part of him, his head resting against hers, as he caresses her with the sensitive left hand that would caress me, if I'd only let it. I can't let him see that I'm jealous of a cello.

So I sit hugging myself to prevent my innards from exploding and shooting from my mouth, turning the floor into an abattoir's dustbin. But there's always the risk the player will erupt without warning, like Mount Saint Helen's, sparks everywhere, uncontrollable conflagration.

'Shit! I'm useless! If I'd any talent I wouldn't have been a pauper at home. I'd have had plenty of money, a big car, a house. I'd have been able to ask you to be my wife with a future to offer you.'

He'd have had a choice too. He wouldn't have had to come with me in order to eat and have clean shirts.

'Nabokov said "in exile one lives by genius alone". I don't have it, Serena. I'm scared. What am I to live on?'

I can't answer him. Same old story. He looks for the answer hiding in the bottom of a bottle.

Dunstaffnage Place, 14th October

Soon after midnight, I hear Max downstairs, fumbling to get his key in the lock. A familiar sound that puts an orange mist before my eyes, and the taste of bile in my throat. He's been drinking more and more, but never before to the staggering and dopey stage. He slams the door too hard, swears in Russian, starts attempting to negotiate the stair.

The special meal I made for his birthday is cold and

congealed in the bottom of the oven. I've been tempted to throw the Arvo Pärt CDs in the fire. It's cold outside, and he's wearing a light jacket. I can hear the blood swishing through my brain, ready to explode with rage and misery, while he climbs the stair on all fours. Animal. Drunken pig. He makes it to the landing, grinning inanely, trying to focus on me, and stands up swaying and hiccupping.

'Where have you been till this hour? As if I didn't know. I could smell it from the door. I'm glad you want the police to lift you for being drunk.'

'Is no crime to be drunk.'

'It's a crime to be an illegal immigrant, you fool.'

'No police. I saw no police.'

'Did you walk along the dockside?'

'Yes. Nice night.'

'Cretin. There's not even moonlight. You could have drowned. You can't put one foot in front of the other. There's deep mud at the bottom of the water.'

He lurches against me and I beat his chest with my fists.

'Selfish bastard. I thought you'd had another accident. You think I want a phone-call in the middle of the night to say you're in a hospital, or prison or something?'

'Shhh, don't be angry, my beautiful Serena. I was quite safe; I wasn't on my own. I was with Tom.'

'Who the hell's Tom?'

'Bernie's husband. He wouldn't have let the police take me away. S'rena, don't be cruel to me.'

He loses his balance and wraps his arms around me, so that we both almost fall. The smell of his whisky-breath makes me want to vomit. I push him back with more force than I intended and he sits down hard in the sitting-room doorway. I'm staging a re-run of my parents' marriage. Their unhappiness is a heavy black ribbon running through the centre of my life, strangling me.

But there's a light in Max's eye as if to say 'Ah! This is exciting!' He pulls himself up, and tries to embrace me again. And though I didn't intend it, my nails find his face on a reflex; a lucky hit. I draw blood. I slam into my room, leaving him bewildered, his hand to his cheek. He slumps on the landing outside my door, scratching at the wood like a puppy, blubbering like a spoilt child.

'S'rena, I'm so unhappy. You understand this? I'm so lonely. You won't be a wife to me. I'm not supposed to be here at all. Every day I wait to hear the police knock on the door. I know I let you down. I'm so unhappy.'

I hear him struggle to get up, belching alarmingly. I bundle him into the bathroom in time, not meaning to help him, more concerned for my carpet. Yet I find myself holding his head and sponging his face and worrying about his pistachio-and-cream pallor. He retches himself empty, while I hug him absentmindedly.

And what the hell did I promise anyway? Not 'for better, for worse', certainly. I can't recall the words.

I have no memory, ever, of Morag looking after Frank when he was drunk. Instead she'd bolt the outside door. I remember her standing behind it, in her nightie, holding the big steel poker in case he tried to break in. He was sick on the landing and she left him to clean it up next day.

Kneeling on the cold bathroom floor, my arms round

Max's waist, trying to take the strain into myself rather than his gut, because I'm still worried about his injury, it comes to me: I don't have to be Morag. So I clean his teeth, help him pee because he can't aim straight, and discover I can't do it without feeling *something* – but I'm not sure whether it's love or pity or guilt. Is this what loving someone is, helping them vomit all the poison out, and still finding them desirable? I manoeuvre him upstairs and into his own bed as gently as I can.

'Will you be all right now?'

He clutches my hand. 'Stay beside me. I want you near me. Please. I'm cold and I'm lonely.'

'I'm angry with you.'

'I know I'm a worthless lout, you should be angry, but please stay with me.'

I can't refuse him. He's shivering uncontrollably, and this is more worrying than anything else because on the coldest nights Max is always warm. I often tease him about being a hot-blooded creature: a shrew or a vole. In retaliation he teases me about my feet. I slide under the covers and hold him. I try to weep silently, so he won't notice.

'Perhaps you're beginning to learn about growing potatoes,' he says. I can hear him smiling, in the darkness.

'Max. Happy birthday.'

He laughs miserably. I'd like to believe we both settle to sleep with optimism in our hearts.

Dunstaffnage Place, 15th October

But I'm a Celt; optimism's not my strong suit. By the time I called him at home in my lunch break, Max had shaken off his hangover. It's evening now, and we're back at Carla's. She watches me closely and enquires after my health. When Dougal begins to frame the crass and obvious question, she kicks him – not bothering to hide it.

'Come through with me, darling,' she says after supper. 'We'll try on jewellery, leave these hard drinkers to their man-talk.'

Carla seats me at her dressing table, takes off the dusky crimson amber necklace she's wearing and puts it round my neck, still warm from her own skin – an amazingly sensual touch.

'Suits you better,' she says. 'It brings out the highlights in your hair. No,' she lays her hands over mine, 'keep it, it's a present.'

'I couldn't. It's beautiful. And it's old, it's valuable.'

'Your friendship is more valuable to me. You should wear amber for your health. Wear it for Max. Slip into bed wearing nothing else and he'll be like a wild stallion.'

I'm not sure I appreciate her visualisation.

'So much tension in your neck! I'll give you a massage. What is wrong between the two of you? Be careful you don't lose him. He's a sensual, passionate man.'

How dare she speak to me like this? Hinting she's seduced my man – then touching me too.

'You didn't want Fergus for sex,' she croons. 'Don't deny it. I didn't blame you. He was a coarse man. Why the hell did you marry him? I wouldn't have let you, if you'd come with us as I asked you.'

'Dougal liked him. Anyway, I admit it was my own fault. I've paid for it.'

'This time you picked a good one. Possibly because you chose him before you knew him.'

I try to stand up, but she keeps her hands firmly on my shoulders.

'I blame you for what you're doing to Max. If you don't enjoy sex you should have found a man like Dougal who can't get it up more than once a year.'

'I hardly think you go without, Carla.'

'It's not my problems we're discussing. I keep myself amused. But if you can't give Max what he needs, you should give him his freedom.' Carla's deft fingers work their way between my shoulder blades. 'You told me you got married, but if you did it in such a short time-frame, I can't see how it can be legal.'

'I'm sure it isn't. The intention to begin with was to provide him with an excuse to stay in this country. Then we could split up, get divorced, whatever, once he found his feet.'

'But you're still together.'

'It's early days. Has he told you he wants out of it?'

'God forbid. He adores you. But it doesn't make you happy, so for both your sakes you should end it.'

She dabs me with perfume while I'm still bemused – sliding her fingers down between my inadequate breasts. 'This is the spot to put scent, if you're intent on keeping him. Drive him wild.'

Drive him to antihistamines, I think. She starts painting me with her make-up. 'You should wear more eye shadow, kohl too. I'd have thought you'd have learned this, being on TV. Your superlative eyes are your best feature, those and your hair – don't ever cut it. Now it needs a little lipstick to balance the effect.'

I'm an easy target: mouth still hanging open. She carries on regardless. 'Max is the type who needs sex. He doesn't just want it; he needs it to be healthy. I can hardly believe he's not the best lover you ever had. He's well-equipped for it, and I bet he has as much talent for loving as for his music.'

'All this you can tell from casual observation? That he's hot stuff and well-hung?'

'I can tell from looking at his feet.'

'What utter crap.' Though you should look at them. They're nearly as beautiful as his hands, toes so long and supple he should be able to play the piano with them. Very possibly he can.

'No, it isn't. I've made a study, over many years. Maybe one day, I'll write a book. It's one of the most obvious diagnostic signs.'

Just as well she's never shared this wisdom with Dee. She'd have been locked up years ago for loitering in men's shoe shops.

'This is better,' she adds. 'You're almost smiling again.'

I try to keep my voice cool and controlled. 'As a matter of fact, I couldn't tell you whether he's good in bed or not. You tell me.'

That stops Carla in her tracks. 'What do you mean?'

'I haven't slept with him at all. It'd be OK by me, but he says he doesn't want a white marriage. Isn't it a quaint expression? It means one with no sex. Would certainly make you think twice about talking about white weddings.'

'What are you saying? I know you told me you were just sharing a house with him, but it's clear to me that he's deeply in love with you. And you with him, I think?'

'Yeah, yeah. What am I supposed to do? Dab on some scent to fix it? It's too late, anyway.'

'You can't go on this way. Tell me what's wrong.'

'So you can write a book about it too?' I'd hoped to confide in Carla. She's the older sister I'd have chosen if I'd been given the choice. I want to be able to rest my head against her well-cushioned shoulder and tell her I'm frightened, I'm miserable, I've never had good sex in my life, I wouldn't know what it is, I'm so lonely, and I started to think Max was it for me, and now it's all gone to hell again.

'You can't blame Max,' she says. 'He's a man. It's a natural urge. You have to sort yourself out.'

'Just like that.' I snap my fingers.

'I know it's because of whatever happened to you when you were young. But you never told me any details.'

'I'd have thought Dee would have given you chapter and verse. She's told just about everyone else.'

The headline above the newspaper photo of Donald John being hustled out with a jacket over his head said: Carstairs for beast who subjected primary schoolgirl to terrifying sex ordeal. *The article mentioned self-mutilation.*

'As if I'd waste my time listening to anything Dee says,' says Carla. 'Were you raped?'

'No. I struggled so much I managed to get away from him before he could do *that*. I was barely ten.'

'Didn't you get counselling?'

'Not at the time. Just my grandmother telling me it was all my fault, and police plus salacious reporters crawling all over the village.' Plus the multiple deaths I caused.

'I wish I could help you,' croons Carla, rocking me like a child. 'But I'm a musician, not a psychiatrist. I don't know how you can fix this. I only know you need to fix it.'

Why does everyone in the whole damn world talk about it as if it's something a man with a blowtorch can mend?

I start to scrub at my face as soon as we're in the car. Max moistens the corner of his hankie, carefully removing most of the black circles I've made under my eyes. Suppose I take Carla's advice, climb the stair tonight, and slide in beside him, naked, except for the glowing necklace?

'Have you been talking to Carla about us?' I ask.

'What about us?'

'You know what about us.'

He swears under his breath. 'You may not think I have much sense, at least credit me with a little pride. You think I'm anxious to shout it from the rooftops?'

'Then how did she know? Why would she say I'm cold towards you?'

'You are. You never touch me; you never come near me in public. You think I'll embarrass you? Get a boner in front of your friends?'

I want to slap the anxious-puppy expression off his face. 'She says our marriage can't be legal anyway. Everyone says so.'

He sobers up at once. 'We did what we did. In front of witnesses. It was speeded up a little, that's all. I want you to be my wife. You *are* my wife. Carla loves you too. She's a kind person, Serena. You mustn't fall out with her.'

Dunstaffnage Place, 17th October

'Look. Your husband's on the telly,' Max says.

The new series of *Learmonth on the Lookout* has started its winter run; he's watching in a fascinated stupor.

'Fergus is a disappointed man,' I tell him. 'He thinks he deserves to be in London, flying the flag for punters who expect Concorde for the price of EasyJet.'

Lookout would represent success beyond imagining for some, but it only goes out in Scotland. It's clear he's offended somebody in the past, because he's superb at his job, meticulous. Each detail has to be just so. Nick says it makes him a *perfect* bastard. But at some stage, he's either hit on the wrong con men, or his arrogance has got the better of him in an exchange with the powers that be, both at the BBC and Albion. He's been walled up in a provincial tunnel like Henry, the engine who was naughty.

'He's just a bloody actor,' I say.

'You've a nerve, accusing your husband of being an actor. You can put on a pretty good act. So you regret it, when you see him? He's a TV star, he must be rich.'

'He's a lot better off than I am. Not the way you read in the papers, the hundreds of thousands a year. Anyway, the best of luck to him.'

'These things signify for you though, money, status.'

'You think I'm impressed because his name's in the *Radio Times*?'

'You need to have luxury, like this house. Better to have a husband who earns a lot.'

I punch a cushion, hard.

'And you loved him,' continues Max, 'you must have. Or do you only marry men you can't love?'

'Max!'

He turns to face me squarely, folding his arms. 'What qualities in me did you imagine you could love? I'm trying to understand.' He sounds weary. 'You should have been less impulsive. You admit you burned your toes the first time, with an unwise marriage.'

'Fingers. Burned my fingers.'

'Whatever. Burned your fanny.' He begins to drum his own fingers on the chair-arm. I ache to yell at him to quit fidgeting. 'I want to be able to fall in love with you, Serena.'

' "I want to be able to fall in love with you." ' I mimic him. 'Why did you come with me then? Just to get away?'

'I won't deny I was glad to leave at the time. Your friends have told you this, Serena. If you'd listened to them you would have understood better. "As well this one as another", I said to myself.' He reaches across and squeezes my shoulder. 'Jesus, I'm teasing you! I wouldn't have gone with just anyone.'

Memory can swallow a lot. But I don't think I'll ever be able to forget the moment when he put it into words: these words.

'The spark was there. But love needs bloody hard work. You're the one who didn't take it seriously. On a whim, you decided.' Max can become impatient so quickly. 'If you'd met me in this country you'd not have given me a second glance. You were obsessed with the idea of falling in love in St Petersburg. Any man would have done. You admit you liked me better – "loved" me, as you prefer to say – before you knew me at all. Now you've had four months of living with me, you've changed your mind, the way you did with this Fergus. You want to walk away from the mess, the same as a dog that's crapped in the street. I can't be bothered with the way you decide it's easier to end it. But if it's what you want…'

The tide of his anger ebbs quickly, leaving me stranded and gasping for air. He stretches his arm along the back of the sofa and strokes my hair cautiously, as if I'm a temperamental and sharp-toothed animal. 'Fergus has another woman?'

'I've no idea. I'm not interested. He didn't leave me for another woman, if that's what you're asking; he wasn't having an affair. Neither was I.'

'You have a lot in common, the same job, the same friends. He's a handsome man. I'll bet he's attractive to women.'

'I'm fed up with the subject of Fergus.'

When the bell rings, I peek out of the window but see no unfamiliar cars in the street. Max pads down the stair, opens the door.

'Can I help you?'

'You can let me in.'

Creeping Jesus. I'd assumed he was at home watching himself on the telly. I storm onto the landing.

'What do you want, Fergus?'

'Ah – the angel of the house! I'm delighted to see you too.' He pushes past Max and strides upstairs. It's why he's so efficient at his job. He could push past a serial murderer, brandishing a microphone. He's on familiar terms with dangerous people: serious criminals. He doorsteps thugs. He says he's never been afraid. 'There are almost as many who owe me a favour as bear me a grudge,' he says. 'It's the only way you can do this job.' And right enough, he's never had so much as a bruise to show for it. A powerful man. That's a large part of why I fell under his spell. The others at Albion are hyenas, snapping and yelping over the carrion. The only killing they're brave enough to face is character assassination. Fergus is a true predator, even if he brings down his prey by stealth and cunning. He nails the real villains. He doesn't bugger up ordinary people's lives just to fill an awkward thirty-second gap in a bulletin. His heart's in the right place. If only someone had snipped the wiring between the gonads and the brain.

'Why are you here?'

'To make sure you're all right, kitten. You look a little flustered. Hope I didn't interrupt hubby doing a spot of interior decorating? Well, perhaps not. How are you? No one sees you now, I hear.'

I can smell the whisky on his breath from several feet away. Max has followed him up, and lays his arm protectively around my shoulders. He has enough pride to pretend not to recognise Fergus.

'Serena, do you know this person?'

'It's Fergus.'

'Her husband,' says Fergus.

'No, I don't think so. I am her husband. What do you want here?'

'Come off it, my friend. "Husband" implies there's a legal contract. So, I'm visiting my wife – OK with you, Boris? I want to be sure you're looking after her. She's not one of your Commie women. She's used to better, a decent standard of living.'

'Why are you here really?' I ask him.

'Social call – remember those, do you Serena? It's what civilised people do. They sit around sipping chilled wine and discussing Schumann. Not that you're up for it, if I recall. You could bring us up to date with the latest opus of the Brothers Gallagher, or the newest thing in diesel-dyke-music.' (This is how Fergus deals with the fact he'd never heard of Melissa Etheridge.) 'Well, witch, how are you?' He holds up his fingers in the anti-evil-eye sign. 'Don't glare at me like that, woman.'

'Leave us in peace,' I say. 'You've had your money back, so shift your arse out of here.'

Fergus throws up his hands and flinches. 'I didn't think you were into using words for any body-part below the neck. What's that in Gaelic, now? I'm sure they have a fine word for arse. Given the variety of wildlife and the looks of the women, they probably have thirty words for it, like the Eskimos with snow. Sheep's arse, dog's arse, goat's arse, duck's arse... Mind you, their sheep aren't such hot shit either. It's why so many emigrated to Australia. Better-looking sheep. What do you, think, Boris?'

'Why the fuck d'you call me Boris?'

Fergus slaps his shoulder. 'What you're all called, isn't it? Where's the cat? I never agreed another man could have it. Where is he Serena – upstairs or through in your bedroom?'

He walks calmly onto the landing and opens the door of my room. Gorby deserted me weeks ago to stretch his lanky frame alongside Max's at night. Cats have no mind-crap about loyalty. When it's a matter of extra paw-room, no contest.

'You're not taking the cat.'

'Cuddles up to Boris here does it? I must admit, there were nights I found the idea of the cat's arse seductive, for want of a sheep. I thought the mail order catalogues were all "beautiful Russian women"? Didn't realise they did pretty men too. Not sure why you bothered to shell out for the fake paperwork before you brought him here. You could have ordered from the comfort of your own home.'

'What makes you think buying came into it?'

'I'm an investigative journalist. The thing you pretend to be, witch, only I'm good.'

'Why the hell do you call my wife a witch?' yells Max.

'Because she is one. Better watch yourself, Boris. Say the wrong thing and she'll turn you into a wood louse. Not a good idea to let her get between you and the door when she has that look about her. Another tip – don't let her play with matches or sharp objects.'

Max stalks towards him. 'Fuck off. Get out of my

house.'

'It's your house, is it? Suffering Jesus, madam has certainly climbed off her high horse. I wasn't permitted to call it my house, no matter that it was.'

'This is Serena's home; you're not welcome here. Get out. Now.'

'Look at the state of the man! I know how you're placed, pal. I recognise the frozen, shell-shocked look. Comes with the realisation that the requirement to thresh your own oats doesn't end with the nuptials. Weird philosophy they have out there in the Isles. Sex is OK as long as you don't take pleasure in it. Am I not right, light of my life?'

'Shut up, and go.'

'Shush. I'm giving this Russkie some valuable advice. Have your cojones docked, why don't you. She'll pay. Anything rather than open her legs. She was like that with me too. You shouldn't shack up with men who have normal appetites, Serena. You should have a government health warning tattooed on your forehead.'

I'm floundering in the hope Max won't understand what Fergus is saying.

'I think this was your problem. Serena says you were useless in bed, even when you managed to get it up.' Oh, nice shot, Maksim Stepanovich!

Fergus's throat puffs out like a capercaillie's. 'If she suits you, you must have more lead than pencil. That's why she gave me such a hell of a time. Too big for her.'

'I think your head's too big for you,' yells Max. 'Perhaps I'll shift it off your neck.'

'She should get herself stretched. They can do all sorts now; there's a clinic in London. Same place does fancy stitchery to make them virgins again; she could have the whole works while she's at it. Can't imagine how she managed to lose it in the first place. Required a general anaesthetic I should think.'

Not quite. A fourth-year medical student and something extremely nasty in my drink when I was nineteen, but there's never been a need for Fergus – or anyone else – to know the details.

Max grabs him by the lapels. I can visualise it all: the police, the handcuffs, the court case, the headlines tomorrow in the local paper. It won't make it onto our morning bulletin. Needs a multiple arrest of illegals before it's news for Albion.

I try to place myself between them. 'Don't touch him, Max. It's not worth it.'

'Oh, I think it gives me such satisfaction it's worth a lot.'

But he doesn't hit Fergus. He gets his hands around his throat and shakes him, then manhandles him towards the stair. I grab Max's arms and hold onto him as Fergus leaves.

'What money?' Max says as soon as the door closes. 'You took money from this creep?'

He's so angry, I'm frightened.

'Ages ago. I borrowed a little.'

'Since you were with me?'

'To get us back here, if you must know. I ran out of cash.'

'This man paid for me to come to Britain?' His laughter

arrives as quickly as the anger did. We both sit on the floor, gasping for breath. It ceases suddenly, as if his throat's been cut.

'You told him,' he says.

'Told him what?'

'That you don't sleep with me. That I'm such a pathetic creature I've accepted I'm not allowed to screw my own wife. This fat pig knows.'

'He doesn't know shit.'

'You think I'm stupid? You think I don't understand enough English? He knows you don't sleep in my bed: "through in your bedroom", he said. Bugger it, I know the difference between through and up. And all the time, you're grinning at his funny jokes.'

'Oh, nonsense.'

He slaps me so hard I fall over against the sofa. I sit up and hit him back with all the force I can muster.

'Bitch.' He catches me by the wrists and grapples with me on the floor; his grip is tighter than a vice. 'And is it true what he said, that you wouldn't sleep with him either? You told me it was because he hurt you.'

'He did. He raped me.'

'What nonsense!' says Max. 'He was your husband. Is he a good lover?'

'What do you want me to say? You want to know if his cock's bigger than yours?'

'His bank account's certainly bigger than mine. I think this is why you let him do it to you.'

I yawn. Nervous reaction.

'Bored, are we?'

He starts to unfasten my trousers, still trapping both my wrists with his other hand. Right there on my favourite rug, in the place I'd imagined cuddling Max, he's going to invade me and hurt me. I twist my head and sink my teeth in his arm. He releases me immediately, and sits with his face in his hands. I feel terrifyingly calm.

This is where he leaves. This is how it ends. I try to stand up, but he grasps my hand again, gently now.

'Let me go,' I say. I never wanted a sappy fairy prince. So this is what I do – I fidget and scratch until the Beast breaks through. I have turned into my mother. I'm a woman who drives her husband to rape her on the sitting-room floor.

'Sweetheart, I'm sorry,' says Max. I can tell without looking; there are tears in his eyes. 'I don't know what came over me. I swear on my father's grave I'll never treat you that way again.'

I want to punish him, and I want to hold him and weep with him. 'I'm tired. Let's talk tomorrow.'

'I need to hear you say you forgive me,' he says. 'I hardly know what I'm doing. Jesus, I'm losing my reason.'

I clamp my mouth shut, but a strangled sob escapes all the same.

'Don't. I won't hurt you any more. Give me a clue. What do I need to do to make you happier? You're always sad.'

'You do make me happy. It's me who makes me sad.'

I want to be able to tell him all the parts of him I love; his muscular shoulders, his beautiful hands, his elegant toes, the way his hair lies in the wrong direction, smooth and sleek as fox fur above the tanned skin at the nape of his neck, his strength, his stamina. But the words are strangled in my throat.

'Tell me things,' I croak.

'What things?'

'I have had one fucking awful, hellish day with Fergus and all the rest, and I need you to tell me something nice.'

'I don't know what you want me to say. OK?'

'See? You can turn even this into a quarrel.'

He stands up and switches on the light. 'I want to comfort you, but you're my woman not my child. I'm sorry I frightened you. I don't understand what you want.'

He leaves, slamming the front door so hard the Chagall print falls off the wall. I sit for a long time, contemplating the shattered glass.

Albion Studios, 20th October

I seek out Fergus, rather than trying to avoid him. He seems to have calmed down.

'I know you're mad at me, but please, help me out on this one. You know the right people to ask.'

'Ask what – don't tell me you've decided to go for the right kind of therapy at last?'

'Ask about what Max needs to do to make it official here. He needs to apply for a visa, doesn't he? Then they'll check he's living with me, and eventually he can get permission to stay legally.'

'It's not so simple! The man's a violent lout. A liability. You said he came in on a stolen passport anyway.'

'I know, but surely we don't have to tell them? We can

just say the people at the ferry didn't check properly, and we hadn't realised there was paperwork he should have had beforehand?'

Fergus snorts. 'Some chance. I don't have any pull at all with the type of people who can sort out this scale of mess! Bloody hell, Serena, I don't know why I bother with you. Well, OK, I know a couple of human rights lawyers. I'll ask them on the QT.'

He calls me in the afternoon. 'I've got a heads-up about someone he can go and see. He'll need to take his passport. Maybe the bit of paper you bought too. The lawyer will advise him whether it's best to burn it and pretend it never happened.'

'Which passport– the fake one?'

'No, idiot. His Russian one, the legit one. Though he'd better dispose of the stolen one too, pronto. He'll need to go through to Glasgow. Have you got a pen?'

He gives me the name and phone number of a solicitor who's reputedly a whizz kid in sorting out immigration and asylum.

'I don't know how to thank you.'

'Yes you do.'

'Other than that.'

'Maybe once you've got shot of this character, you'll think better of it, kitten.'

Best keep him in this mood for a bit yet. 'Maybe I will, Fergus.'

I wait impatiently for Max to come home.

'I've found a way to start sorting it out so you can stay legally, get a proper job, a driving licence, all that caboodle.'

Short intermission, while we sort out the misunderstanding over caboodle and canoodle.

'You need to go by train to Glasgow. I'll come with you, if you can get an appointment for a day I'm off or on late shift. All you need take is your passport – your proper one, the Russian one.'

'Ah,' he says.

'Ah what?'

'I don't have it.'

'What do you mean you don't have it? You showed it to me.'

'I showed it to you in Petersburg. I didn't bring it with me.'

'Of course you did. You had it on you when we went to the registrar's. Bloody hell, Max, are you trying to tell me you've lost it since you've been here?'

'I gave it to Zhenya for safe keeping, when he gave me the other one.'

I rant at him for half an hour, how could he be so stupid, what made him think he'd ever see it again, did he imagine there could be a logical sentence with both "Zhenya" and "safe keeping" in it?

'Do you have an address for him?'

I know, even as I ask, it's a silly question, and it would be an even sillier idea for him to write to Zhenya asking him to post it, in the event he did have an address. He shrugs in his maddening, offhand way.

'I did it because I didn't want to get you into trouble,' he says. 'If I'd been searched at the borders and they'd found it, they'd have known the other one was a fake. If they knew you were with me, imagine what could have happened to you.'

I call Fergus again. 'He doesn't have it.'

'Doesn't have what?'

'His Russian passport. He left it in Russia.'

'Fucking hell, Serena! Well, there is absolutely nothing else I can do for you. Please don't even contact the solicitor; I don't want to find myself dragged into whatever shit-storm your Russkie's got himself into. And if you have half a brain left in your head, you'll send him on his way without buggering about any longer, and deny all knowledge. He latched onto you on the ferry, you believed his tale about being an Englishman who'd spent most of his life in Russia, whatever. Just get *rid* of him.'

Dunstaffnage Place, 24th October

'Serena!'

Max has a catalogue of different inflections for my name. This is the mock English upper class one, the one that means he suspects me of activities not entirely on the level. It has a tinge of contempt in it.

'Call for you, *darling.*' He's holding the phone by the tips of two fingers, as if it has shit on it. His eyes glitter. 'Not your husband this time. Different man every day now. This one calls himself Captain Cunti.'

'Bugger!'

'No, I'm sure he said Cunti. You don't want to speak to him?'

I snatch the phone. 'Hello?' I snap.

'Serena?' Paolo's voice: warm and worldly and

affectionate. I conjure up his pleasing face. For the briefest moment I contemplate whether I can forget the bloody *Fortuna* sailing away while he wouldn't look at me, plus the fact I've made a few spurious wedding vows Max wants out of.

'I thought I'd dialled the wrong number. Who was that?'

'Max.'

Silence fit to split wood at the other end of the line. 'You told me you were divorced.'

'I am. Max is Russian. Maksim Grigoriev.'

'You brought home the man you picked up in St Petersburg? I thought you were a lady.'

'Where are you phoning from? It's a very clear line.' Ground control to Major Tom...

'A hotel near the corner of your High Street and – let me see – North Bridge? I was looking forward to having you show me around, but it doesn't matter.'

I couldn't feel more guilty if I'd sent him a written invitation. Max is next door in the kitchen performing Krakatoa impressions with pots and dishes. I'm sure Paolo must be able to hear, and press my hand more closely round the mouthpiece.

'We'd be glad to show you the city. Please – you must come and visit us.'

'You and your Russian stud? No, I don't think so.'

'Don't take that tone. I didn't ask you to come.'

'No, you didn't. It's my own fault. They tell me I should have come a few weeks back for the Festival. I see I didn't need to catch the comedy shows to get a laugh.

What's your address again – 6A Dunstaffnage Place, isn't it? Maybe I'll speak to your immigration authorities. I need *something* to amuse me.'

He hangs up on me.

'Boyfriend in town?' says Max, coming into the room, 'Kapitan Polo Cunti. You made a date with this man before the ship sailed?'

'You know I didn't. I've no idea know how he found my number. I never gave it to him.'

'Passenger list.' His tone is less hostile. I look up. He's smiling, and holding out my Prada jacket. 'Wear this. It looks good on you. Go to him.'

'I don't want to go to him.'

'Go to him, Serena. He can buy you lunch if you hurry. Handsome man, good job, plenty of cash, crazy for you. What more do you want? He can take you out to a smart restaurant. Italian. One of the good guys. They don't need visas: fill in a form you can probably get in the greengrocers, as simple as buying potatoes. It's all right, Serena. I release you from whatever you promised when we got married.'

'He's threatening to shop you to the immigration people. Not so funny now, is it?'

He turns a little paler.

'I don't have time to worry about it now,' I say. 'I must go to work. Stay in and don't open the door or answer the phone to anyone. Do you understand?'

'Fuck your work. Call in sick.'

'I can't. It's not fair on the others.' Every week there's a new batch of rumours that Albion is being taken over.

We're all shit-scared for our jobs. 'It's your own fault for being so stupid as to leave your ID documents in Russia. I'll come home early. We can talk, and think about how we start to sort this out.'

My mind's spinning with crazy ideas. Maybe I can go to St Petersburg on my own, find Zhenya and get his passport back? If I fly both ways, I could probably do it in a couple of days. With a good stock of food in the house, Max and Gorby would be OK. Damn – it would mean applying for another tourist visa though…

He puts his arms around me and sighs. 'I'm sorry. The last thing I wanted was to cause you all this trouble.'

As soon as I reach Albion I phone the Embassy and request a form. If I get it back to them quickly and pay a stack of money, I could have it in a week. I opt for the standard processing speed. After all, it'll take Max a little while to put in some calls and track down his friend.

'Nice wee job for you tonight,' sings out Anita, at teatime. 'You're needed at Linlithgow. It's the memorial service for the latest brat who was raped and murdered. Starts at half eight. Candle-lit vigil – the punters love them. The whole country's still in sob-mode after the Di thing. You've loads of time. You can go in the Volvo with Dennis. You made such a good job of reporting the Henrikson case a couple of years back. You're good with kiddie stuff.'

Unemployed building worker Joss Henrikson has pleaded guilty to a series of "depraved" child sex offences, including admitting to two charges of attempting to rape a baby, Edinburgh High Court heard today. In court, prosecutor Thomas Smith QC described Henrikson (35) as a "determined and committed paedophile".

The court heard that he lured his seven-year-old victim, who cannot be named for legal reasons, to woodland on Corstorphine Hill. Some of the evidence was too extreme and distressing to report.

Henrikson also pleaded guilty to attempting to rape the 11-month-old baby of his former partner. Detectives recovered the footage of this incident which Henrikson had recorded in which he talks about how he intends to use the baby for sex.

Mr Smith also told the court that when police raided Henrikson's home following his arrest in September last year they found a box of camcorder cassettes. These proved to hold recordings of filmed sex acts with another unidentified under age girl.

Mr Smith added that the video evidence recovered showed Henrikson to be "a violent and controlling man" who treated his victims as "possessions" which he used for his own sexual gratification…

The breakthrough in catching him only came because the seven-year-old had scratched him so hard. They recovered his DNA from under her nails. She defended herself…

My brain freezes. Not that I'd ever confide in Anita, but it was being sent as court reporter for Henrikson's case that made it all flare up again.

'You can't justify sending a reporter as well as a cameraman. All it needs is a read. I'm not going. It's too late. God damn it, it's Friday. It's dark. It's freezing. It's October. Why can't Nick do it? He covered the murder.'

'Kiddies aren't really a man's thing. You look the part,

sweet and funereal in your navy blue rig-out. Is this Prada?' she asks, clawing at my jacket. 'We're paying you too much. Possibly you could shed a tear or two? I'll tell Dennis to make sure he catches that.'

Terribly preoccupied with form, Anita. She has a theory that the bereaved should always have the manners to indicate dress code in the funeral notice, to avoid the embarrassment of turning up in black to a fuchsia-tee-shirt-and-shorts one, or vice versa.

'I've hardly been home before nine once in the past fortnight,' I say. 'This is the weekend'

'Getting restive, is he? Never mind. I'll switch you to day shifts every day next week, put someone else out. Come on, Serena, it's not as if you have kids you have to get back to. Nick does.'

'I have a home to go to, just as much as the ones who've bred successfully.'

'And you have a job that needs you to put it first,' snaps Anita.

'Stuff your job. I'm up to here with your fucking job. This is sick. It's not news. A child was raped and murdered, and they haven't caught the animal who did it, so why are we covering some self-indulgent memorial event? Why can't we be as honest as they were years ago? "There's no news today, so here's Elgar's Cello Concerto"? No, we mould it and shape it and pretend we're alchemists converting thin air into nuggets of news. I'm done with being in your secret society, Anita. And you can tell Roger that too. Tell him he can bloody well sack me.'

I log on again, type out a resignation letter and hand it

to her.

'Don't be so stupid. Take this back.'

I ignore her. She tears it up and tosses it into the bin.

'Take a candle. You want to show respect.'

'I can't hold a candle and the mic. I'll burn myself.'

'Look in the canteen for an empty jam-jar to put it in. Tie string round the top – didn't you ever do that when you were a kid?'

'Why do we have to cover it at all? This is beyond tacky. You're always saying we don't have the luxury of covering human-interest crap, like the papers.'

'There's bugger all else around tonight. If we don't have input from this end, we can all kiss our jobs goodbye. You knew when you came here it was no nine to five set up. We go where the news is, when it is. The Albion philosophy.'

'I'm not wasting my time doing this. It won't get used. I'm sick of this place thinking it can fuck up my life and not use the product.'

But my life's already fucked up. Maybe she's right. If I want to swan around pretending to be a news journalist, I have to be willing to make up news with the best of them.

'The Beeb'll have a camera there. They won't have time to cut it for the Nine, or even the regionals. You can get back here and have it cut for the Ten. Top marks for Albion.'

'Media hype. The papers put the parents up to doing it so they can have a two-page spread.'

'Kit yourself out with a candle, there's a doll. I'll give you the money for it. I wonder if you should take a wee posy too?'

'For fuck's sake, Anita! All right, I'll go. What do you want? I'm not talking to the parents.'

'There'll be a token worthy there from the politzei. Do a "what lessons?" line. And that minister, or some other professional do-gooder's bound to show. "How it's brought the community closer", da-da-de-da. How a few more of the mothers take note of where their kids are after dark now, that sort of crap. This is your piece. You decide. Use your initiative, for Christ's sake, if you have any.'

'Who writes your script? Your pal Fergus?'

'Fergus Learmonth is no friend of mine,' she says, too quickly. 'You're the one who married him, poor little cow.'

'Is that what you all say about me? I'm the poor cow who was daft enough to marry Fergus?'

She shrugs. 'I'm not aware that "we" discuss you. But since you ask, yes, most people are sorry for you, because it didn't work out. *I* wouldn't have married him.'

'He wouldn't have asked *you*.'

We glare at each other, and laugh (though on my part it's hysteria, not amusement). All the years I've worked with her this is the closest to a conversation we've ever had. I call home to tell Max to tape the late news, so I can keep it and watch it when I'm old and wonder who I am and where this media whore reporting from Linlithgow has vanished to. I let it ring for ages. No reply.

I travel with Dennis the cameraman, my eyes wide open for the whole journey, so I cut out the visions from Ollasdale Wood. I carry my night-light in a jar, and lay it in the park where they found the small, broken body, and try to work out how it'd feel if it had been a child I know,

Bernie's kid for instance, and I feel nothing, nothing, except resentment. And fear.

So I corner the minor celebrity the police have appointed because he's a forensic psychologist (he's often on TV; I recognise him at once), and lay into him on why kids are still getting abducted and raped and murdered in broad daylight while the police sit on their arses gawping at monitors and counting their brownie points for promotion. I ask him why his self-proclaimed expertise in 'profiling' means they're not one iota closer to nailing the bastard who did it. I'm way past polite; he isn't getting off the hook. I go straight for the jugular.

Afterwards, I find I can't stop the tears. I don't want to get straight back in the car with Dennis.

'You head off with the VT,' I say. 'I'll come in a wee bit later.'

He puts his arm round me. A kindly soul. 'I'm not surprised you're upset. But I'd rather you came back with me, so I know you're safe. How on earth are you going to get back from such a Godforsaken place at this time of night? Tell you what – I'll drop off the tape, and let Anita cut it herself, then I'll take you home. Deal?'

'Deal,' I say.

Dennis drops me at the head of the street. I feel unusually calm. I know what I need to do. I'll offer Max his fare home, plus the cash he earned; it's still sitting in my account. No hard feelings. We've both been over-optimistic. If he uses the fake again, he'll only need to sort out the passport business at their own border, but no doubt there are ways round it, if he's carrying cash.

The house is in darkness.

I sit on my sofa with the lights still out.

He drove me to the woods at Ollasdale in his father's car. I was aware even as he started the engine that I wouldn't have been allowed to go if I'd asked. Donald John had been there all my life, except for the times he was in hospital. His father was an elder in Granda's kirk. I knew the grown-ups said he wasn't right in the head, but I was desperate with longing to find Kilmeny, and anyway, I'd heard my mother say it was small boys who weren't safe with Donald John.

It was a retired teacher from Aberdeen, up on holiday, who stopped for me when I found the road, and ran out blindly, waving my arms. I should have asked him to take me in the opposite direction. Anywhere but home to Granda's house. I should have stopped to wipe the knife-handle clean.

Dunstaffnage Place, 25th October

When I come to from dozing, it's half one in the morning. I can't believe he's being so selfish and reckless as this. He's a grown man. I can accept the fact he has decided he wants to end it. I at least want to end it properly: handshakes and consolatory words and some semblance of dignity. *Is fheàrr teicheadh math na droch fhuireach*, as my Grannie would say: Better a good retreat than a bad stand.

I find Colquhoun's number in the book. Of course, there's no reply. He could be at Marjorie's, but I'm confident he'd never go there without saying, or carry out the threat to stay over. I don't dare ring her at this hour and risk giving her a heart attack.

So I ring a friend with a strong heart. Dougal's surprised, sleepy voice says, 'No, haven't seen him since the last time you were over. Carla's not here. She's taken a gaggle of kids to a concert in Glasgow. They're not due home till this afternoon. Are you all right, Serena?'

I fight down the picture in my mind, trying to control the waves of nausea. Maksim and Carla in bed together? Too tame for them; somewhere semi-public and risky, a women's toilet, her legs wrapped round his waist so only one pair of feet shows, stifling his mouth against her neck.

I wander round the house, trying to gauge if anything is missing or different. All his best gear is still in the wardrobe and the chest: the sweaters and sexy Levi 501s I've bought him. I draw comfort from the coarse denim, holding it to my cheek. I decide to look among his mementoes for clues. There's only one photograph left: Max and Zhenya in uniform. Apart from that, nothing but an army logbook. His diploma from the Leningrad Conservatory is still on the wall in the gilt frame I bought for it.

But I've known from the start Max travels light. He could pack a bag in ten minutes, and if he wants to vanish he'll leave a cold trail. He's not thirled to possessions the way I am. He comes from a rainy country, yet he's never owned an umbrella. When Dougal lent us one, I had to show him how to put it up.

I perceived his former lifestyle as squalid, so I failed to notice that he was happier in one small room. His temperament would suit life on a boat, or in a cave. A single pan for cooking, a pair of jeans, a bucket to wash in, and furniture plucked from skips. To him, clutter is anathema to art and empty rooms gestate inner visions. 'Humble living does not diminish,' he used to tell me. 'It augments.'

I huddle in the armchair, my duvet round me, jolting fully awake every few minutes, imagining I hear footsteps upstairs. Then I take a notion to look inside the stove. The UK passport cover is still recognisable, though he's made sure the inside is completely burned. Stupid, stupid man! There are several sheets of paper, letters perhaps, which disintegrate into dust as I try to extract them. Only one has writing and print I can decipher. It's our marriage certificate.

Around three, I hear a taxi draw up outside, and Ursula's door opens then closes. I run downstairs.

'I don't suppose you happened to notice what time Max went out?'

She looks distracted. 'Max?'

'It's just that he hasn't come in, and he hadn't mentioned he'd be this late.'

'I haven't been here since early afternoon. My aunt in Stirling's died.'

'God, I'm sorry. I didn't mean to disturb you.'

She smiles wearily. 'It's all right. She was over ninety. She'd just gone in her sleep. The police came for me, because the neighbours hadn't seen her for a day or two. They couldn't get in, so the local bobbies came here. It would have been about four in the afternoon – and I know Max was here then, because they knocked at your house first. They weren't sure of the address. I could hear him moving about, though he didn't answer the door.'

We gaze at each other.

'They were uniformed ones too,' she says, her hand at her throat.

I put on a coat and walk along the river path. In less than twenty minutes I spot him heading towards me, unsteady on his feet.

'Come for a walk with me,' he mumbles, clutching at my arm.

'It's the middle of the night.'

'You like to walk. There are friends I want you to meet.' He gives me a wobbly smile, and his eyes gleam like an animal's.

'I'm not interested in meeting a crowd of drunken bums. Max – we have to talk.'

'Walk with me.'

It's an exceptionally fine night, though the cold is biting. I fall into step beside him, back in the direction of Leith.

'Talk to me then,' he says.

'It'd be easier if you were sober. Why did you destroy our marriage certificate?'

'They came for me. I'm so worried I'll get you into trouble.'

'They were looking for Ursula. Her aunt died.'

'That's what they'd say. I know they were looking for me.'

He has a bottle of vodka in each pocket, the genuine product, not a Western imitation; it begins to dawn on me who these friends are. He keeps offering me a swig, but I only pretend to drink. One bottle is three-quarters empty by the time we've reached the area where my gentle river's hemmed in with dank walls and becomes a caged, vindictive beast.

'Let's turn back here,' I say.

'Just a little further. They leave tomorrow, or the day after. I want you to meet them. I'm bursting for a pee,' Max says, heading for the edge of the embankment.

'For God's sake be careful. If you think I could go into that water to save myself, never mind you –' I turn on my heel, disgusted, and start to walk back along the path.

I turn to check he's following me. It can't have been more than a minute, I'm sure of it. The path is completely empty. It takes a moment before I can bring myself to look over the edge. Suppose Max's beautiful hands are breaking the surface for the third time, reaching towards me, pleading? But the dark water is smooth, barely a ripple. It's impossible he could have fallen in and drowned. It hasn't been anything like five minutes. I've read it takes five minutes to sink, at least, and Max is young and fit.

He's hiding, to tease me, playing his irritating trick of being able to sober up instantly. Frank was just the same. Perhaps it's a skill men acquire in the services.

'Max!' I call softly. My voice echoes off the walls. I call again, a little more loudly. 'Max – stop fooling around. I'm going home.'

A flashlight shines in my face. There are two of them, around a hundred yards further along the bank. They look like thugs. Not in uniforms, as far as I can see. God, Edinburgh's getting as bad as St Petersburg. I shade my eyes.

'Lost my dog!' I call. 'Max! Max! Here boy!' I try to whistle, but my mouth is too dry. I turn and move away as fast as I can without running.

I sit up until the beginnings of dawn. Surely he'll have had the sense to lie low for long enough for them to move on, then leg it home? When it gets to seven, and still no sign, I phone Fergus.

When I tell him, he *laughs*.

'It's not funny.'

'I'm sorry you got a fright. You weren't meant to be there.'

'What?'

'I mean, you shouldn't have risked walking alone in a place like that in the middle of the night. What do you want me to do about it anyway?' he says. 'Bloody hell woman, you said you wanted shot of him, you should be happy. Why are you waking me at this time weeping and wailing – you expect me to care?'

'I have to find out what happened to him.'

'What are you trying to tell me – you pushed him in?'

'Of course I didn't. Fergus – I don't know what to do.'

'Nothing. Are you listening, Serena?'

'I can't do nothing. Suppose he did fall?'

'Hell, witch, I still hanker after you, but I can't sort out all your messes for you. You sit tight and zip it. He'll be perfectly all right. Even if he did take a dip, he'll just have swum to the nearest steps, feeling puzzled. If he was so drunk, he wouldn't even have noticed.'

'He can't swim,' I say in a small voice.

'Nonsense. All rats can swim. Now – stop this. Go to sleep for a while. I have to head down to London again today – fuck it! It's time to go to the airport – I'll call you once I'm there. Now, kitten, concentrate – listen to what I'm telling you. If the politzei nabbed him, you'll hear soon enough. If he fell in and drowned, there'll be a body. They don't just lie at the bottom, you know. Not unless it's well weighted-down – you didn't, did you? Shush. Stop wailing. Just kidding. Serious again. Who else have you told about this?'

'No one. Well, I told Dougal I was looking for him last night. And Ursula. I'd spoken to them before he turned up.'

'Good. Neither of them should be a problem. How good a look at you did these cops get?'

'I don't think they were cops. They looked more like nightclub bouncers. Big oafs. They could have been private security men. I suppose they could see it was a woman. Not much else. I had my hood up.'

'But you didn't meet anyone else while you were with him?'

'There was no one else around at the time.'

'So this is the story. He wasn't there when you came home from work, and you haven't seen or heard from him since. If anything happens, I'll say you were with me most of the night. Do you understand, Serena?'

'Yes,' I say obediently. 'But Ursula knows I was here.'

'Right. But I was there with you, till early this morning – OK? You left me snoozing in bed while you spoke to her, then came straight back. Who else have you told about this ridiculous marriage thing?'

'Just you. And Carla. Oh, and the woman who lent him the cello.'

Fergus swears under his breath. 'Carla's not a problem; presumably she'll keep quiet if you ask her to. What do you know about the cello woman?'

'She's rich. She has influential friends. She likes Max.'

'Fuck. Well, you could always just tell her you made it up because you thought she wouldn't approve of you sharing a house with him otherwise?'

'I suppose so.'

'Suppose nothing. I'm telling you, this is what you do – do you understand? Now – is there anyone else? How about your aunt?'

'I was going to tell her when we went up to visit. But a lot of people know he lives here.'

'It doesn't matter. Here's the story, Serena. You were delayed in St Petersburg because you and Dee got lost. She doesn't know by the way, about the marriage bit?'

'No.'

'Good. She's just the sort of bitch to drop you in it for a laugh. Right – you decided to come back overland because you hate flying. This guy picked you up on the ferry, and you got talking. He said he was going to Edinburgh to study, and was looking for a room to rent. You were looking for a flatmate, and you thought it was handy because you'd be able to practise your Russian. You with me so far?'

I mumble agreement.

'So just sit tight and keep shtum. If he doesn't turn up dead or arrested, you're home and dry. If he does, you get yourself off the hook. Look – as soon as I'm back, come and stay with me for a few days.'

'No, Fergus.'

'I don't have time to argue. Hopefully by then you'll see the sense of what I'm suggesting. You can have your own room, witch, for now at any rate.'

Albion newsroom 25th October

By eight-thirty I'm at my computer. No one else is in – Albion doesn't work a Saturday morning shift unless there's something juicy on the go. I scan feverishly through the overnight police releases on the wires. A handbag snatch in Oxgangs, and six cars vandalised in St Mary's Street. I ring their information room. 'Just doing the check-call – anything fresh with you? Not much of a haul for a Friday night.'

Everywhere I try, I draw blanks, as I'd known I would.

'She's not home yet,' says Dougal. 'They're due back at noon. Hasn't there been any sign of Max at all? Look – are you sure you don't want me to come over? You must be worried sick.'

'I'm at work. I'm OK.'

I head home, just in case he decides to turn up, and make some more calls.

'Why didn't you phone sooner?' Marjorie says. 'He must have had an accident. You poor girl. Shall I drive over? Is there anything I can do then?'

I almost break an ankle when the phone rings.

'Loved your Wee Lorraine piece last night!' Anita bawls into the receiver. Jesus! Was it really only yesterday? 'The way you nailed that sanctimonious geek and shaved his balls for him. Forensic psychologist! What do they know about villains? Roger saw it too. He's been bending my ear about why I don't use you more often for a piece to camera. Why indeed, Serena, when you look so good? The camera loves you. With your skinny wee figure it doesn't matter if it puts a few pounds on, lucky bitch.'

'It turned out OK then?'

'I thought you might not have had a chance to see it.' I can tell she's smiling. 'I taped it for you. Hey listen – what we were talking about yesterday; I really hope it works out for you this time. It wasn't your fault with Fergus. He's a creep of the first order. I was married once you know, and it didn't work out. It's not for everyone. Are you still there?'

'I'm a wee bit preoccupied,' I say. 'Max has gone AWOL.'

'Shit! Is there anything I can do?'

'Not really. I'm just telling you.'

'You've got my home number, haven't you – and my mobile?'

Never would have believed I could find Anita's throaty voice comforting.

Carla doesn't phone. She turns up on the doorstep.

'So – you've obviously made all the usual checks. You'd had a quarrel? He's gone to stay with a friend then. Give you a fright. Men are bastards.'

She studies my face and becomes ferociously angry. 'My God – you thought he was with me did you? Bad enough you believe I'd steal another woman's husband –

but that you'd believe I'd steal *yours*. I'm hurt, Serena, wounded to find you think I'd stoop so low.'

'I told you before, he wasn't my husband, except on a piece of paper, and it was a fake, which he's burnt. Anyway, I knew he wasn't with you.'

I tell her the whole story. 'Fergus says I should keep quiet about having seen him. He says Max couldn't possibly have fallen in.'

'Of course he couldn't. Even people who can't swim don't just drop like a stone.'

'I wish – '

Carla strokes my hair.

'I have to apologise to you,' I say. 'I suppose you're just about the only woman I know who's absolutely normal. I mistook it for something else. Forgive me?'

'Nothing to forgive. Shit happens, between friends. Now – who else does Max see?'

Dunstaffnage Place, 26th October

All of today I've sat beside the phone, willing it to ring.

At midnight, I change the message on the answering machine. 'If it's you, Maksim, please leave a message. I love you. Come home.'

Then I realise Peigi might call, and I haven't warned her, so I phone her and almost make her ill with nerves, getting her up long after she'd gone to bed.

I lie down in the big bed, on Max's sheets, surrounded by the scent of his body. I lie on his side of the bed, nearest the door, where he could have protected me from mice. I sleep fitfully for several hours, hearing his voice in my head: *And I will come again my love, though 'twere ten thousand mile.*

Albion Studios, 28th October

I drag myself into work at noon, wild-eyed through lack of sleep.

Fergus is perched on the corner of my desk, hair newly cut, tremendously pleased with himself. He's wearing the dark grey suit I've always particularly liked; I'm vulnerable enough to find it makes me nostalgic.

'Sorry, later than I expected getting back yesterday. I thought you'd be asleep. I want you to come and stay with me from tonight onwards.'

'Have you heard something?'

'About your Russkie? No. But I have some other news for you. Got a minute to talk to me? In private.'

I follow him meekly through to an empty studio.

'I wanted to tell you before it's all around the place. Prepare yourself for a surprise, kitten.'

'You're getting re-married?'

He gazes into my eyes. 'Not a bad idea. But what I wanted to tell you was that I've finally got it, Serena, what I've worked for all these years.'

'Early retirement?'

He laughs, catches me up in his arms and whirls me round.

'London, and an absolutely obscene amount of loot. I'm off in a month.'

'Congratulations, Fergus. No matter what's happened between us I could never say you're not brilliant at your work. You deserve it.'

'Kiss?'

I give him a desultory peck and attempt to extricate

myself, but he holds me tighter, burying his face in my hair.

'We need to talk about us, now I'm leaving Edinburgh.'

'There is no "us". You walked out on me, and we got a divorce. Remember?'

'I didn't walk out. You kicked me out.'

'Out of your own house? You left, Fergus, because you said you couldn't stay with me on my terms.'

He spreads his hands and looks helpless.

'No couple could stay together on those terms.'

'Max has, for months now.'

'There is no comparison. You and I were married, then suddenly you didn't want to be.'

'It wasn't suddenly. You just didn't listen to me.'

'Come with me. We can make a fresh start.'

'Och, why do you even ask? You know I can't.'

'Of course you can; this Russian thing was nonsense all along. I'll have a considerable amount of pull down south – I can get you any job you want. And there are better doctors down there, Serena. I'll do whatever you ask. If you want me to put myself in the hands of a trendy shrink too, I'm willing to make the sacrifice, for you. You used to make me so angry and frustrated I didn't know what I was doing. I've learnt to control it. If it's important to you we'll have another wedding – they'd probably be happy enough to do it again in a church, in the circumstances. I suppose we should, so you'll get my pension. You're bound to live a lot longer than me.'

This gives me a jolt. Fergus looking boldly in the eye of mortality – where does it leave the rest of us?

'It's too late to think like that,' I say.

'I love you, witch, I need you. Come with me and we'll have the most wonderful life you could dream of.'

He's familiar with the worst of me, my warped unfeminine body with a mind to match. His soul's as black as my own. I'm almost ready to believe we truly do belong together.

He's holding me so tight I can hardly breathe. He has an erection like a prize stallion. I can't keep my mind off the idea that he could take whatever he wants here and now, and no one would even hear me scream, because of the double-soundproofed doors.

He must have noticed me looking in that direction, and thought I'd spotted someone through the porthole, for he relaxes his grip enough for me to wriggle free.

'I'm not coming back to you, no matter what. Help me find Max, Fergus.'

He does a strong line in theatrical laughs. 'You want me to have the docks dragged? Oh, don't start again. There's no way any such thing happened. He's just taken himself off. It was on the cards, wasn't it? He thought he was onto a good thing, conning you into bringing him here. Now he's found out getting to stay isn't a stroll in the park, he's decided to take the easy way out. It's not as if you had a *relationship* with him.'

'I'm very fond of him.'

'But you hadn't started sleeping with him?' He holds me at arm's length and studies my face.

'No, I hadn't.'

'Well then. What are you getting so het up about? Your flatmate's buggered off. So what?'

He leans his forehead against mine and closes his eyes.

'Just tell me there's been no one since me.'

'No one since you, Fergus.'

He sighs.

'You have the contacts,' I say. 'You're always telling me how good you are at finding out stuff. Find Max for me. I need to know he's all right, nothing more.'

Fergus studies me artfully. 'If I do this for you, will you come and stay with me. As my wife again?'

'Of course I won't. Why are you even asking?'

'Because I don't want to remember how it was when we split up. I want to remember the good times – and we did have some good times, Serena, didn't we?'

'There's a lot of water under the bridge since then.'

'I need it, to give me closure.'

I don't comment. He scampers off, eyes gleaming. I swear I can see the tips of the wee horns poking through his curly hair.

PART THREE: DIMINUENDO AL NIENTE

Dunstaffnage Place, 28th October, evening

I thought it would take Fergus days to unearth any useful information, and he'd have forgotten most of our conversation, he'd be so caught up in his promotion. But I'm no sooner home from work than he's at the door.

'Not a word or a sign of your precious Russkie. Not arrested or deported or picked up for chasing skirt or fished out of the water. But there was a Russian ship in Leith Friday right. She sailed on Saturday. The *Chaika*. Home port Murmansk, and that's where she was supposed to be headed. They had to get a freebie from Mathers Mechanical to patch up the engines and the pumps so the safety lads would let them sail. Bob says he has no idea how far they'll get before it breaks down again. He says they hadn't enough fuel anyway. Might make it home for Christmas. But I imagine it's where your precious Max disappeared to.'

He stops pacing the room and rubs his hands together. 'Now – the arrangement we made. Have you packed yet? We'll go to my place.'

'What arrangement?'

'Tonight. I want you to move in with me tonight.'

'Och, Fergus, I didn't take you seriously. You didn't actually believe I'd sleep with you? I never agreed to it.'

'You didn't refuse either. You were cuddling and necking with me till I was ready to burst, and you were hot for me too.'

'I was never hot for you, if you want the truth.'

'You promised me. Come on Serena – I've played fair by you. Why do you want to condemn me to just having this to remember, us rowing and calling each other names? Bugger it, I put up with a lot when we were living together, having to cajole you and bolster up your puny fucking ego and play house with you.'

He picks up one of my favourite Habitat cushions and flings it across the room.

'You don't want to be anybody's wife, do you? You just want to play-act with your fucking pine furniture and your naff fucking pictures and your Scandi-sodding-navian décor.'

'This is why we got divorced, remember? I don't want to go to bed with you, and you don't want me under any other terms.'

'I keep my promises, and I promise you, if the bastard's still in this country, I'll have him in a detention centre then shipped out to Siberia before he can blink.'

This is bad. Damage limitation called for.

'It's all too sudden,' I say. 'You said you wanted to spend time with me. Well then, spend time with me here. But no bedroom stuff. I agree, we need to say goodbye to each other in a more civilised way. Because, yes, we did have good times together.'

He leaves, mollified, promising to come back later.

I decide it'd be politic to call on Bernie to ask if Tom has seen him. Her face crumples with concern. And this woman, so much younger and more competent than me, brings me into her home and gives me coffee well-laced with brandy, and is thoughtful enough to chase her pyjama-clad child to his own room and speak to him sternly when he tries to come out.

'He's had an accident,' she says, without hesitation. 'But you've tried the hospitals, of course? He'd never leave you. It's all he ever talks about, you, and your work, and the children you'll have together. He's so proud of you. I don't think he was with Tom on Friday. Wait and I'll phone him to see if he has any bright ideas.'

Tom has no more idea than I have of where Max could have vanished to.

Dunstaffnage Place, 30th October

As things have turned out, I'm glad I've allowed Fergus to visit me in his old house.

Tonight, after we've eaten and I'm trying to think up the appropriate words to persuade him to go back to his own place without an argument, there's a knock on the door. He stands up to answer it, but I'm already half way down the stair. Max is forever forgetting his keys.

John Seaton is on the doorstep.

'Archie asked me to call round,' he says. 'Maxie hasnae turned up for his work since last week.'

I look at him blankly. 'His work? What work?'

He's equally amazed. 'What sort of work does anyone do in a pub? Clearing tables, washing glasses, cleaning the toilets. I thought you were his wife?'

'No,' says Fergus. 'I'm Serena's husband.'

Johnser looks a little taken aback. I can see he recognises him.

'Max was just lodging here for a while,' adds Fergus.

'Oh. Right. It's just that we were worried about him. It's no' like him no' to turn up. We thought mebbe he was ill or something.'

'Not as far as I know,' I say. 'He's gone away.'

'Without saying cheerio to anyone? Where's he gone?'

'He didn't say,' says Fergus, his arm reassuringly round my shoulder. 'You probably know he was here illegally. We only discovered this after we'd said he could stay here for a while. My wife's always been far too soft-hearted. She loves to help the under-dog.'

Johnser regards me curiously, seems about to say something, then bites his lip.

'You think he's been lifted?' he asks after a moment.

Fergus shrugs. 'I think we'd have heard.'

'He was always worried about it,' says Johnser, glaring at him. 'He was frightened he'd get Serena into trouble. He's got a phobia about uniforms. The pigs used to come in the pub, you know, just put their heads round the door, and Max would do his Houdini act. Disappear before your eyes. Even seen him pull that trick a couple of times when the Sally Army came round. Anything in a uniform.'

'Does anyone else have his address here?' asks Fergus.

'Doubt it. I knew because I used to visit him the odd afternoon when Serena was at work.'

I know now who was responsible for the days when I used to come home to the certainty that Max had been smoking pot. (He'd smile gently at me and say, 'A friend had some.' Then I'd get very angry and yell that I wasn't working my butt off so as he could slum around with his pals smoking dope.)

'I know how to contact you either at the pub or your recording studio,' I say. 'I'll be sure to let you know if we hear anything.'

'You don't have an address for him in Russia?'

'Sorry, no. It's partly why I took pity on him. He didn't seem to have a place to live.'

I want to shrivel and die for breaking faith with Max so badly.

'He's going to go to the police,' says Fergus the minute Johnser has left.

'You reckon? I wouldn't have thought his type like the police.'

'Well, either he will or one of the others will.' He smiles to himself. 'I don't think the police'd find him though.'

'Why not?'

'I told you. I reckon he left on the Russian ship I told you about. He'll be well away by now.'

'If the people at the port reckon it'll only get as far as Aberdeen, couldn't we ask there? All I want is to know he's all right.'

'We're not asking anyone or anywhere else. OK? You said he'd burned some papers? Have you had the fire on since?'

I shake my head.

Fergus rolls up his shirtsleeves and cleans every grain of ash from the stove, double-bagging it carefully.

'We'll dispose of this on our way home,' he says. 'Don't

look at me like that. The only sensible alternative is if you come home with me for a while. You can have your own room, witch.'

Then he lights a fresh fire, and sits on the sofa beside me, the cat on his lap.

'Just like old times,' he says fondly.

But I know in my heart it will never be like old times. Never again.

Pitt Gardens, Edinburgh, 6th November

I have been staying with Fergus since last Friday, and he hasn't protested over the fact that I'm sleeping in his spare room. I can see he believes patience will pay off. Gorby shares his bed. Maybe this is enough for him, for now.

I go to work like an automaton and semi-sleep like a zombie, after checking my own house every day to see if Max has been there. I chant his name inside my head like a mantra as I try to doze off. Then I'm wide awake, wondering if I've dreamt him too.

'Where would someone like Max go?' I ask Carla. 'Where could he lose himself?'

She doesn't hesitate. 'If he's still in this country? London.' I feel she knows what she's talking about. 'But you know, Serena, I think it's likely he did leave on that ship.'

'Why would he do it without telling me?'

'Because he realised it would never have worked out for you two,' she says gently. 'You looked wonderful together, but you weren't well suited. You need a man with a gentle temperament.' Carla lets me cry myself dry.

'Well, you're right anyway,' I say. 'But I know Max isn't far away. I can feel him breathing.'

His breath is soft on the nape of my neck, the way it was when he used to draw my hair aside and nuzzle me there while we stood at the sink washing dishes.

Carla looks at me pityingly. 'If he wanted you to find him, he'd have left clues.'

'I need to have a last try at finding out what happened to him. I made him come here. I'm responsible for him.'

I go home to my own place and lie in his bed, as I did on the night he left. On an impulse, I get up again, and look at myself for a long time in the wall mirror he used when he combed his hair. Then I undress and put on the Stone Roses Spike Island tee shirt he particularly liked, before lying down again, my head on his pillow.

Chelsea, London, 8th November

I should see Dee while I'm here. I miss her. Maybe not this time, though. She won't understand, and I'm not ready for a blow-by-blow account of all her latest encounters with uber-capitalists, so this has been a boon: Marjorie was willing to arrange with some of her friends to give me their spare room. It took a single phone-call and I was on my way south for a long weekend on the cheap.

Carla's right; one of the few times I saw Max really happy in Edinburgh was when he hung out with the buskers on the Royal Mile. Winter makes it easier to find them. I haunt the underground, going from one station to the next, listening for the sound of a cello among the Bob Dylan wannabes. Time after time I'm certain I hear him, but when I trace the music either it's a stranger or there's no one there at all. Hide and seek.

Then I have to gallop to the nearest Ladies and splash cold water on my face, and glower at myself in the mirror until the floor stops heaving. Sometimes I have the urge to bang my head against the glass and keep banging until one or the other shatters. I'm numb, disoriented, the way you are when you're wakened suddenly from a bad dream. I'm viewing everything from a distance; voices sound as if they're at the end of a tunnel. I have become invisible.

I finally admit the truth: I wouldn't have been able to recognise Max's playing anyway.

Albion Studios, 12th November

I feel calmer now I'm back at work, though Anita still casts worried glances in my direction when she thinks I'm not looking.

'You want sick leave?' she asks. 'You're entitled to it. Compassionate leave, anyway.'

'I'm not sick. But I'll need to take some of the holidays I'm due.'

'Look, I don't know if I should ask you this, but Sure Foundations – you know, the charity people? – they've persuaded Albion we should send a reporter on their next aid trip. They asked if we had a Russian speaker. They're going to the Ukraine. But in the circumstances…'

'They speak Ukrainian in the Ukraine. But I guess you won't find many people here who speak Ukrainian. Anyway, Russian is more understood than English there. I'll go,' I say. 'When?'

'Not till nearly Christmas. The weather'll be hellish. You have to get more camera training in short order. And there'll be six thousand bloody risk assessment forms to fill in. If you're sure. Maybe we should persuade them to take aid to Mexico this time. Better weather.'

I've been toying with the idea of resigning once and for all. I've psyched myself up to it. But she believes in me. I break into a cold sweat of relief. I suppose the square peg feels the bruises for a while too, until its shape re-adjusts. I can do this.

'I have somewhere I need to go before then. That's why I'll need some time off,' I say.

When I get home, my Russian tourist visa, valid for thirty days, is waiting for me.

Carla is unsympathetic. 'You're trying to give yourself a nervous breakdown. The last thing you need just now is to hear the Russian language, or anything about the damn place.'

'I need to try to know what's become of him.'

'Accept it,' she tells me. 'He doesn't want you to find him. It's not only that he hasn't been in touch; he's covered his tracks as carefully as any criminal. I was wrong about him. I can admit this freely. He's not a good man. He's a wicked, thoughtless bastard, to do this to you.'

Max used to say this about himself. He said it was a consequence of growing up in a disintegrating country. 'It's affected us all,' he'd say, 'even the young people. You can't twist and distort a sapling and expect it to grow up straight and strong. I am not a good person. I'm bad for you too.'

But in the street I still find myself waiting to see him

come hurrying through the crowd, his collar turned up against the rain, his shoulders slightly hunched, eyes searching for me too, my fine-featured mate among the river of dour, uncooked-pastry faces; the only figure in colour in a black and white film, like the cute kid in Schindler's List.

I book to travel out in nine days' time.

To keep myself busy I've bought a book on downsizing, and piled up the boxes of Morag's ornaments. By good fortune rather than foresight I take them to Phillips instead of the PDSA shop. I'd never heard of Clarice Cliff or Susie Cooper. 'Bizarre' meant nothing more to me than a good description of the violent oranges and greens and awkward angular shapes of the *Fantasque* pots and plates. There's also a box of Art Nouveau trinkets; those are pretty, particularly the small mantel clock with a turquoise enamel dial – though it doesn't work. I'll keep it, and some of the earrings. I'm appalled to find they predict I'll have more than two thousand pounds to show for a clean attic and mantelpiece. All these years I've despised her taste, and she's left me what would have been a small fortune to her.

St Edmund Avenue, 13th November

One more major task to accomplish: I can't bring myself to weep as I haul it up the front steps. I've lost the capacity to feel. My nostalgia is for what seems like the memory of a fairy-tale with an unhappy ending. The prince doesn't arrive in time to save Snow White. The ivy covers the windows and Sleeping Beauty suffocates. The shoe doesn't fit.

'You might as well sell it, Marjorie,' I say. 'I don't think Max will be back. I can't ask you to keep it on the off-chance.'

She's in tears. 'I won't sell it. It'll be here for when he comes home.'

Fergus has tutored me in the line I've to feed her: how I'd lied about Max being my husband. I can't bring myself to raise the subject. She doesn't feel like a threat.

But I mention that I'm sure she was aware he was here illegally, and that I'm keen not to make too much of a fuss. She nods sympathetically.

Mornings are the worst. The time Max loves best of all, never happier than when he's up early and has a purpose to his day, out of doors at daybreak.

'Why don't you go to your aunt's for a couple of days?' suggests Ursula tactfully, as I wake her at six, adding to the heap of black bags for the bin-men. I know she believes I'm losing my mind along with my clutter.

'What if Max phones? He always calls me on my mobile, and I can't use it in Balvaig, the signal's not strong enough.'

'Leave it with me. If he calls, I'll find out where he is, explain about the police.' It's a scenario as futile as the scientists hunched over radio receivers, waiting for messages from outer space.

I've left Gorby with Fergus meantime, since I'll be away so much.

Balvaig, Isle of Soma, 15th November

A stranger would easily miss the village road's sharp turn off the main route that funnels the caravans to the street lights and chip shop at Portmore, or the lush, improbable plantings of Colonel Crichton's garden just beyond Balvaig on the road to Red Point. There's a hairpin bend into a cantankerous bridge that smashes exhausts and guards a narrow, ferny road. Baby burns vanish under the tarmac in an impotent gurgle and the roadside rocks drip diamonds of water in the hottest weather; sweat on Gaia's face. In summer the ditches are full of yellow flags. Through low-grown stands of birch and rowan and gorse the road twists past unfenced rushy fields and bedraggled, uncooperative sheep, out of sight of the sea until it swings abruptly to the right, climbs steeply and tops the brae. Balvaig Bay's laid out below like a postcard, and beyond, the wide sweep of Loch Olla, hugged by its headlands, and the low, crouching silhouette of Barra. Next stop – America.

The summer after Donald John showed me the fairies, one of the Balvaig fishermen took me out on his boat on a summer's evening. He'd none of the daft superstitions about women or rabbits. A minister wouldn't have been encouraged to step aboard, but it was a personal preference, one my father shared. Coming back into the loch, the engine slowed to walking pace and he pointed to the scattering of light-filled windows against the dark braes. The gilded sky was at our backs, and the sea bright; dusk had settled on the land. The points of light reminded me of fallen stars, or tiny candle-flames to draw moths. The loch was filled with the keening of eider duck, and the air was a spider's web against my face.

'God's own country, if there is a God,' he said. 'Wherever you end up, Serena, this'll always be your home. Hold to it, and you'll never know poverty.'

I've only to close my eyes for the picture to come up: the small lights that signify home as night falls on Balvaig and Lonemore and Douglastown. I knew who I was then better than I do now.

A little past the first cattle grid beyond the village, there's a pair of improbably grand gateposts, built by my great-grandfather, with a neat blue and white signboard:

MacKenzie
Kingdom

Fortress MacKenzie. By the time I reach it darkness has fallen. The taxi driver from Portmore is dubious when he sees the potholed track.

'It's all right. I would know my way down with my eyes shut.'

I can hardly wait for dawn, for the panorama of rock and sea and minuscule islets. The landscape that possesses me. Is it aware too? Do the stones and the trees and the burn sigh and think: she's home? I'm scarcely aware of my surroundings these days though, the way you can't see your own face without a mirror. I wish I'd brought Max here so *I* could learn to appreciate it again. Autumn's most beautiful:

the season of metals, when everything, even the moon herself, turns to gold and copper and bronze. I've missed the best of it. The leaves are sere and faded. Grey upon grey upon grey.

Kingdom hides until the last minute. It's as dour as its builder; Peter MacKenzie's father raised the house with his own hands, upon the thin sour ground his ancestors had wrested back from the moor, high above the machair. 'The last to drown and the first to burn,' Grannie would say. It doesn't turn its shoulder to the hill but faces the wind, its two dormers like eyebrows raised in perpetual questioning. It's roof was never marred by a TV aerial for the old man condemned it as the devil's own work, and Peigi says she'd rather have a good book. On either side of it, two Scots pines, wind-sculpted into oversized bonsai, their trunks salmon-pink and silver, heart-breaking in a rosy dawn, and at the front a couple of stunted apple trees.

The original croft house still stands, a black house, its thatch replaced with corrugated iron. In Ollasdale wood, Granda once showed me the stumps of the trees cut for its roof-timbers. My folk were like Max's. They built their homes from the materials they could carry home.

We have our own stretch of shore below the steep fields, and an ancient rickle of stones we optimistically call a jetty. Granda used to clear the boulders and the slimy brown sea wrack alongside it. After he died no one bothered.

There's an islet you can reach dry-shod when the tide's out, not ours strictly speaking – I believe it belongs to the Crichtons, but no one else ever bothers to use it. It's perhaps a hundred metres by thirty: my Green Isle of the Great Deep. Hours I spent there as a child, building playhouses with white pebbles marking out the rooms and the glutinous green seaweed we called mermaid's hair for carpets, never lonely. On the seaward side is the incongruous wreck of a wooden structure – too fanciful to be called a shed, but we don't go in for gazebos in Balvaig. I was always afraid to go near; its ghosts didn't want company. I asked Peigi, more than once, what it had been. 'Haven't a clue,' she'd say, lightly. 'It was there before my time. Something to do with the fishing, I suppose.' And she'd play with the pendant she wore always; a golden halved heart with a viciously jagged edge.

When Morag and I sifted through the debris of Frank's house, I realised where the other half of the pendant was, but I've never understood why. Instinctively, I hid it from my mother. I kept it at the time, but it's one of those precious objects that has vanished over the years. I've never asked Peigi about it, and I won't now.

I'd lie on my isle, looking up at the sky through birch-leaves or the green and gold bishop's croziers of bracken shoots, catching grasshoppers in my hands, and butterflies; tickly sensation of the frail wings, fairy-dust on my skin. And I'd imagine I heard the laughter of another child, until I became fixated with the idea of a missing sibling.

Mammy, did I ever have a wee brother or a sister?

God, no. You were quite enough, thank you very much.

But still I'd search furtively in the photo drawer for the faded, creased snapshot of a smiling, toothless forgotten baby, in case I'd murdered him too.

Peigi's in a fluster with waiting. 'You've a face on you as white as a dish-clout.'

'I've not been sleeping.'

She regards me sadly, this stunningly good-looking woman who's probably never been with a man, but has spent her days patiently collecting the broken shards of others' marriages. I'd say Peigi sleeps soundly every night, because she never did a single bad thing in her life.

She's depute head at Portmore Primary now. What a waste. She has inherited the MacKenzie height gene. I used to tell her she could do some modelling, but she'd just laugh and say, 'Och, Serena – what on earth would I model?' Talented too. She can play the piano and the violin. She and Max could have played together.

In my earliest memories, she's like a butterfly or a migratory bird. She'd arrive from Canada every summer – smartly dressed, soignée, glamorous – and my mother would glare at her with loathing.

Grannie railed at her too, but she always seemed to rise above it with the faint smile that told me she was thinking 'Fools!', and remembering the return air ticket safe in her bag. The only adult in the family who spoke kindly to her was my father.

Fragments of conversations I must have heard in the days before they thought I could understand bubble up:

What did you marry for Morag, if you don't like that side of it?

Everyone marries. Most women don't enjoy it.

Most women? You can't judge the world by Mammy. Men want

it – you knew that, obviously, or you wouldn't have got yourself in that predicament. Women have to get used to it. No good'll come of it. He'll go with other women.

I wouldn't care. I wish he would.

As long as his pay packet doesn't.

I wouldn't have done it, except for her. You think I was going to be lumbered with a kid on my own?

And more than once my mother said something else I didn't catch; what etched it in my memory was the look Peigi threw me, big-eyed and scared.

Then, after the Donald John incident, suddenly she was back in Scotland full-time. She taught in Glasgow for a year or so, then moved back to Balvaig after Granda died.

We both go to bed early, and I'm to sleep in the room where I was born, with its minute gable window framing a glimpse of hill and sea, like stained glass. I stand by the window brushing my hair, listening to the familiar voice of the burn, seeking out the moon-path on the darkling sea. When I was a small child they found me down there at our bay in my nightie, up to my knees in silvered water and bawling my eyes out because it turned to liquid under my feet.

I look at my reflection in the small, foxed hand-mirror that's lain on the chest ever since my earliest memories, and I find I don't know who this person is.

I leave the lamp on, as I have at home too, since Max left. But I wake again in the small hours. Too much light:

lamplight and moonlight and the outside of the window plastered with the furry brown bodies of moths. I rise and switch it off. Mine is the darkened window after all.

Kingdom, Balvaig, 16th November

I've finished unpacking my case. 'Can you keep these here for me, Peigi? I didn't want to leave them at home.'

I've put the photos, and Max's Conservatory diploma, still in its frame, in a box.

'So this is Maksim? Such fair hair. I'll put these with the others in the album. Here's one of your father,' she says. There they are, the two of them, squinting into the sun, arms round each other's waists; laughing, young and carefree.

'This isn't my mother, is it? It's you, Peigi. I haven't seen that one before.'

'I've been rearranging them a wee bit. He was a handsome man.' There's a saw-edge to her voice.

'Your brother-in-law?'

'Not when the picture was taken, before they married. He was at school with me, you know. Not a church family.'

'I don't remember ever meeting Frank's parents?'

'You wouldn't. They were not welcome in Dadda's house. Frank Stuart's parents were travelling folk who settled on the island after the war.'

I can feel myself turn red, then pale, and I lose the battle to keep the distress out of my voice.

'So I'm part gypsy? Tinker, anyway?'

Peigi makes a non-committal noise.

'You're your mother's daughter,' she says after a pause.

'That's probably the thing to hang onto.'

I look at the photo again. You couldn't make any mistake: the pair in it are a couple. I glance at the date scrawled on the bottom of the photo. September 1966.

'Morag had another boyfriend when this would have been taken,' my aunt adds lightly. She's clearly forgotten that the date's written there. 'Eamonn Maher. Glasgow Irish. She wanted to marry him, but he was a Catholic. You can imagine the fuss.'

'And did he want to marry her?'

Peigi smiles sadly. 'It was never very clear.'

'Is there not one of Eamonn?'

'Even Morag wouldn't have dared bring a picture of Eamonn Maher into Dadda's house.'

'What did he look like?'

'Not unlike you,' says my aunt. Her voice is calm. 'Same colouring. But then, so had your mother.'

Silence lies heavy on the room.

'So she stole your boyfriend?' I ask.

'She didn't steal. I gave. I was used to having to give Morag whatever she asked for. "Don't be so mean," Mammy would say to me, "you'll get it back." I suppose she was their favourite because of the time she nearly died of the meningitis.'

And did she get Frank back when Morag tired of him? And when was that anyway? Was she ever not tired of him? Is it why Peigi went away to Canada – because she was tempted to take her man back? What happened in the first year of my life, when Mammy and I lived here, and Peigi was teaching in Glasgow, where Frank worked?

'You know Serena, I always wondered if she had a wee bit of brain damage from her illness? It's not unusual for meningitis to cause that.'

'A *wee* bit! And what became of this Eamonn Maher?'

'Haven't a clue. We never saw hide nor hair of him again after your mother married Frank.'

A truth too awful to dwell on is twining its roots through my brain.

'He never tried to get in touch to see how Morag was?'

'Not that I know of. Why would he?'

What is she playing at? Telling me half a secret, then challenging me with those steely dark blue eyes? And why did Morag get to marry whoever she wanted, but the whole family ganged up to stop me going with Gregor McIvor after I went off to uni, because he was just a policeman? Unfair.

My aunt unfolds the yellowing newspaper cutting from the Free Press. She has always been the family archivist.

'And do you still never sing, Serena? I often wondered why not.'

To spite your precious sister. She never took the least interest in my singing, until I won my medal. Afterwards, she'd nag me the whole time to do my party turn. So I shut up and haven't sung since.

'Where's my Mod medal nowadays?' I say.

'Safe in my drawer through the house. You should take it with you.'

I've been looking forward to showing it to Max, proof that I have *some* musical credentials.

'Do you remember however early you woke in summer

Grannie would be at work in the garden already, singing in Gaelic?' I say.

Psalms, love-songs, everything under the sun, while she forked in manure or kelp, or fed her hens.

Peigi nods, and brings out more pictures of Frank. He was handsome right enough when he was young, a real hunk, with his laughing eyes and wavy brown hair, eyes the colour of ripe hazelnuts.

'He was a good man, your father. Just foolish, and too fond of the drink. He had a good heart. I should never have left you on your own with Morag and the parents. God forgive me, but my mother was a nasty, wicked old bitch.'

I still have a clear memory of the day, the year after Morag and I moved to Glasgow. I came home from school, let myself in, and stood in the hall, listening to my mother screaming like a vixen caught in a trap. I raised the courage to push the sitting room door ajar, then I ran across the landing. Within minutes the house was full of neighbours, a couple of policemen arrived, and my father was red in the face yelling, 'Rape? This apology for a woman's supposed to be my wife. As for you, you interfering brat...' But he didn't dare hit me in front of the law.

Morag was even angrier with me. 'What a showing-up, you silly wee bitch! I'll never dare show my face to yon nosey bisom across the landing again.'

'Dee says you do that with no clothes on. You were both dressed. I thought he was murdering you.'

The next week, Frank moved out again. My mother never tired of telling me it was my fault.

Fairy Hill, Balvaig, 16th November

I climb the hill behind the house, and lean against a rock to watch Hector McCrae at his winter ploughing in the field to the north. His land is much better than Kingdom's. Primitive people used to roll on the ground in autumn to take its fertility into their own bodies for safe keeping until the spring. They asked permission. Now the ploughs gang rape the soil, and the seed's sown by cold metal, so the earth's holding out on us.

I've lived it in my head over and over; sitting beside Max on the heather, looking down on the loch with the tiny islet where they sacrificed bulls to Mourie a millennium after the saint they'd replaced him with was dead; ageless water, tiers of wee lochans on the hill, scraps of lapis-lazuli sky dropped on the moor, glints of sun on wet rock, prayer-flags of mist on the hill. And the wreckage of a plane scattered across it like confetti, the plane his namesake died in. Frail rocks that'll be dust one day, when there are no more stars to see.

The island's stark beauty terrifies the tourists from the soft south. A few days of sunsets and benign weather make them say they'd love to live in the West. They lie. Off they go on the ferry after their fortnight, and rare the ones you ever set eyes on again. They never find the winter that falls overnight, when you wake to find the three Beinns covered in pristine white icing.

You can see the fish farm clearly, tucked in against the

north shore of my islet so it fades into the background, because the folk who run the Balvaig Inn made such a fuss.

Max would have valued this place as I do, for its small imperfections (like the crescent-shaped silver scar he has on his left side, just below his heart, the one he'd never talk about beyond saying it was almost his ticket to heaven). He would have loved the juxtaposition of hardness and fragility, the flowers that'll come in spring, the small bright blue butterflies of summer. The shells on the beach at Ollasdale, translucent lilac like babies' fingernails.

I pick idly at the grey and ochre lichen. Lichens thrive best in places where other life falters. A mutual dependence of algae and fungus, intertwined metabolic processes. It was the same with my ancestors, in this island and on Skye; mutual support wasn't optional. In the forest, Max told me lichens signify pure air. I'm so selfish I've never really thought what such things must mean to him. Such a huge country, so much pollution, rusting subs on the Neva, right in the middle of town. Not a good place to raise children. But he used to look so wistful when Bernie wheeled her pram down the street, and when I teased him about helping her up the steps with it he laughed; 'just getting in some practice'.

And if I'd been a normal woman, my body could have been carrying within it at this moment the tiny clump of cells that bears the imprint of features, a personality, quirky characteristics: my slightly crooked pinkies, Maksim's incomparable toes, perhaps his amazing talent that'd bloom against all odds, like a flower bursting through concrete. Would he have left me then? Would it have had brown eyes or blue? It makes a difference to how you see the world, they say, especially in the spectrum between blue and green. I can't see colours clearly at all, without Max. I roll on the hill's stony lap and howl for want of my man, for want of his baby.

I don't know how to talk to my aunt about what's wrong with me, any more than I could to my mother. I don't believe the MacKenzie women have the knack of it. Who could Peigi and Morag have talked to concerning men and loving? Certainly not Grace Robertson, their mother, or the terrifying grandmother, the Seer whose husband never laid eyes on her except clothed from the neck to the ankle.

Peigi told me once she'd been deployed to give her wee sister a pep talk before she was married, on the grounds that she was a teacher and she'd read a book. She seemed to find it funnier than I did, but it wasn't until I found Morag and Frank's marriage certificate I realised why. It was dated 25th November 1966: less than six months before my birth. She must have been hot for him once. Or hot for someone, anyway. I steer my mind away from what my aunt told me earlier.

The sun is setting as I get home: a copper-peach sky slashed with vivid green across the horizon. Only seconds it lasts, the emerald drop, which is supposed to bring luck. I tell Peigi, 'I won't be home for Christmas. Albion is sending me on an assignment to Ukraine.'

Then I break my more immediate news. 'I'm taking a wee trip to St Petersburg later this week, Peigi. Just a few days.'

She's glaring at me every bit as eloquently as Carla did.

But she wouldn't understand, so I don't try to find the words to explain this need I have to know what the other people in Max's life – the ones before me – look like. The need to know that he won't be back in two days or two months or two years so it can all start over. The need to be certain he meant what he said about releasing me.

I fall asleep reading Peigi's poetry book; it falls open at the pages I've memorised since I was able to read.

It wasna her hame, and she couldna remain;
She left this world of sorrow and pain,
And return'd to the land of thought again.

Baltiyskaya District, St Petersburg, 22nd November

It's surreal to be back beside the canals and the bridges. I've always wanted to see it under snow, but there's only a thin scattering. I book into a cheap hotel and within forty minutes I'm climbing the stairs to Max's flat, my heart in my mouth. Maria answers the door.

'Hello!' she says. 'Isn't Max with you? We heard you'd set up home together. Zhenya came to take anything he'd left.'

'You haven't seen Max?'

'Not since June.'

'Where does Zhenya live?'

She shrugs. She has no ideas about who else or where else I can try.

I decide to retrace our steps from the night we met.

Zhenya is in the first bar Max took us to. He's smartly dressed, and when he smiles at me, his eyes are steady and calm. He no longer looks like a madman.

'Kuzkuz!'

He laughs and plucks me off my feet to swing me round. 'I never thought to see you again so soon. Where is he, then?' He gazes expectantly in the direction I've come.

'Gone.'

'Oh God, don't cry. Let's find a quiet place to sit. What are you saying – is he dead?' I shake my head. 'Ill, then?'

'He went away. I thought maybe he'd come back to St Petersburg.'

'No one here's seen him,' says Zhenya. 'I'd have heard.'

'What about his mother? I wondered if he'd gone to her?'

He grimaces. For a moment, I think he's going to burst into tears. 'He was like a brother to me. He couldn't come back and not tell me. I wanted so much to take both of you to see the white cranes,' he says. 'I've dreamt about it, how we'd go for a long journey into the forests, just the three of us.'

His grief's much harder to bear than my own.

'I'm sure nothing bad has happened to him. Maybe we'll make the journey yet. But how about you? You look so different, Kuzkuz.'

Indeed, I can scarcely believe it's the same man. I used to blame him for being a bad influence on Max. Maybe I've had things the wrong way around.

'I'm clean now. I have a job.'

Not as a musician, apparently, but running a flower shop. I find this amusing, but he's so earnest as he describes his daily work, I know I mustn't laugh. At least it has cheered him up to talk about this rather than Max. There's something else I need to know.

'Did Max do drugs?'

A naïve question, but I have no yardstick here.

'No, just a little pot from time to time. He has more sense than me.'

I tell him about the *Chaika*. I give him as much information as I've been able to glean about when it sailed from Leith, and the prognosis there about how many stops it might have had to make. I ask him to find someone in Murmansk who'll know about ship movements.

'I can't manage to go there myself,' I say. 'I wouldn't have a clue who to ask in any case. Do you still have his passport? He said he'd given it to you for safe keeping.'

'Of course. Do you want to take it with you?'

'I can't see much point – I have no idea when I'll see him.' And of course, if I'd had it – or if Max had it – weeks ago, the entire outcome could have been different. 'I was angry when I found he'd left it behind. I still can't understand why he'd do that. If he'd had it with him in Scotland, we could have got a proper visa for him.'

'He thought you'd be in trouble if he was stopped with both passports on him,' says Zhenya.

I know I should feel gratitude towards Max, but I'm still too stressed and angry.

Carla and the others are right. He doesn't want me to find him. But Zhenya's his *friend*. I write down my addresses for him, in Edinburgh and at Peigi's house. I write down his shop's address.

'Please, I really have to know he's safe,' I say. 'You'll let me know?'

'Give him time. He'll come back to you. Time's different for us. It doesn't run in a straight line.'

'It's all right,' I say, patting his hand. 'I don't think he wants to come back to me. I just want him to be happy.'

I persuade him to take around half of the cash that Max earned, so it's available as soon as he gets back.

'The girl who sometimes stayed with him – Katya. Do you know how I can find her?'

'She's from Odessa. She went home, I think. I didn't hear she came back.'

'Do you know her other names? Or an address?'

'I can find out.'

Arcadia, Odessa, Ukraine, 24th November

'She married,' says the elderly violin teacher whose name Zhenya gave me. 'Quite some time ago. Possibly ten months. She has a young child.'

He writes down her address for me.

My heart starts beating far too fast as I climb the stairs to her door. I keep having to stop and catch my breath. It's a smart building. Katya and I stare at each other. The baby in her arms is tiny, though it has a good head of fuzzy black hair.

'Mitya,' she says proudly. 'Dmitri. He's almost four weeks old.'

'Zhenya Kutozov gave me your address,' I say. 'I think you used to know Maksim Grigoriev?'

'Max? I haven't seen him for ages. So – you're a friend of Grishkin's? You speak excellent Russian.' She has the same knowing, gap-toothed smile as Maria. A pretty face, though she'll run to fat before she's forty. Maybe a lot of it is because she's given birth so recently.

'He was sharing a house with me in Scotland for a few months. You say you haven't heard from him?'

My mind floats up to the ceiling. I observe myself talking calmly with this woman who shared Maksim's bed and his body and his music.

'Not for a year. No – it must be longer.'

The flat is large and elegantly furnished. She's so proud of it, I have to accept a guided tour. The kitchen is well equipped, even down to the huge American larder fridge. In the sitting room there are elaborate chandeliers, and expensive rugs on the newly refurbished parquet floors. ('No one would want to marry me,' Max said. 'I have no money, no prospects.') Katya tells me her husband is a 'businessman'. I don't want her to elaborate, and she's clearly happy to leave it at that.

In the corner is an antique carved wood music stand, and a violin lying on a chair beside it. So much of what Max plays was originally scored for the violin.

'You used to be his girlfriend?' I say.

'This isn't his baby,' she murmurs, not unkindly. 'I can see in your eyes that you're wondering. Look – he's the double of my husband.' She fetches a gaudily-framed wedding portrait. The baby's features are a miniature duplicate of the swarthy man at Katya's side, almost embarrassingly so. I've been imagining how it could have been if I'd had Maksim's children. They'd be scale models of him, and people would look in the pram and laugh slyly and say, 'No prizes for guessing who *his* daddy is.'

'Grishkin will come back,' says Katya. 'He always does, eventually, like a tom-cat with his ears torn.'

'How long did you know him?'

'Since we were students. He'd be around for a while, then off again. It wasn't a love affair. I was a convenient place to leave his bag and take messages for him.'

'So the flat he stayed in – it was really yours?'

'Originally. Have you asked his mother?'

'I don't know how to contact his mother.'

She shrugs. 'I don't imagine he'd have gone to her. He hated her, and his father both.'

This draws me up with a jolt. 'I thought he seemed to admire his father. But he's dead, isn't he?'

She looks taken aback. 'Is he? What happened?'

'Wasn't he killed in a car accident years ago?'

'No! He used to find Max and try to tap him for money. I don't think he'd had a job for years. Max won't stay away from you for long. You have a good job?'

I pull a face.

'Grishkin can't commit himself to anyone or anything,' says Katya. 'He'll be thirty in a couple of years, and he behaves like an adolescent.'

'A year, surely? It was his birthday last month. Twenty-nine?'

'No, I'm sure he's the same age as me. He'll be twenty-eight now. He's a drifter,' she adds, a little sadly. 'Nobody to love him.'

'His grandparents did.'

She looks vague. 'Perhaps.'

Here's the answer then. Two people starved of love — what did we imagine we could give each other? Max and I are more similar than I cared to admit before.

I like Katya, no point in denying it, but I can't bear to be here any longer.

I stand in the street feeling giddy, gazing up at the sky and taking great gulps of air as if I've been reprieved from a death sentence. It's a big risk I've taken. If Maksim had been with her I'd have wanted to harm both of them. I look up at Katya's window. She's watching me. I wave to her almost cheerfully as I turn to make my way to the station for the Petersburg train.

Hours later, as we trundle through darkened countryside that could be anywhere, I pull a face at my reflection and lean my forehead against the cool, grubby window.

White cranes are practically extinct. The chances of seeing one are slight. The chances of seeing two dance together are not computable within my lifetime. As bad as believing in fairies.

Dunstaffnage Place, 28th November

I'm glad to be home, though no one seems to think the Sure Foundation idea is anything other than folly.

Carla tries distraction tactics. 'All three of us can go to Brittany, if you don't want to stay in Edinburgh. That's the best idea of all. You can spend your Christmas holiday flirting with a handsome Breton fisherman.'

'Perhaps, next summer.'

Fergus has left. I walk along his street and look at the

'for sale' sign. I feel an unexpected pang of nostalgia. He's won anyway. He has custody of the cat.

Poland, 23rd December

We're on our way to Ukraine. I'm not at all confident I'm as multi-skilled as I pretend to be – this is what comes of disregarding the NUJ's advice. The Sure Foundations director, Garry, doesn't buy into doubt. 'God will guide your hand,' he says. As long as God has the instruction book.

The journey is getting more hellish by the day. All my good intentions are as frozen as the roads, and I'd sell my soul to see a real toilet that's clean.

Kiev, Ukraine 31st December

It's a little better now we've reached our destination and I can get out of the bloody van. But the suffering is confusing. All of it moves me. It's impossible to judge what will move potential donors: which story to champion over another.

'I don't know how to film it to bring out the scale of suffering,' I tell Garry. 'Everyone in the West has famine-fatigue. What's another sick child on TV. How do I show their humanity?'

I can't summon up much enthusiasm for Kiev, although it's the root-stock of all I thought I admired. The ancient capital of Rus is just another city, with kids begging in the streets. The Russia I've craved all these years is a mirage; they carry it with them in their hearts, all of them, Max and Zhenya and Katya. I could never have been part of it. And three weeks is all I have to figure out ways to convince plump Scottish hands to reach deep into their pockets and write large cheques made out to Sure Foundations.

Garry finds a doctor to show me around the biggest of the main hospitals, an elegant, blonde woman called Tania.

'I would leave,' she says. 'I've tried, but I can't. Maybe one day. Or I'll be carried out in a box.'

Hospital Number Three is worse than I'd anticipated. Corridors where the floors haven't been washed in too long, nurses without uniforms. But when I comment on this, Tania produces a twisted smile.

'They're not nurses. The relatives come in when they can. This is intensive care here. A mother or a sister or a wife. Plenty of people; no equipment.'

'Are babies born here?'

'Of course.'

'You don't have a specialist – gynaecology and obstetrics – called Yulia Grigorieva?' I ask. 'She may use a different surname. She came here from Petersburg about nine years ago.'

She shakes her head. 'None in this hospital with Yulia as a first name.'

'Is there someone who might know?'

She leads me to a ward with beds in the corridor, up the centre of the room, so close we can scarcely walk between them. Silent women with sad-eyed babies.

She hails another white-coated figure. 'The English journalist is looking for a gynae specialist called Yulia. From St Petersburg.' She turns to me. 'What age?'

'Possibly mid-fifties. She's Ukrainian. She came back here when her husband died.' Unless everything her son has told me was a lie. Katya certainly hinted as much. I realise with a sinking heart, I can't vouch for a word of it.

'Yulia Tarenteva?'

'I'm not sure of her name. Her husband's name was Grigoriev. I think.'

'She's the only Yulia I know. She's at Sarny hospital.'

'Is it far?'

'Five hours' drive. The road's not too good.'

'Would I be able to get there by bus?'

They both smirk. 'Better to find someone who's willing to drive you.'

I write down both the woman's name and the hospital's. 'I'll do some filming in all the hospitals around Kiev, Tania. Where would it be best to start?'

'The children's cancer hospital,' she says at once. 'You have a strong stomach? You could film in an operating theatre.'

'Wouldn't they mind? I've no sterile clothing.'

She laughs and shrugs.

The scene is so terrifying I can scarcely hold the camera steady: two operations going on simultaneously in the same theatre, people in ordinary street clothes wandering in and out, the absence of a hospital antiseptic smell. And in the midst of it, a calm, green-gowned figure creates a pool of tranquillity, sewing up what looks like a lump of raw steak.

He works with a total concentration that reminds me painfully of Max.

He finishes what he's doing, and straightens up, stretching his back and wincing slightly.

'Come on. I'll introduce you,' says Tania, with a strange catch in her voice. 'This is Dr de Bourka. Our best surgeon. From Ireland.'

I groan inwardly. I've always despised the ones who call themselves by pseudo-Norman names rather than admitting they're common Celts like the rest of us. He walks towards us and pulls down the face-mask, hands the goggles to a nurse. Vivid cobalt blue eyes, dark-lashed, behind neat gold-rimmed glasses. He's smiling; there's a cat's cradle of laugh-lines at the corners of his eyes. A fine-boned, intelligent, alert face, that's reminiscent of Nick's peregrine falcon. A powerful man. He looks at me very directly.

'You're making a film?'

His accent is as tuneful as Bernadette's. I smile at him.

'I'm travelling with the Sure Foundations team.'

'Please – go ahead. I'm sure my patient won't mind. Let me go and get cleaned up, and I can tell you more.'

He smiles at Tania, who is lingering by the door. 'How are you? See you later.' It's a dismissal. She hesitates for a moment, then leaves.

'So,' I say when he comes back, 'you use a lot of surgery here?'

'We haven't the drugs for as much chemotherapy as I've been used to. There's an awful lot more treated by surgery than in the West. I count myself fortunate we'd enough anaesthetic today.'

'You've had to work without? I'd heard rumours, but it's hard to grasp.'

He's leading me down a long corridor; there's no smell of blood here.

'I'd not have let you watch one of those operations. Though there's a lot I've learnt from the surgeons here. It's not everyone who does well with chemotherapy. Maybe we depend on it too much in the west. OK? Got what you need? Sure Foundations – and what have you brought us this time?'

'Everything from paracetemol upwards.'

He grins and holds out his hand. A broad, blunt, capable hand. 'Tania didn't introduce us properly. I'm Danny de Bourka. What do they call you?'

'Serena… MacKenzie.' I've never got around to calling myself Serena Grigorieva except in my head.

We walk along the corridor side by side. Tania is nowhere to be seen. I try to gauge his age – about the same as me. Certainly not much more. And while I fiddle about pretending to report news, he's saving lives.

'That's an awful neat wee camera – you can make a film with it?'

'It's the latest thing. Digital – you can get broadcast quality. You're a long way from home, Dr de Bourka?'

'Danny, please. Donegal. You're Scottish? Highland?'

'There's not many people notice. I thought I'd lost the accent. I've lived most of my life in Glasgow and Edinburgh.'

He has strong-looking, regular, very white teeth. I like his ears too; they sit fine and close to the head, as does his neat, curly black hair. Everybody we pass greets him; he seems to have the capacity to make the world love him.

'We can have what's allegedly coffee here,' he says, steering me into what looks like a canteen. 'Though possibly not quite the standard you're used to! It's the one thing I miss most. A cup of really decent coffee.'

'Are you married?' he asks as soon as we sit down.

Not a man to beat about the bush then, or waste his time. 'Yes. No. Well – kind of. Are you?'

'Now, I can give a straightforward answer. No I'm not. How can you be "kind of" married? You mean you're separated?'

'Something along those lines. It's a long story. And what are you doing here, Dr de…Danny?'

'I'm with a medical aid society. A Catholic thing, though I'm not much of a Catholic. I'm the only foreign doctor here. Fish out of water. You're not a Catholic?'

'Can you tell just by looking?' (Granda would have drunk to that, if he'd been one for drinking.)

'I could tell your entire history and temperament at a glance.'

We drain our cups and head back along the corridor.

'You've been here a long time?' I say. 'You speak good Russian.'

'Nearly three years. I learnt quite a bit before I came. It'd have been better to learn Ukrainian, but I couldn't find anyone to teach me. It's not so different anyway. And you? I heard you talking to Tania.'

'I learnt it at school. Can I film in here?' We're passing a ward full of cheerful bald kids. Their faces are eager, though most of them look like skin-covered skulls, as if smiling might split them open. But the room's full of chatter and laughter. I wipe my eyes discreetly with the back of my hand when we leave.

'You never get used to it,' Danny says, his voice throaty and full of sadness. 'An awful lot of thyroid cancer in the kids. What's the film for?'

'To help with fund-raising; to let people see there's more folk in need of aid than the ones in Africa. Not that I don't think the people in Africa deserve aid too,' I add, tripping over my words.

'Don't feel you have to say so. It's why I'm here too. An awful lot here feels familiar. People who're fatalistic, superstitious, and either get religion or hit the booze. They could be the folk you'd see on Grafton Street. They've had an awful lot to put up with. The memories are still raw. So you're a professional film-maker?'

'I'm a journalist. I'm doing this as a special project.'

'So you'll be moving on to film other places?' I can hear the disappointment in his voice. It's balm for the bruised soul. I manage a genuine smile.

'We're based in Kiev for three weeks,' I say. 'I'll film around the town. Other hospitals, and so on.'

I've heard there are kids living under the railway platforms in the main station because the paedophiles won't come after them there. Every now and again, one gets mashed by an unscheduled train.

'There's a children's home they want me to cover too, on Christmas day, their Christmas. And I'm keen to go to Sarny, to the hospital there. Do you know it?'

'It makes this place look sophisticated. You won't try to drive yourself there?'

'I daresay some of the others will come with me. I don't mean to go till near the end of our time here.'

Hospital flats, Kiev, 18th January 1998

I've seen Danny every day, for they've put us up in a flat in the block where he lives, beside the hospital. After just over a fortnight he feels like an old friend. I know he doesn't have a woman; though I've had my suspicions from the way Tania looks at him. I know it might have mattered to me if he had, even though I'm trying to learn to be sensible.

I know from his colleagues that he gets scarcely any pay, and when patients' relatives bring him gifts of eggs and vegetables and the odd chicken as payment, he gives them to the nurses.

'They have nothing,' he tells me, blushing, when I ask him about it. 'A lot of them haven't had their salaries for a while. I can afford to pay for my food.'

He's at the end of the three-year stint he signed up for, and he doesn't think he'll stay on.

'I'm burned out,' he says. 'I hope I've been able to do some good here, but it's been long enough. It's begun to get to me, seeing so many people die, and nothing I can do about it, and so much of the equipment banjaxed. I'll look for a job where I can go on learning. Everything's moving fast in cancer treatment. And maybe I can teach a little too. If I can pass on what I know to other doctors, it helps the work more than another burned-out surgeon in Kiev.'

He's heard about an interesting job in a specialist

cancer centre in Cheshire.

'I'm lucky enough to have a house there already,' he says. 'My father had a huge win on the Irish Sweep a good few years back, and he shared out the money equally between my brothers and me. I got a house with my share. I've rented it out the last three years, but I'm keen to get back to it.'

As he tells me, I can sense he's watching for my reaction, and I don't need to force it. I'll be happy to think he's in the same country as me.

A thoroughly good man. Too good for me. And a Gaelic speaker – it's not so unlike ours. Not so much as the differences between Russian and Ukrainian. Another swan freak too.

'Swans! When I was a kid, I used to nag all the time to visit my aunt in Galway, because her house looks out on the Corrib, and there are hundreds of them. I loved to watch them arriving, with their big feet down like a plane's landing gear, throwing up spray. And they'd fight, they'd stand right up on the water and go at each other like avenging angels, defending their space.'

'Did you know,' he adds, 'the biggest single colony of mute swans is in the Volga delta. They say there's thousands. Maybe we could go and see them some time?'

'Serena,' he adds suddenly, 'I've been thinking – how about if I drive you up to Sarny tomorrow? I know the area and I can get hold of a decent car. It's only a few hours' drive.'

'I'd be very grateful, but I have to come clean; I do want to get some filming done, but mainly I'm trying to contact one of the doctors there.'

'What's his name? Maybe I know him.'

'Her name's Yulia. I'm not sure what surname she uses. Either Tarenteva or Grigorieva. She's a gynae specialist.'

'Doesn't mean anything. Why are you trying to find her? Is there something you have to tell me?'

He grins and punches me lightly in the belly.

'Mutual friend. I promised I'd look her up.'

Sarny, Ukraine, 19th January

For what feels like weeks, we trundle through countryside bland and tasteless as desert-grown fruit. I feel guilty, having lied to Danny, so as we're approaching Sarny I tell him about Max, and the circumstances of being *kind of* married.

'This is the only good thing I've done in my life,' I say, 'helping a charity. And even now, it's not for the right reasons. But I have to know what happened to him. He may have been in touch with his mother.'

'Does she know he got married?'

'I shouldn't think so. I'm not even sure we *were* married. Everyone at home said it couldn't be legal. I'm sorry – I should have explained all this before you offered to bring me.'

'I'd still have wanted to keep you company. By the by, I don't think you should tell her. Just a gut feeling I have. Say you're a friend of his. You don't need to let on about the rest. How long were you with him anyway?' he adds after a moment's silence.

I can hardly bring myself to answer truthfully. It sounds

so ridiculous, so illogical, so immature.

'Five months in total.' I laugh ruefully. 'And we fought just about every day.'

Danny sighs. 'I suppose it's why I've given entanglements a wide berth. I never wanted to get hurt. I can see you're hurting a lot.'

This is what it must be like to have had a limb amputated. I'm desperate to reach out with some part of me, because Danny's reaching out to me, but it isn't there, though I can still feel it. I've seen books about this in Waterstones. Soul retrieval. I need the services of a shaman, not a doctor. How can I find a soul-mate when I've mislaid so many bits of my soul?

Yulia is much as I've visualised her. An inch or two taller than I am, dark brown hair well-peppered with grey, cut in a severe bob with a fringe, and her eyes are Max's eyes but with a glitter of mica rather than gold. I don't know if I'll be able to stay lucid.

'My son? Oh yes, I used to have a son. Haven't heard from him in years. The last I knew, he was still living in Petersburg, moving around from one run-down hovel to another. My son! All the money I wasted in fees, and he lives like a gypsy. What do you want with him? What trouble is he in now?'

'I met him there briefly last summer. Just wondered how he is.'

'I've never known him stay more than a few months in

one place. Twenty-seven years old, and he's never done a real day's work in his life.'

'Twenty-nine,' I say mechanically. 'Last October.'

She glares at me. 'I think I know what age my son is. I've had long enough to wonder where I went wrong since his father left.'

I'm confused, but ask anyway, 'You don't think he might have gone to his father?'

'His father! His father wouldn't know him. The drink rotted his brain years back, though I don't suppose he's dead. They'd have come after me for the cash to bury him.' She looks at me calculatingly. 'My son hasn't left you pregnant, miss?'

I shake my head. 'Nothing like that.'

'I'm sorry – I have to get back to my patient. A difficult birth. The mother's very weak.'

The place needs aid as desperately as any I've seen. 'Listen,' I said, 'what does your hospital need most? Perhaps we could come here on the next trip.'

'There's nothing it doesn't need.' She looks very tired all of a sudden, and sweeps the hair from her forehead with the back of her hand; such a familiar gesture. I flee.

Yulia has promised to get in touch if she hears from Max. We both know neither of these eventualities will occur.

Danny is waiting in the car, reading a magazine. He lifts the camera case and looks at me expectantly. I'm angry that

Max lied about his father, about his age, that his mother doesn't know how old her son is, whatever; either way, I'm losing my grip on the details of the man I lived with for almost half a year.

'She didn't have any news then?'

I weep helplessly against his chest, making a damp patch on his shirt. He kisses the top of my head. When I look up in his face, his eyes are full too. The things he sees day to day, his patients dying after he's spent so much effort trying to make them live, all these children; these he observes dry-eyed, yet he'll well up for me.

'I didn't know him,' I snivel. 'Every damn person I speak to, there's more proof I didn't know the least thing about him.'

Danny detaches me gently and starts the car.

'Let's get away from this place. We can come back later if you want.'

He drives out of town and we find a snow-covered parking place in a small forest, with a frozen waterfall and icicles several feet long. In summer, it must look like the waterfall at Ollasdale, the one deep in the woods. Danny keeps the engine running so that the heater works, and draws me close. I slide my arms round his sturdy, comforting body, under his jacket, and we sit this way for the best part of an hour.

'I don't know who made you believe you're not a good person,' he says. 'I hope some day you'll tell me about it. I've known you for less than a month but I can see you've got it wrong. You've just had your heart broken. It'll mend. Trust me – I'm a doctor.'

'Well, doctor, I've been listening to your heart for forty minutes, and I can tell you, it sounds fine.'

He laughs, and tickles my neck. 'You'll get through this. You're a strong person, though you don't know it. And I'm here for you, for what it's worth.'

I kiss his cheek in reply.

'You really still feel you're married to him?' he asks.

'God knows why. He burned our marriage certificate, but it wasn't worth the paper it was printed on anyway. We'd to bribe someone to get it. It might as well never have existed. No trace now except some dodgy paperwork in a Russian registry office. In fact, there probably never was any paperwork. We weren't married in the other way either,' I add. 'I didn't ever sleep with him.'

The only nights of unbroken, refreshing sleep since I was ten were the ones I spent in the safe haven of Max's arms. But it's easier to use the common euphemism to explain.

'He's hurt you a great deal, I think.'

'I've hurt myself. I realise now how little I knew him. It was all a dream. Crazy. I'm supposed to be a grown-up, but I've behaved like a gullible child.'

'Don't change because of this. I think you're fine the way you are. If you find this Max, will you stay with him?'

'No! I only need to know he's safe.'

He sighs. 'I wish I knew how to help.'

'You do. Just being here, you help.'

'Serena…'

'Let's go back now. I have to get ready to go tomorrow.'

'Home,' he says.

'Well – Edinburgh. The past few years, it's felt like home, but I'm not so sure I want to go back there now.'

For half an hour, we trade stories of our real homes.

Peat-reek. Oiled wool. The smoke from driftwood that's lain in salt water. The smells that signified home for our ancestors. Clove-scented honeysuckle, queen of the meadow, seaweed crisping in the sun, bog myrtle. Turned earth. Tiny white wild roses you've to bury your nose in

to catch the fragrance. The sharp green scent of new bracken that burns the nostrils like pepper. Flowers of broom that can make you drunk without liquor. The taste of salt on the lips when you've been walking in the wind. Mountain-cold spring water. Blaeberries bursting against your teeth. Hair-fine thorns in your fingers. Oystercatchers rising up from under your feet screaming abuse if you walk on their beach at sundown. All these, and we're still on common ground.

Back in Kiev, he cooks cheese omelettes for supper, then tells me he has a surprise for me.

'Shut your eyes.'

He pops a couple of berries into my mouth.

'Are these brambles?'

'I had them in the freezer since autumn. They're probably radioactive, but such a small quantity won't hurt us.'

We spend the night together in his room, but he's too gentle to try to ask for what I know he wants. We just cuddle a lot.

Hospital flats, Kiev, 20th January

He walks out to the van with me, and gives me a single sad, friendly kiss. 'The phones here are hardly reliable,' he says, 'and the postal system's hopeless. We'll send each other e-mails.'

'Mind what you write. I only have it at work. There might be someone looking over my shoulder.'

'We'll write in our native tongue then, I'll write in my Gaelic and you write in yours and we'll see how much we understand. I don't think I'll be writing anything very incriminating. I learnt my Irish from my grandmother and the Christian Brothers. I have a dictionary, but it's an old one. I don't suppose it has the words for body-parts between the neck and the knee, never mind what you do with them. That's better. I prefer to see you smile.'

Because I'm not a good person, I'm hardly wondering if he's as sad as he looks. I'm thinking: How weird to come all the way to the roots of the country I was besotted with for all of my life, and find a man who wants to send me e-mails in Gaelic.

I leave Danny my rose geranium soap and my toothpaste, luxuries here. Little enough.

'I won't wait,' he says. 'I can hardly bear to see you leave. I'll just keep imagining we're about to meet again. I'll be reminded of the scent of your skin every time I wash.'

His eyes are sad, though he's pretending to grin. I don't know if I'm strong enough for the burden of having the power to hurt such a thoroughly good man. I watch as he climbs the steps and goes through the swing doors. He gives me a small, lonely wave just before he disappears from sight.

Albion Studios, 28th January

Anita and Roger are beside themselves with glee at the way our film has turned out.

'You really *have* got the hang of this,' Roger says. 'The men love you because you're a sexy wee thing, and the women love you because you look like everyone's perfect daughter.'

They grin at me like conspirators and tell me about the job going in London, on the mother ship, for a health correspondent.

'We don't want to lose you,' says Anita, 'but it's a super chance. Throw your hat in the ring anyway?'

All too neat to be true.

'Did Fergus set this up?' I ask.

They both look at me blankly. I don't think it's an act.

Sandringham Terrace, Edinburgh, 20th February

Carla is unhappy about it, I can tell, but she puts a brave face on it.

'It's just what you need, and it's not a chance you can pass up. We can visit you. As long as you promise to keep away from that pig Fergus.'

'I was thinking of bunking up with him,' I say straight-faced, but she isn't fooled for a moment. Not that I've even told my ex-husband about my promotion.

'Like hell you were. When will you have to leave?'

'Not till the end of March. Let's spend all the time we can together until then. It's not so far anyway – a few hours on the train.'

She looks at me speculatively.

'You've met a man?'

'How do you know I didn't find Max?'

'Your eyes. When you were with him they were either full of anger or full of misery. My God, I felt sorry for both of you. Now you look – contented. Fulfilled. I never saw you look this way, ever. Contented is best, believe me. Who is he?'

'Och, nonsense. I'm pleased to think maybe I'll have a real career at last, rather than just a job, that's all.'

Carla smirks.

Yes, I met a man. We write to each other most days, and we speak on the phone when we can. He's due back in the UK in less than four weeks. He's the very best person I ever met, but I don't know yet if I can manage to fall in love with him. And I harbour a small fear in my gut, because I suspect he wants to possess the inside of my skull as well as the softer bits of my body, and a benevolent dictator's still a tyrant.

'It doesn't happen like an explosion,' says Carla. 'Remember I told you. It's more like a fire in a haystack.'

'It's an explosion for some people.'

'Love at first sight's for people with their heads screwed on wrong.'

I glare at her.

She laughs. 'What are friends for, if they can't tell you the truth? For God's sake, this time make sure you fall for one with plenty of money and a good job.'

'I want romance. I'm not a pragmatist.'

'Bullshit,' says Carla. 'You can only afford to be romantic after you've done the cost-benefit analysis in your head. Nothing kills romance faster than the wrong education or the wrong bank account.'

Or the wrong temperament. Or the wrong childhood. I wish that, just for a change, I could have found romance and pragmatism on the same menu.

Kingdom, Balvaig, 21ˢᵗ February

I'm spending a long weekend at Balvaig, to compensate for Christmas, but I'm afraid my aunt derives little comfort from my presence.

'I don't understand you,' she says. 'You're tearing round Europe looking for one man, then you're hankering to get back to Edinburgh to see if another's sent you a message on a computer.'

I think electronic love is the best it can get for me.

'Well, what are you doing?' Peigi doesn't give up easily. 'Are you going to go on seeing this Irish doctor? I hope to God you're not thinking of going back to Fergus.' (She's furious because a postcard from Fergus arrived for me this morning. A view of Tower Bridge and the message: *Come on in – the water's lovely*. She understands neither why he sent it, nor why it makes me angry, nor why he knew I was here in any case.) 'Or this Russian, this Max – what if he turns up?'

'He won't,' I say, decisively. 'Actually, I'm very worried about him. I'm sure Fergus knows something about what's happened to him, but of course he won't tell me. Max has the address here anyway, as well as the Edinburgh one. If he's OK, he's aware how to find me.'

'Why do you feel you need a man anyway?'

She's always asking me questions with no solution:

sound-of-one-hand-clapping stuff. My aunt, the Zen priestess. When I have the answer to that one: Enlightenment. What *do* I need a man for? Why do I require the same lesson over and over? What have I ever needed a man for, when it was clear none of them ever had a need for me, other than the crass and obvious? Except one. I summon up the courage to try to tell Peigi about my problem, though without any hope that she'll understand. She just sighs. Ah well.

'I've often wondered if any of the women in our family are cut out for it,' she says. 'Even my own mother. She should never have married. All these miscarriages. And she hated sex. Maybe we should all have been nuns.' She gazes pensively out of the window, and then walks around the room with folded arms, peering over my shoulder at the email I printed out at Portmore library this morning. 'What's "réalta eolais"?'

'Guiding star,' I say. I've bought myself a second-hand copy of Dinneen's Irish dictionary.

'He's very romantic then? "*You are the guiding star of my life...*" – he's a poet. But I still think you should stay quiet on your own for a while. You've just newly divorced Fergus.'

'I'm not my mother,' I say. 'I'm done with beating myself up because she didn't love me and neither did Frank. I've had a couple of false starts, I admit, but I want to be with a man. With the right man, one who's there for me, and understands the way I am. I'm nearly thirty-one.'

'Don't give me the old "biological clock" nonsense. And you're just going to work your way round the world till you find this right one, are you?'

'If I have to.'

'You could always come back and live here,' she says. 'You used to love the island.'

'I still do, but I couldn't live here now.'

'You could if you wanted to.'

'There's no work. What would I live on?'

'You could rent out your flat. I'm hardly going to charge you. You could go back to teaching.'

'There's no secondary school here.'

'Well, you could always convert your qualification to primary, and teach in Portmore. It's served me well. But maybe you think a life like mine's not good enough for you, Serena.'

'I'm different from you, that's all.'

My aunt shakes her head in despair, but she's smiling now.

'Let's walk down to the shore,' she says.

Kingdom's small scrap of beach makes me nostalgic. In summer, a solitary pair of wild swans used to settle here, when I was a child. The cob would stand guard over his mate as if she was the most precious object in his world; they never seemed to have young. Then one year he arrived alone. He'd stand on the same rock, as if he could conjure up her memory by being there. He became more mellow and tame. He didn't hiss and raise his wings when we took him bread. 'His mate must have died,' said Peigi. I wept for pity. Another season the same. Next year, there was another swan with him. 'It's not his wife,' I said: judgemental, even as an eleven-year-old. 'He's found a new one. Isn't he lucky?' 'How do you know she didn't just find a new husband?' 'I don't think swans do such things. Not the female ones anyway. It's men do that. Women keep the faith.' My aunt glared at the swans. But I thought he looked wistful. He didn't love the second wife as much. But birds need to be in pairs, like shoes and bookends and people.

'You remember the swan who was left on his own?' I ask Peigi as we reach the water's edge.

'I do. But it wasn't the male who was left, the way we thought it was. Hector MacRae knows about these things. He said it was the female. A swan widow.'

'Do you know what Grannie told me? She said the girl swan had gone away because she was so disgusted by my behaviour.'

'She never said that!'

'She did. After the thing with Donald John Munro.'

Peigi's face closes like a clam shell.

'Did they ever let him out?'

She shakes her head. 'He died there years back. He'd have been about fifty.'

'Remember the police found the knife in the grass – why did they never take prints off it?'

'Well, in the circumstances… It wasn't the first time he'd lured a child away, you know. He was a paedophile. It just got hushed up because of his father, and because he wasn't quite right in the head.'

'He didn't threaten me with it. And he didn't cut himself. He didn't have a knife at all. It was me. I took Granda's knife from the kitchen, the one he used to open mussels for bait. I had it in my pocket. It's why Donald John had wounds on his hands as well as – elsewhere. You see what this means?'

Peigi stares at me.

'It means I must have known. In the back of my mind.'

'Don't be daft. You were only a wee girl. You might just have taken it for devilment.'

'Do you think I should tell the police? I lashed out at him, and I certainly knew what I was doing then. I meant to cut it off, if I could. But the blade wasn't long enough. Should I tell?'

'Of course not. If you did it in self-defence, what difference does it make? Why did you never tell *me*?'

'You weren't there. No one was there except Grannie and Granda, and no one asked me about the knife. No one noticed it had gone. Granda didn't have time to notice. I was going to confess to the policewoman in Oban, but I was frightened I'd be put in prison. I never told anyone, till now. Morag wouldn't let me talk about it afterwards. It was as if I'd done something so bad it couldn't be mentioned.'

Peigi wipes her eyes. 'You carried that burden all these years?'

'Maybe he'd not have been arrested and put away if I'd confessed. Then Granda wouldn't have had a stroke, and Donald John's father wouldn't have shot himself.'

'The lad had been in and out of mental hospitals since he was a teenager. And the father too. He'd some sort of religious mania. The whole family would have come to a bad end no matter what.'

'Grannie said it was all my fault.'

'It was my fault if it was anyone's,' says Peigi. 'I was to blame for trying to sort out people's lives, then leaving you with the likes of my mother and my feckless sister. Come on back into the house. It's cold.'

Margaret, my aunt Peigi: pearl of great price. She's still a very attractive woman. Her dark hair's fading to a stylish silver, at the nape and the temples. She's kept it long, and she wears it swept up, old-fashioned, like an Edwardian lady. She was always the beauty in the family. Not a conventional, easy beauty, hers. Good bones. I used to take comfort from the fact I've inherited those at least.

I walk up to the old burying ground. I push open the creaky gate held onto its hinges by nothing more than rust and faith. I run my fingers over the inscription in both languages, so familiar I see it in my dreams:

In loving memory of Flying Officer Prince Maksim Michaelovich Chaliapin, born 22 April 1922, died March 15th 1944. "He sought the stars, and found in them his heaven."

'Please let my Max be all right. Let him just have left because he decided he couldn't live with me in this country,' I whisper. I lay my bunch of scarlet Dutch hothouse roses against the stone, sheltered from the weather. I know in my heart it will be the last time I visit my Russian Prince.

Just one more trip to make before I start my new life.

St Petersburg, 28th February

I have to blink hard before I can believe my eyes when I see them. A gaggle of kids – the eldest what, maybe ten, twelve?

– have set up a stall directly opposite St Isaac's, in the bitter cold, and draped it with plastic to warm a mini-hothouse with their breath. They're selling pot-plants, and the ploy is working, passers-by are stopping to look, and to grin at the incongruity of it. Pot-plants! But already my hand is in my pocket.

The building where they lived burned down, they tell me. Part of it had been deliberately set alight to show off new fire-fighting pumps, but the pumps didn't work, and the ordinary fire engines took too long to arrive. They came home from school to see mothers, baby brothers and sisters, aunts carried out on stretchers, unidentifiable cuts of charred meat. So they ran away, because they didn't want to be taken to the orphanage where children's bodies are sold to friends of the management. They hid, then crept back to the basement, which was still habitable, once it had dried out. After a council of war, to see what they could live on, they stole a packet of coleus seeds, and started their nursery. In the smoky darkness, along with hopes, they have germinated a new generation of plants with gaudy leaves. I have no idea whether one word of their story is true.

What do winter tourists or commuters want with plants? Clever kids! They'll get the money anyway, just as they have from me, and their stock won't ever deplete. Such beautiful children. From the southern republics, I should imagine. Dark curly heads and lustrous eyes, the same almond shape as Zhenya's, smiles flashing like bunny-tails, voices shrill and tense as startled birds. They are wary, watching out (as I am too, I confess) for anything in a uniform (and there are so many, even now).

Perhaps they won't outlast their plants. I don't know whether to be angry or optimistic. Tomorrow morning, I'll find them again, if they haven't been moved on, because I've remembered the name of the local doctor who runs refuges for street-children. Or maybe I just need to introduce them to Zhenya. He could sell their stock for them at a fair price.

I've strolled around the city once more. This time, it's different. My steps are purposeful. The Neva's sleek under ice, and the streets glint and glitter with frost. All the Summer Garden's statues are sheltering in their miniature wooden houses. Oh yes, it's still every bit as lovely as the postcards, the loveliest city on the planet, and still they come in busloads to see it sparkle, and hold their breath, and wipe their eyes: 'The cold! The beauty!'

My cure is well advanced. I can tell myself, 'I am in Max's city', and I stay clear-headed, though I can't forget that it holds his heart in a way I never did. This is where he'll be if he's anywhere, back among the unbroken white of midnight streets, radiant islands, snow-carpeted bridges and cool high rooms with tall windows. But I'm also learning that Max's St Petersburg isn't the real one, any more than the Catherine Palace is. The truth is somewhere in between, and it's a less depressing truth than I perceived before.

I tried to give him what I thought he wanted – memories, security, sentiment. But his needs all along were more basic: a woman to be there for him. He never wanted to be my companion. He wanted what I couldn't give; now I understand – no one's to blame. Now I'm fighting not to forget details like the precise timbre of his voice, and the script of the last real conversation we had.

Several times, since I've been here, I've spotted Max ahead of me on the street, his lanky, elegant frame and his pale hair, and I've run after him, only to find myself having to apologise to a stranger who looks askance at me, as if I'm a madwoman.

And, of course, I've realised, too late, that probably the consequences of making a clean breast of it to the authorities in the UK wouldn't have been anywhere near as serious as we'd feared. There are already thousands of Russians living quite openly in London. Fergus is right. I'm not any kind of investigative journalist. He is though, and he obviously knew I'd vastly over-estimated the risks. He was just winding me up, and I fell for it. Again.

Maybe it would have made no difference anyway. Maksim. I think I fell in love with the name as much as with the man. Elegant and urbane and beautiful. The name for a fairy prince with hair like flax. It took longer to see there's a coldness in it too. Maksim. A brittle, evanescent name, a pattern of frost-crystals.

I've thought a great deal lately about words, how we betray each other with words, and judge each other, how a single one can cripple a relationship that held promise and pull the plug on hope and burrow deeper than bullets and burn more than fire. Frank was right about words. They can kill or cure or corrupt.

I've seen Zhenya again. The *Chaika* made it home to Murmansk by the end of January, but Max wasn't on board. They denied all knowledge of him, but Zhenya thinks they were lying. As predicted, they only got as far as Aberdeen, and were detained again there for a month, because the ship was deemed unseaworthy. So while I was fretting over him, he was less than three hours' drive away. I am angrier about how he has betrayed Zhenya than I am about how he has betrayed me.

I make him take the rest of Max's money, for safe keeping. He'll need it once he gets back. I make sure he still has Peigi's address, because I don't know yet where I'll settle in London – or even *if*. It's a city I've never been able to conjure up any affection for. And Fergus is there now, and Danny isn't…

Zhenya is awkward, because he used the cash I left with him before Christmas to help set up his own flower shop. It's becoming very successful – he's pouring all the creativity from his music into composing beauty from flowers. What a team he and Dee would make now!

'I feel bad about using Max's money,' he says, 'but I can afford to pay him double now, to make up for it – or give it back to you. It's yours, really.'

'No, Max earned it, and I know he'd have given it to you if you needed it. Keep it, for when he finds you again.'

I am a free woman. I have no promises I need to keep. My passport's secure at the hotel, and all I have in my pocket as

I stand on the bridge they named for Pyotr Schmidt, is some change and a hankie and the poem in Gaelic that pinged into my inbox before I left. I lay my fingers around it again, feeling how the paper's nearly disintegrating from being folded and unfolded.

I'll never see the white cranes dancing. But the swans on the Corrib in Galway city – I may get to see them, one day. Swans are good. They don't come out of a fairy tale, they're real and available, and I won't need a miracle to be able to watch them scrunching up the water with their enormous feet as they land and take off and fight for the right to Lebensraum. I understand now why the swan widow at Balvaig took another mate.

Carla was right. The spark's never enough if there's no fuel, but the fire in a haystack arrives by magic. The heat builds and builds and builds until it's unbearable. Then the flame comes, and before you know it the whole stackyard's gone up, and there's a blaze visible from the neighbouring county. So it's possible she was right about other matters too. For some of us, strong affection is as good as it ever gets, because passion's too dangerous.

Tomorrow afternoon, I'll go home. I have choices to make.

I could go along with Peigi's idea of a good way to live my life. But I'm not my aunt and I'm not Ursula. My mindset doesn't lend itself to being alone.

I could go back to Fergus – it would be an easy route. It'd be what my grannie called "the flat, wide and pleasant path to Hell". He and I have more in common than I've been willing to face, but there was something sordid in our relationship from the start. I felt like the kept woman of an overweight, sleazy Edwardian lothario.

There could be another option. Danny has blossomed into a good friend to me. We're already planning a holiday in Ireland, but I know in my heart he won't rush me into anything I'm not ready for.

I've faced the same crossroads as Bonnie Kilmeny, and I think I'm ready to opt for the route I know in my heart is the more cowardly one. She was brave enough to decide to turn her back on the real world. I'm not.

And yet, and yet…

Occasionally, in my dreams, I'm back there with Max, in the Land of Thought. And always, always we're in a wood like Ollasdale.

WHITE CRANES DANCING

If you enjoyed WHITE CRANES DANCING, you'll love
CONTAINMENT
the second book in the Balvaig series
and
THE SWAN WIDOW
the third volume, which is Peigi MacKenzie's story

Visit **http://www.fionacameronwriter.com** for exclusive updates & additional material

Follow Fiona on Twitter @fionacamwriter

http://www.flyingswanpress.com

www.ingramcontent.com/pod-product-compliance
Lightning Source LLC
Chambersburg PA
CBHW021232060726
47590CB00005B/1736